TERA LYNN CHILDS

Straight Stalk

For Crystal, a rock star in every way

PROLOGUE

"YOU'RE A TURNER," Lydia declared, her voice carrying crisply despite the noisy crowd in *Cafe Frais*, my favorite SoHo teahouse.

Intrigued, I regarded her over the gold rim of my teacup.

Next to me, Fiona choked on her Earl Grey. "Is that anything like a spinner?" she sputtered as she dabbed a napkin to her chin.

I wasn't sure what Fiona meant, but odds were it was obscene. Her mind lived forever in the gutter.

Carefully setting my own teacup on its waiting saucer without a clatter—some Southern manners were hard to lose—I considered the conversation leading up to Lydia's odd statement.

We had been discussing my romantic past. Not exactly my favorite subject, but with new beau Evan on his way to join us for brunch—meeting the girls for the first time—they seemed intent on rehashing history. I had just finished telling them about seeing my latest ex shopping at Gracious Home with his new boyfriend.

Sad, but true.

Which did not explain Lydia's bizarre declaration.

"What precisely do you mean?" I asked.

"Well," she began, resting her elbows gently on the floral tablecloth. "David is gay."

I nodded politely at her statement of the obvious. "Yes."

"And before David there was Jon. He's gay, too."

Also true. Two for two. With a sinking feeling about the direction of this conversation, I nodded again.

"Tell me, Bethany. How many of your ex-boyfriends are gay?"

"Just the—" *two*, I started to say. Then I remembered Tad. But that was all—oh. And Richard.

Four?

How was it possible that I had blocked out the glaring reality that my last four beaux had since burst forth from the closet? That was the sort of pattern a girl really ought to notice.

What did this say about me? Was I the kind of girl who only attracted men of uncertain sexuality and repressed urges? Was I a ... closet cleaner?

My face must have fallen because Lydia leaned even closer and smiled sympathetically. "A turner," she repeated. "See what I mean?"

Yes, I did. All too well.

This was probably all my fault. How depressing. Oh, not that I made a conscious decision to only date un-outed gay men, but there must have been signs. Little indications—or big ones, as in the case of Tad's "roommate" in his West Village studio apartment—about a man's true sexuality.

That I had overlooked these signs in the past might mean I

was only looking for unavailable guys. I couldn't get hurt if rejection was beyond my control, right?

Sounded like something a therapist would say.

Deeply psychological.

I read once that girls only sought out men either similar to or the opposite of their fathers. Since none of my exes were the strict, overbearing, ultimatum-giving type, I had to assume I was seeking out the latter.

I sighed, lifted the teacup of English Breakfast with two sugars, and took a fortifying sip. Over the porcelain edge, I caught sight of Evan making his way through the crowded café.

A welcome sight.

"Evan's here," I announced as I set my cup back on its saucer. "He's different. Not a gay bone in his body."

Fiona snorted again but turned with Lydia to get their first look at the new man in my life. Well, he wasn't new to me. We'd been dating for almost six months, but I kept him tightly under wraps. After my previous disasters I'd wanted to wait until I was sure before introducing him to the closest thing to family I had in the city.

Seeing me, Evan waved enthusiastically.

He dressed so well. In a non-gay, purely heterosexual way, of course.

Simple black leather jacket. Flat-front black trousers. Shiny black loafers. Lavender paisley shirt?

I scowled.

Fiona and Lydia exchanged a less-than-inscrutable look before turning back to me.

"Good luck with that," Fiona said.

Lydia added, "I'm so sorry."

I did not need sympathy. Evan wasn't like the others. Lydia had already found her Mr. Perfect. Fiona was working her way through the entire male population of New York before settling on a favorite. And I, despite my questionable track record and my friends' initial impressions, had found mine.

I was certain.

We talked about everything. He made little romantic gestures like leaving a single red rose on my pillow and sending me chocolates at work. The sex was—well, the sex was mediocre at best, but the rest of the relationship more than made up for that lack.

Just as I had that affirming thought Evan reached our table. He came immediately to my side and bowed down to kiss me on the cheek. As he leaned in I noticed the silver and leather jewelry adorning his neck and wrist.

"Evan, I've put a lot of time and effort into you," I said before I could stop myself. "If you turn out gay, I'll castrate you."

ONE

WALK-IN CLOSET WAS DOING OKAY. Not great. Not fantastic. Not an overnight success. But for a relatively new SoHo boutique, it was doing okay.

Two years in business and going strong.

Still, it could be better.

Things could always be better.

If a great windfall fell my direction, I wouldn't step out of the way.

The bell over the front door tinkled just as I finally found a home for a box of shantung neckties in the overcrowded back room. Quickly dusting off my *toile* skirt, I pushed through the sage green damask curtain separating the showroom from the storage to find my mail carrier walking to the counter.

"Good morning, Fred." I smiled even as I cringed at the thought of another delivery. If he had anything bigger than a clutch purse I would have to start turning the boxes into displays.

Or he might have bills. Bills would be worse.

"How was your weekend?" I asked.

Fred answered with a terse, "Fine."

One word responses were his forte.

He was never much for conversation. In fact, in the two years since Walk-In Closet opened, I couldn't think of a single time he had actually spoken more than two words to me. And those were usually, "Sign here."

I only knew his Christian name because Albert, the Saturday mail carrier, was a friendly older gentleman who loved taking the time for a chat. Fred seemed to resent the fact that I had learned and called him by his name, but I took a perverse pleasure in being friendlier than his behavior warranted.

Eventually the honey would sweeten him up.

Without another syllable, he handed over the small stack of envelopes—all disgustingly bill-shaped—and walked back out the door.

Sometimes I felt he would prefer my absence so he could leave my mail on the counter. But I was convinced I must be the only pleasant interaction he got all day and that he needed all the help he could get. One day I would break through that gruff veneer. One day he might even say, golly, *three* words.

A girl can dream.

Quickly flipping through the pile, I saw two bills that absolutely had to be paid by Friday and several more that could be put off another week.

This was not how I had imagined running the store. A financial balancing act between downright necessities and necessary improvements. I downright *needed* to pay the rent. But I also needed to order better quality padded hangers before another careless shopper left the floor around the lingerie display littered with slinky camisoles and lace garter belts.

Footprints didn't wash out of pastel silk.

The SBA loan that jump-started the shop had gotten me the lease and the décor and the initial stock with a little left over for advertising. But that was gone. Now that I *knew* what I needed.

Too soon old, too late wise.

I pulled the portable file tote from beneath the register and filed the vital bills in the "Pay Now" file and the rest under "Pay Someday." The "Pay Now" file was a little plumper in the pants than I last remembered.

With the business bank account hovering precariously above the red, I had to bring in some bill-paying cash soon.

Whenever I needed extra cash flow there was one easy answer. Well, two, but I wasn't about to call and ask my father for help. His opinions on my choice to stay in the city and start my own business rather than return home and marry a nice, successful Southern boy were unequivocal: he would neither forgive nor assist me.

So, it was time to hold another trunk show.

They always brought in a crowd of fashion hunters desperate to get the newest, hottest couture. When they found the perfect piece, they usually bought an item or two from the shop to go with. When they didn't, they usually bought *some*thing from the shop so they didn't leave empty-handed.

Thanks to Lydia's connections, I could always get a Ferrero Couture trunk show when I needed one—occasionally with an appearance by Ferrero himself. And the last one had been nearly four months ago.

Right around the time Evan and I broke up. *Le sigh.*

At least that relationship had dissolved over another woman—not another man.

I had the card for the Tri-State sales rep tacked up in the storeroom. Pushing back through the damask curtain, I hadn't taken two steps into the cardboard maze when the doorbell tinkled again.

I groaned.

At least it couldn't be more bills. Unless one of my creditors had resorted to couriered delivery or repo men.

Maybe it was a customer.

Actually, I noted as I stepped into the showroom, it was two.

A pair of well-dressed-if-a-little-on-the-West-Village-artistic-side men stood inside the doorway, scrutinizing the store. Though Walk-In Closet carried both full men's and women's wear, most of the men's wear was bought by women shopping for men. Hiding my surprise, I stepped forward and greeted them.

"Welcome to Walk-In Closet, gentlemen."

Their attention turned to me, assessing me as avidly as they had the shop.

"My name is Bethany. How can I help you?"

One man, the taller of the two, stepped forward and asked, "You're the owner?"

Not usually the first question out of a customer's mouth.

If not for their generally professional appearances, I might have reconsidered them for repo men.

"Yes," I answered.

They smiled. The tall one nudged the blond one in the ribs.

"I need a shirt," the blond announced.

The tall one nodded in enthusiastic agreement. A well-dressed bobblehead.

"Wonderful," I cooed. Clapping my hands together, I led them to the men's shirts. "What kind of shirt are you looking for?"

"Oh dear," the blond said, "I hadn't thought of that."

This seemed an odd comment from a man who had presumably entered the shop with a purpose. But after two years, very little walked through that door that still surprised me. I'd seen much, *much* stranger things.

"All right. Let's start with type. Dress shirt, sport shirt, or t-shirt?"

The two men looked at each other, conferred for a moment, before deciding on a dress shirt. Making a mental evaluation of the blond's style—youthful, energetic, a little flamboyant—I headed for the latest shirts from Vanny-O, a talented young designer who lived in my building.

I took every opportunity to promote local designers. It had to be good karma to help someone on the way up.

Pulling three of the more colorful designs off the rack, I wagered with myself that he would choose the one with bright yellow, purple, and lilac variegated stripes. I was rarely wrong.

For a moment, when I held the shirts up, his eyes brightened like a schoolboy. Then the thrill banked and he approached my outstretched hand cautiously.

"I'm not sure," he mused, taking the pale green shirt covered with bright turquoise pinwheels and holding it up to his chin. "This seems awfully bold for the office. I'm not sure I could carry it off."

The tall man stifled a snicker.

"Nonsense," I assure him. "Of course you can… I'm sorry, what was your name?"

Small business success hinged on relationships. The first step to creating a relationship with a customer was an open, friendly atmosphere. That was why I always introduced myself by name to new customers and asked their name at the first opportunity.

That was how I had regular customers today who had first walked through my doors two years ago.

"Steven," he answered with a grin.

And that was how I would get and keep Steven as a customer.

"Pleasure to meet you, Steven." I took the pinwheel shirt out of his hands and handed him my choice. "Office fashion is overwhelmingly relaxed these days. Even many professional workplaces have eliminated ties from the dress code. That leaves a man little room for color in his wardrobe. The dress shirt, whether worn with cargo pants, dress cords, or a pinstripe suit, is your canvas. You don't look like a man who's afraid of a little color, now are you, honey?"

Steven beamed. Nearly ripping the hanger from my grasp, he held it beneath his chin and turned to admire himself in the full-length mirror. "What do you think, Trevor?"

The tall one, Trevor, nodded in considered approval. "I think we have a winner, Steven."

Steven clapped his hands in unrestrained glee. "Wonderful." He grabbed Trevor's wrist, pulling him to the mirror. "Now do him!"

Between them, they tried on nearly every item in the shop —including some pieces from the women's collection. By the time Steven and Trevor left, their purchases rang up at nearly three-thousand dollars.

What a way to start a Monday.

Looked like new padded hangers might make the cut. One more sale like that and the new mannequins for the storefront would have a chance, too.

Coming down from the euphoria of an excellent sale, I knew not to let one successful sale eclipse a thin bank account. I still needed an influx of cash if I wanted to pay the bills *and* make all the improvements on my list. Heading once again through the damask drape, I wound my way through the maze of boxes. I finally reached the bulletin board next to the restroom. Just as the doorbell tinkled.

Another customer, I hoped.

Determined not to navigate the maze again, I quickly snagged the business card and tucked it in my only available pocket. My bra.

Back through the boxes and the curtain.

I found the shop empty.

That was strange. I knew I'd heard the bell.

I stepped into the shop, the periwinkle heels of my peep-toe slingbacks clicking on the parquet floor. To my right, a head of tight black curls popped up from behind my display of men's shoes. Followed by a cheery round face I recognized instantly.

"Cassie!" I cried.

"Bethany!"

She darted around the display, throwing her arms around me with abandon when I met her halfway. I returned the hug with equal enthusiasm—though perhaps a bit less abandon. Southern women always show a little restraint.

"Cassie, good Lord," I exclaimed. "What are you doing in New York?"

"Didn't you hear?" she gasped. "I've got a new job."

No, I hadn't heard. And why hadn't she called me?

"In the city?"

She nodded emphatically. "I've been back nearly a week, but haven't had a spare moment outside work. This job is keeping me on my toes."

"I'm glad you found time today."

She bit her lip, the pencil she habitually chewed on noticeably absent. "Actually, this is work, too."

"What do you mean?" I asked.

The last time I saw Cassie Bishop was graduation day at Columbia. Ten years ago. I'd stayed in New York and laid the groundwork for opening Walk-In Closet. She'd headed for California and a career in television.

Over the years she had risen through the ranks from coffee gopher to second assistant production manager to assistant production manager, mostly on soon-canceled TV shows and movies of the week. The jobs weren't always the greatest, but by Hollywood standards she was a resounding success.

Seeing her again made me feel a decade younger than my thirty-two years.

She hadn't changed. Still the same riot of black curls framing her fair, heart-shaped face. Still cherub-cheek-popping bright smile and light blue eyes that sparkled with possibility. Still dressed entirely in black—I had hoped the bright colors of California style might have rubbed off on her just a little bit—not even a pastel accent piece.

At least Hollywood hadn't changed her.

Though we hadn't seen each other in all that time, we had worked hard to keep in touch with more than the occasional email. We spoke on the phone at least once a month.

It felt like we had never been apart.

"What I mean is," she explained as she headed for the floral chintz settee in the corner, "I'm not here for social purposes. This is business."

She collapsed on the settee, grabbing my hand and pulling at me to sit next to her.

"I'm here to offer you a job."

With my legs crossed at the ankles, knees held chastely together, and skirt smoothed into place, I let her guide me down onto the settee.

"A job?" I shook my head at the nonsensical notion. "Cass, I don't know anything about television."

"Of course not, silly," she admonished. "But you *do* know about fashion."

I couldn't argue that point. For the better part of ten years I had been working in fashion retail, even before opening the shop. My resume included a stint as a buyer at Bradford's, a display designer at Louis Jewelers, and a sales associate at more than half a dozen clothing stores.

Since the shop opened I'd kept on top of all the latest, subscribed to all the trade and fashion magazines, even got interviewed once for a small feature in *Lucky* titled "Southern Gals in the City."

But what did that have to do with television?

Cassie tucked one foot behind the opposite knee and turned to face me. Her eyes widened as she settled into a more serious pose.

"Have you heard of *One Straight Guy at a Time*?"

I shook my head.

"It's a new makeover reality show. A cast of five gay guys with various specialties—culture, fashion, cuisine, grooming, decorating—take a disaster dude and turn him into the perfect man. A whole life make-better." She leaned back with a self-satisfied smile. "I'm the production manager."

"How wonderful! Very impressive title."

"It is," she agreed without modesty. "And as production manager I'm in on all the creative meetings. At the last one, the producers and director were talking about outside consultants we need on the show."

I listened carefully, still not sure how this related to me, but happy to see Cassie so enthusiastic about this new job.

"When they said they needed a fashion consultant with loads of real-world experience, I recommended you." She leaned in close. Placing a hand on my shoulder, she explained, "Bethany, they love you. They love your shop. The job is yours. If you want it."

"A job?" I repeated. "As a fashion consultant? What does that mean?"

"It means, babe, that the show pays you for your expertise. For your advice. And, if the contractual agreements with the other consultants are any indication, they'll dress the cast in clothes from your shop whenever you want, list your shop in the opening and closing credits, and use your shop on the show a minimum of four episodes every season."

After the full sixty seconds it took for this information to sink in my lungs failed. I couldn't breathe. Couldn't speak.

This was everything my shop needed. Exposure. Advertising. Customers. *Income.*

This was my windfall, and it fell right in my lap.

My ecstatic shock must have shown on my face because Cassie hugged me close and exclaimed, "We'll have so much fun working together!"

When the doorbell tinkled I barely noticed the UPS man prop the door open and load up his hand truck with boxes.

TWO

"MISS LANGE, welcome to T+S Productions."

From the moment I walked through the rusty steel door of the warehouse occupying the address Cassie had given me, I had been in a state of shock. The entire interior had been renovated and converted into a full-service production studio.

Offices lined the length of an entire wall, their stainless steel doors regularly interrupting the rows of TV and movie posters documenting the studio's moderately illustrious history. High above the polished concrete floor, dozens of lights crowded the massive grid hanging ten feet below the warehouse ceiling, ensuring they could light any area within the several thousand square foot space.

From the front entry, I could see three different television sets: a kitchen I recognized from a popular homemaking show, a news desk belonging to Channel 17 Action News, and a cozy living room with an easy chair and twin loveseats clustered around a low coffee table.

Busy people, dressed mostly in black—no wonder Cassie

hadn't been inspired to break her habit—bustled in every direction, many talking into wireless headsets.

But nothing surprised me more than to turn to the sound of that rugged voice and find Trevor of yesterday's shopping duo addressing me.

"Trevor," I began, unsure how to finish.

"Surprised to see me?" he asked, his rugged features relaxing into a smile. "We had to check you out. You can't blame us for a little subterfuge."

"A little...? You mean Steven works here, too?"

"You could put it that way."

He extended a hand along the bank of offices in a walk-with-me gesture. As we strolled backstage, he explained.

"Steven and I *are* T+S Productions. Our little shopping expedition yesterday was a test."

"A test?" I echoed, even as the light began to dawn.

"We couldn't very well hire a fashion consultant without being certain of her expertise. And to make the test honest, you couldn't know you were being tested."

I pressed my lips together, a long-standing nervous habit that three generations of Lange woman had tried to abolish from my behavior.

"But why? I mean, you didn't have to... All those purchases!"

"Why did we buy so much stuff?" Trevor voiced the question I couldn't. "Because the stuff was fantastic. Because you sold us. Trust me when I say we are finicky about fashion, but you keyed in on all the right elements. You passed the test, Bethany. With flying colors."

"Oh," I exclaimed quietly.

In all my years in retail, I had never felt more proud of

myself. I'd always believed I had a knack for fashion, for finding just the right outfit for any given customer. But validation was a magical thing. I instantly walked a little taller.

We reached the end of the row of offices and Trevor turned down another row of doors—these polished maple with large gold stars at eye level.

"These are our dressing rooms and offices." He tapped the star that read *Avilla* as we passed the first door. "Gives the talent a real kick, like they're big-time movie stars."

I nodded, at the same time thinking that if I were an actor I would want a gold star on my door. What girl didn't want to feel like Grace Kelley?

We passed several racks of clothes—wardrobe pieces—and I marveled at the array of designer clothes. Everything from Armani to Versace to Calvin Klein and back again.

"And this," Trevor announced, drawing my attention away as we approached the last door, "is your office."

Following the wave of his elegantly manicured hand, my gaze landed on the gold star with *Lange* proudly engraved on its shiny surface. My very own star?

"An office?"

"You'll need one," he explained. "Our production schedule is very tight. We'll be shooting three episodes in as many weeks, plus there will be photo shoots and public appearances. We need your input on all of that. And as soon as the press releases go out we'll be bombarded with free wardrobe offers, samples, *bribes*. Anything fashion-related is under your purview—and yours to keep, if it's anything good. I once got season tickets to the Yankees. Unfortunately for that designer I'm a Mets fan."

I laughed nervously.

This sounded a lot more involved than I had imagined. I pictured popping in a couple times a week, ordering clothes, making sure everything arrived on time and fit as expected.

From Trevor's description, this would be a full-time position. I was going to need more help in the shop than the occasional sick day I could con out of Fiona and Lydia. Besides, Fiona usually ended up driving the female customers away and going home with the men.

But with the generous signing bonus the contract included, hiring a sales associate was not a problem. For the thirty-seventh time in the last twenty-four hours I thanked the Lord and Cassie for this opportunity.

Trevor waved me forward. I bravely opened the door to my office—*my* office. The interior was a delicious shade of deep cream, nearly the color of an almond latte, with filigree wallpaper and gold accents.

An antique writing desk stood to one side, a harlequin-upholstered desk chair at the ready. Six valet hooks lined the far wall, beneath wooden letters—A, B, C, D, E, and SG—waiting for the first wardrobe selection for the cast and the pilot episode contestant, I assumed.

I couldn't have designed a lovelier office myself.

"Our design guru is responsible for the décor."

"It's beautiful," I assured him.

"It should be. He's the best."

An expansive vanity mirror on the right wall caught my eye. Surrounded by dozens of round light bulbs it reminded me of the original Max Factor studio rooms Cassie and I had toured on our spring break trip to Los Angeles. Very old school, Hollywood glamour.

"I can't wait to meet him and thank him." And kiss his feet.

"Good." Trevor looked up as a brown-haired man in a royal blue Miles Davis t-shirt appeared in the doorway. "You're about to get the chance. Time to meet the cast."

My heart fluttered.

I hadn't expected to meet them so quickly. I'd hoped for a little time to adjust to my surroundings. To explore the office and maybe get a peek at some of the clothes on those racks outside.

No such luck.

"Bethany Lange," Trevor said by way of introduction, "meet Adam Avilla. Our culture expert."

And with that, Trevor politely excused himself and slipped out of the office, quietly closing the door behind him.

With a deep breath, I realized this must be a sort of test, too. Not to get me in the door, but to make sure I could get along with the guys. And maybe make sure I could keep my head above water in a flash flood.

I steeled myself against nervous panic. These Yanks couldn't find enough water to sink a Lange.

"A pleasure to meet you, Adam." I extended my hand in greeting and stepped forward.

For a long moment he just looked at me, dark brown eyes scanning me from head to toe in evaluation. When those espresso depths—the rich color calling out for earthy greens and beige-y neutrals—returned to meet my expectant gaze, he smiled.

"Nice to meet you, Beth," he said as he took my hand on the pretense of a handshake and lifted it for a kiss instead.

I pegged him instantly as the charmer.

Straightening, he held his arms out wide in a gesture of welcome. "Clothe me as you will."

From Cassie's brief run-down of the show, I knew that his duties entailed broadening the cultural horizons of the Straight Guy. That could involve anything from giving him a lesson on contemporary art to teaching him how to introduce romance in his life. His role seemed like the least defined, but—to me—the most important. He was responsible for making the Straight Guy a better human being.

What could be more important?

But, while I knew what he did on the show I didn't know anything else about him—or the rest of the cast for that matter.

"Before we get to that," I explained, "I'd like to get to know you a little better. Can't dress the outside until I know what's inside."

His brown eyes sparkled.

"Thirty-something Scorpio. Former member of a boy band that shall remain unnamed. Youngest of six children. Favorite color: Blue. Favorite food: Tamales. Favorite Streisand song: *Don't Rain On My Parade*." Adam flopped onto the gold couch next to the desk and folded his arms behind his head. "What else do you need to know?"

Laughing, I leaned one hip against the desk, carefully smoothing the full skirt of my floral sundress. "What else is there?"

"Well, there is a tattoo." He grinned, the very picture of the devil. Then winked as he added, "But I don't think you'll ever be in a position to find it."

"You'd be surprised," I returned. "There isn't much a man can hide from his costumer."

Adam laughed, seemingly surprised that a daring comment or two didn't scare me off. Sometimes it was an advantage to cloak the spitfire beneath a veneer Southern charm.

My unease dissipated and I knew this was going to be a wonderful experience. The cast was just a group of regular guys. And dealing with guys—straight or not—had never been a problem for me.

Dating them? That was trickier.

But handling men was a skill every Southern-bred lady possessed.

A sharp double knock sounded at the door an instant before it burst open. A tall blonde man dressed in burgundy velvet jeans and a pale pink polo shirt over a white oxford stood in the doorway, surveying the room.

His studded belt broke up the preppy tone of the outfit.

"Is this her?" he asked Adam.

"Yeah," he answered. "Cute, isn't she?"

"She's adorable." The blond moved into the room, walking to my side and immediately reaching out to feel the sateen fabric of my dress. "Ooh, high thread count. Anna Tomo?"

"Y-yes, but—"

"Love her new line." He—I still didn't know his name— pouted out his lower lip. "Too bad I can't wear them."

Adam, apparently realizing I had no idea who the man currently petting my clothing was, said, "Beth, this is Bryce Gibler. The fashion expert, if you hadn't guessed."

If Bryce was the fashion expert, then he was the one I would be working with most closely. We would decide together on how to dress the Straight Guy, scout shopping locations for the shoot, and plan how to wardrobe the cast. He would be the on-screen representation of my consulting work, and I could tell he would do it with flare.

"Shame on me," Bryce chastised. "I didn't even introduce myself. Just walked right in and started pawing."

"Sounds like my last date," I joked.

Bryce turned to Adam, grinning deviously. "Oh, I like her."

"Me, too."

"Have I missed the party?"

I turned at the sound of a deep voice. In the doorway stood one of the handsomest men I had ever seen—in real life or otherwise. Tall, broad-shouldered, with nearly-black hair that curled around his forehead and temples in deliciously tempting waves. Dressed in a yummy, distressed denim Western shirt, chocolate brown cords, and brown leather loafers.

My heart swelled.

Then he stepped forward, his pant leg lifting to reveal a sliver of crimson between the browns of his pants and shoes.

My heart deflated.

Months of boning up on the telltale signs of a gay man had led to one undisputed truth: Straight men don't wear colorful socks.

Why were the best looking ones always gay?

Mr. Yummy smiled, the gesture illuminating his crystal blue eyes. My heart threatened to re-inflate. I punctured it with a sharp pin.

"Chris Thompson," he said, extending his hand in greeting. "Food and wine."

Cast member number three. *Gay* cast member number three.

Forcing air in and out of my lungs—no call for going all breathless over a man as openly unavailable as that—I pasted on my best steel magnolia smile. "Bethany Lange. Fashion consultant."

His hand was warm and strong and it took all of my strength not to visibly swoon.

"A pleasure."

For a brief second, he held my hand, his eyes burning into me. I had to resist the urge to fan myself. Then Chris shook his head and, holding only my fingertips, daintily shook my hand before dropping it like last year's hemline.

"Can I make one request?" he asked.

Anything, my mind screamed. "Certainly."

"Make sure everything I wear is stain resistant." His eyes sparkled like a little boy proud of the havoc was about to cause. "I tend to get a little messy in the kitchen."

I smiled politely, but my eyes lost focus. I remembered an old wives tale Fiona had once told me about men who made a mess with food. Which led to an image of Chris making a mess in my kitchen. Then gasped as the fantasy progressed to Chris, chocolate sauce, and a can of whipped cream hovering over my body.

No, no, no, no, no. No!

Four gay exes was more than enough for any girl to claim. At least none of them had been openly gay before I dated them. Only after. Not a terribly cheerful thought, but it was something.

Lusting after a man already out of the closet, however, was a new low. Even for me.

I tried to focus on work.

Chris was the food expert. His primary duty included teaching the Straight Guy how to prepare a meal. On any given episode, though, he might recommend a good wine, give the guy a lesson on world cheeses, or share the secrets to a perfect ice cream sundae.

My mind snapped back to the whipped cream image.

What if—

No! Off limits, even to fantasies.

I had just admonished myself with the final word on the subject when Bryce called out, "Danial, get your tight little butt in here."

"You called, My Queen?"

The brunette in the doorway looked like a cross between a Hell's Angel and a Calvin Klein model. Black biker boots. Tight black leather pants. Tight white t-shirt that sculpted every inch of muscle on his upper body.

If his meticulously spiked hair was any indication, he was the grooming expert.

He would see to the Straight Guy's hair and skin—getting him a flattering haircut, addressing specific skin care issues, and teaching the guy how to shave properly. His mission was to eradicate razor burn and spread hair product throughout the world.

"Act like a gentleman and introduce yourself," Bryce chastised. "This is our fashion consultant."

"Bethany," I offered. "Bethany Lange."

"Danial-with-an-A Malino. Stylist of the stars."

"Maybe Starr Jones," Adam teased.

Chris laughed and added, "Or Ringo Starr."

I fought the urge to melt at the sexy rumble of his laughter.

"Hey," Danial argued, "Ringo has excellent shaft health."

Bryce pursed his lips and tsked. "I'll bet he does."

Unable to hold it in, I burst out laughing along with the

rest of them. Mother always told me ladies didn't laugh out loud in public, but she'd never met this group of guys.

"Thank God you've got a sense of humor." Bryce walked over to the vanity mirror and pushed a stray lock of blonde into place. "Otherwise we'd be sunk."

"Might be anyway," Chris said as he lowered into the desk chair and swung back and forth. "Where's Evie?"

"She was right behind me," Danial said.

I saw Bryce's focus in the mirror shift before he instructed, "Look in the doorway, silly."

We all turned to the doorway.

I gasped.

Behind me, Chris started to introduce us. "Bethany, this is our interior designer, E—"

But his introduction was unnecessary because we were already acquainted. *Well* acquainted.

Suddenly my dream job was looking like a nightmare.

Sucking up a breath of courage, I forced a humorless smile. "Hello, Evan."

THREE

"THAT'S *YOUR* EVAN?" Cassie exclaimed.

"Well," I said diplomatically, not looking up from stirring every last sugar crystal into my tea, "not anymore."

"Don't be obtuse. You know what I mean."

I sighed over my plate.

"Yes, unfortunately I do."

Cassie chugged the remains of her triple shot café Americano. I set my teaspoon on a napkin and lifted the sweet tea to my lips. I could almost hear the gears creaking into motion in her mind.

"Didn't David—"

"Yes," I preempted.

"Oh." She removed the lid and licked the watered-down droplets of coffee. "And wasn't Jon—"

"Yes."

"Oh." Grabbing my teaspoon off the table, she swirled it around the bottom of her cup, scooping up the last half-ounce sitting in the crease. "And Tad—"

"Yes!" I plunked my glass on the table with a resounding

clack. "Yes, David and Jon and Tad and Richard. All gay. Can we just establish that fact and move on, because this is not exactly my favorite topic of conversation."

I tried—really, I did—never to lose my temper. But I was at the end of my tether. Four gay exes was bad enough, but now the one straight guy in my recent romantic history was passing himself off as gay on national TV. I was not exactly in a restrained mood.

Shocked by my outburst—a rarity she had only witnessed one other time in our fourteen years of friendship—Cassie stared at me, lip gloss-less mouth agog. Her bright blue eyes sparkled and I knew she was thrilled by my emotional exhibition.

Cassie was the sort who thought it wasn't healthy to keep anything bottled up inside—which may explain why she'd always had a tough time hanging onto a job for more than a few months. She'd been waiting years for me to pop my cork.

"Lord, Cassie." I gingerly rubbed my pounding temples, desperate to quell the ache that had begun the moment Evan Riley walked into my office. "I'm sorry, I just can't—"

"Whoah! Don't apologize." She waved off my explanation. "You have every right to be upset."

That didn't dilute my guilt. I had no reason to yell at her when she was only trying to be supportive.

"I mean if even *one* of my exes popped out of the closet before my eyes," she continued in the rapid-fire, New Yorker way she always did, "I'd punch him in the nose. Knock his little gay lights out. You two were so serious, Evan could've had the decency to call or—"

"Wait a minute," I interrupted. She was missing the most important point. "Evan isn't gay."

Taken aback, she blinked three times and froze. "What do you mean he isn't gay? He's on a gay makeover show and—"

"I don't care if he's the LGBT poster child. Evan Riley is not gay. He cheated on me with another woman."

Despite his slightly-too-fashionable taste in clothing, Evan had been all man in our relationship. He watched football. He talked about cars. He was a thoughtful and considerate lover. And if he hadn't started cheating on me with some bimbo from his fledgling design firm we would be halfway to the altar by now.

He'd even *confessed* to the affair.

But there was a more recent reason to believe he was faking. "He denied our relationship."

"What do you mean?"

"I mean when the rest of the cast saw we were already acquainted and asked how we knew each other, he lied."

Cassie leaned in conspiratorially. "What did he say?"

"That he had decorated my shop."

She blinked. "He did."

"*Yes*, but he implied that our relationship was *purely* professional." In truth, it had started out personal and become professional when I needed an interior designer for my shop—I couldn't have afforded one otherwise. "Don't you see? Why else would he deny our past? He wants to hide the truth from the producers. He must be getting a pretty good deal for himself and his firm with this show. He'd have a lot to lose if he was inned. They'd probably fire him on the spot."

"Bethany, sweetie, maybe he's just—"

"No. Evan Riley is heterosexual." I grabbed my purse from the floor and pushed out of my chair. "He's faking gay. And I'm going to prove it."

♥

"HAVE you worked in retail apparel before?"

The too-young girl with blue hair and a silver hoop through the fullest part of her bottom lip shook her head, jangling the mass of jewelry decorating her left ear.

"No, but I used to work at this shop in the Village that sold latex bondage costumes and studded dog collars."

Not precisely the same clientele that patronized my shop. Mentally wording my response, I carefully nudged the stack of applications into a neat pile.

"Thank you for interviewing—" I checked the name on the application "—Tegan. I have your application and should make my decision by the end of the week."

The left side of her mouth pulled back in a smile-smirk. "Yeah, whatever."

As she walked out the front door I released a sigh of relief. That was the fourth interview of the day. They had *all* been equally unsuitable.

One barely spoke above a whisper. Another knocked over two displays on her way to the counter. And another could only work from eight to ten in the morning to fit around her meditation schedule.

I guess I shouldn't have expected any less for putting up a *Help Wanted* sign in the window. The foot traffic in this part of SoHo was either affluent shoppers with no interest in something as demeaning as gainful employment or neighborhood residents on the bizarre side of artistic with little experience in upscale retail.

Trying not to bang my head on the glass countertop in frustration, I reached beneath the register and pulled out the

Yellow Pages. Flipping to the Employment Agencies section, I thumbed through looking for a firm that staffed retail.

There was no other option. Time was running out and I needed to train a full-time employee/manager before the show went into production. I had already closed the store three mornings this week to order samples for the pilot wardrobe. What good was this opportunity to promote my shop for free if it went under in the process?

Starting next week I would need to be at the studio from eight to five, Monday through Friday for two weeks straight. If I didn't have a reliable employee by then, Walk-In Closet was sunk.

The doorbell jingled, and I looked up from perusing the tiny print.

"Chris," I exclaimed, his familiar handsome face welcome after the stream of strangers that had been dropping off applications all morning. "What brings you into my neck of the woods?"

His face broke into a genuine smile, with little craggy laugh lines around his eyes and dimples in his cheeks.

Le sigh.

In the few days we'd known each other, Chris and I had become fast friends. He called daily to bounce off ideas for his segment of the pilot. I called to complain about the mass of emails and phone calls I'd had to field—Trevor had been right about the offers and samples and bribes, but he'd underestimated the volume. Chris and I had met for lunch or coffee several times, usually near the studio.

He had become a regular presence in my life.

One I only wanted more of. In all the wrong ways.

"Wanted to check out my favorite girl's place of business."

He moseyed into the shop, his long-legged strides bringing him to the counter in three steps. "Nice digs."

"Thank you," I replied.

His arm slipped around my waist in a comforting embrace.

I laid my head on his broad shoulder. "Hope I can keep her afloat."

He leaned down to look me in the eye. "What do you mean?"

"I mean,"—I extricated myself from his embrace and returned to the phone book—"if I can't find someone to run the shop, she'll either close or I'll have to quit *One Straight Guy.*"

Chris scowled, distinguished worry lines forming between his brows. "Neither."

"What?" I asked distractedly as I found a staffing firm that fed from the Fashion Institute. Surely their students knew their way around a retail shop. I jotted down their number on the pink pad next to the register.

"I choose neither option," Chris continued.

"Me too," I agreed. "But I may not have a choice."

"I've got it!" He clapped his hands together in an excited outburst.

The joy in his clear blue eyes instantly filled me with spontaneous hope. "Got what?"

"The perfect solution. Here, give me the phone." He took it from me before I could hand it over.

Quickly dialing a number without uttering another word, Chris winked at me as he waited for an answer.

"Hey, it's me," he said familiarly. "Can you come to Walk-In Closet, at the corner of Prince and Wooster, right away?" He paused, listening. "Just come already. I'll be waiting for you." He rolled his eyes. "Fine. Just hurry. Love you, too."

My heart plummeted. Yes, I knew Chris was gay. Yes, I knew I had less than no chance. But still, knowing there was someone he loved on the other end of that line drove the nail home in my heart.

Le sigh again.

Chris closed the phone book and threw away my note with the Fashion Staffing phone number.

"Your salvation will walk through that door in under five minutes." He looked extraordinarily proud of himself. Dimples deeper than I'd ever seen them. "While we're waiting you can show me around."

His joy was infectious, I couldn't stop grinning as I gave him the ten cent tour—including the disaster area that was the back room. I had just tripped over a carton of cashmere socks, sending me flying into Chris's sturdy arms, when the doorbell jangled.

"Ah," he sighed like a Chinese monk, "interrupted by salvation."

A woman, foot impatiently tapping on the parquet floor, stood waiting by the counter. Fully expecting to see Chris's boyfriend, I was shocked to find a woman waiting. If a dinosaur had walked into my shop and asked to try on a pair of size thirty-six stilettos I couldn't have been more surprised.

I shook my head. She was a customer. I was about to tell Chris that salvation must be late when he jogged forward and swung the woman up in an embrace.

In return, the woman kicked him in the shins.

"Ow, Kit," he cried, dropping her and bending over to rub his injured legs. "That hurt."

"Good," the brunette replied. "Why did you order me down here? You dating the owner, or something?"

"*This* is the owner." His voice was tightly laced with warning. "*She's* the wardrobe consultant on the *show.*"

"Oh," Kit said, then added with feeling, "Ohhhh."

I wondered at this strange interchange, but stopped short when Chris turned to me and made his introductions.

"Bethany, meet my angelic baby sister, Katherine Marie." Throwing a glare her way, he continued, "Kit, this is Bethany Lange."

His sister. Of course! The resemblance was obvious. Same dark curls, same clear blue eyes, same dimpled cheeks. But there was a little more of a hard edge to Kit than her brother could ever claim.

This was a woman who could—and would—kick butt without conscience.

A good person to have on your side, but heaven help anyone who wasn't on hers.

We met halfway, shook hands, and exchanged confused looks. Neither of us knew what exactly was going on. The cryptic nature of men defied the bounds of gender.

"Bethany's looking for a full-time sales associate to run the shop while she's working on the show. Interested?"

Kit looked from her brother to me and back again. "This is about a job?" She smacked him hard on the shoulder. "Why didn't you say so? I would've pulled on something more presentable than jeans and a T-shirt."

"Actually," I interjected, "I carry the entire line."

Following the wave of my hand, Kit eyed the Thalia Rose display. I only had one tee left in the same pale teal she wore—

and an extra small at that—and had been waiting weeks for a restock shipment. Clearly, she had an eye for trends.

Her face relaxed into a dazzling smile, another feature she shared with her brother.

"Miss Lange, I—"

"Please, call me Bethany."

"Okay, Bethany." She clasped her hands in front of her. "I worked at a retail chain for six years after college, earning my way up to associate manager. Three months ago, when upper management basically confessed that I could never climb any higher in the ranks without upper management experience, I quit. Can't stand hypocritical catch-22's. I know how to run a store; everything from stocking to managing shipments to working the sales floor. If you need someone to rely on, I'm your girl."

What a sales pitch. If she could sell clothes half as well as she sold herself, the shop would be out of inventory within a month.

Bottom line: I was desperate, she had the qualifications, and I trusted Chris.

"When can you start?"

Rather than answer, Kit leaped forward and pulled me into a joyful hug. "You won't regret this."

Over her head of brunette curls, I met Chris's proud eyes. He smiled in silent thanks—as if I were doing him a favor rather than the other way around. No, I shook my head, and mouthed, "Thank *you*."

💜

"I DON'T WANT A DOZEN," I argued into the phone. This was

like arguing with a tree stump. "I want one. Just one. Medium. In gray."

Lord, I'd been on the phone for an hour. After scouring catalogs and websites and magazines in my studio office I had finally found the perfect jacket for Adam to wear in the pilot. Dove gray. Surf-inspired with a skater twist. Simple, stylish, and 100% cotton twill. Perfect for Adam's edgy-but-polished personality.

If only the man from the surfwear company would let me order one. Instead, he insisted on sending me a dozen. For free. I insisted I only wanted one, though the free part was entirely acceptable.

Finally, giving up, I said, "Fine, send a dozen. But only one will be worn on the show."

"Excellent, Betty," he drawled, sounding like a Southern California stereotype.

With only the greatest restraint, I stopped my face just inches from colliding with my desk. A lady does not walk around with a big red impact splotch on her forehead.

"Tough day at work, sugar?"

Yes, but it just got a whole lot better.

"Hello, Chris," I managed with a resilient smile.

He moved his long-legged form across my office and fell into one of the chairs in front of my desk. "Tell me all about it."

"Well, let's see ... We start shooting the opening montage for the pilot next week and so far you've each got about half a wardrobe."

His blue eyes glittered with mischief when he asked, "Which half?"

"For you? The bottom."

"That's okay," he assured me. Then proceeded to lift up the

front of his navy blue sweater, revealing his sculpted abs. "I have a fabulous chest."

Lord, I knew it. We had a fitting session the day before and I'd gotten to know Chris's body in almost every intimate detail. There wasn't a single inch I hadn't drooled over or dreamed about.

How on earth a chef—a profession rumored to have the highest obesity rate of any field since taste-testing was virtually a job requirement—wound up with the body of an Olympic swimmer, I had no idea.

It was a cruel, cruel joke on the unsuspecting heterosexual female population of the planet.

"Put that six-pack away," I teased. "There are ladies present."

He lurched out of his seat and spun in a head-first survey of the room. "Where?"

"Very funny. Shouldn't you be out hunting down the perfect wine or ordering fresh goat cheese from Outer Mongolia?"

"They don't have goat cheese in Mongolia," he replied as if I'd been serious. "Most of their dairy comes from sheep or mare's milk."

Hmmm. Interesting. But not relevant.

I rolled my eyes—*not* a ladylike reaction, but one I surrendered to often.

"You are such a food geek."

Chris grabbed a pad of sticky notes off my desk and threw it at my head.

"Deny it all you like." I returned my attention to the towering stack of catalogs. "Doesn't make it any less true."

To my great surprise, he let out a plaintive sigh.

"I know. Kit's been trying to get me to broaden my interests for twenty-five years."

"Isn't she twenty-six?"

"Yeah, but for that first year she couldn't talk." He leaned back in the chair, arms folded behind his head and face softened in blissful memory. "I miss the peace and quiet."

"I'll tell her you said that."

His eyes snapped to mine, clearly hoping I wasn't serious.

I rolled my eyes again and thumbed through glossy pages full of polos and dress shirts. "Did you come in here just to bother me," I asked in a bored tone, "or did you have a particular reason?"

"Oh yeah." He sat forward in his seat and leaned his elbows on the desk. "Wanna go out tonight?"

My heart nearly leaped out of my chest.

Every fantasy of the last few days exploded like fireworks in my brain. Going out—on a date—with Chris—tonight. Images of chocolate sauce and whipped cream filled my mind.

For about half a second.

Then I remembered ... Chris was gay.

Double drat.

FOUR

"GO OUT?" Eyes glued to a two-page spread of candy-colored T-shirts, I kept my voice as detached and reasonable as possible. Fairly difficult considering my near heart attack of just moments ago.

"Yeah," he explained enthusiastically, "some of the cast and crew are going to the Red Hook. Wanna come?"

My heart started pumping again and I wasn't sure if I was relieved or disappointed.

The Red Hook Brewery, an ancient institution in this part of Brooklyn, was just around the corner from the studio. I had a feeling many Friday nights would begin at their famous two dollar Happy Hour.

Beer wasn't really my thing—more like Mojitos or Mint Juleps—fine, I'd never actually *had* a Mint Julep, but as a Southern woman I felt honor bound to list that as a favorite—but a night out sounded like a good idea.

"Sure. I have a few more calls to make first."

"Great," Chris said as he jumped up from the chair. "Swing

by my dressing room when you're ready. We can head over early and get a good table."

Just to get one last tease in, I called out, "Which room was that again?"

He turned in the doorway, lifting his sweater once again as he backed out into the hall. Patting his stomach, he returned, "Just follow the sound of the washboard."

With a wink and a grin he was gone.

And I collapsed in a heap of hormones onto my desk.

I needed therapy. The kind they advertised, thinly veiled as a "dating service," in the back pages of the Village Voice along with pictures of bondage equipment and remote controlled massagers. I'd never thought four months was too long to go without, but considering the recent direction of my thoughts, my situation was obviously desperate.

Because only a desperate woman would knowingly lust after a physiologically unavailable man.

The phone rang, saving me from dragging out the phone book and looking up escort services.

"Hi Bethany," the extra-cheery voice on the other end of the line said, "it's Kit."

"Hey Kit, is something wrong?"

"No," she denied immediately, "of course not. I'm calling to give you a report."

"Great."

In the week since Kit had taken over running the day-to-day at Walk-In Closet, she had turned the store upside-down. In a good way.

The first day she had called to see if she could rearrange the displays. *Just a little.* When I stopped in to check on things that night, she had swapped sides with the men's and women's collections, giving the men's wear more floor space and setting it closer to the register. A logical choice considering all the upcoming free advertising for that side.

The new layout put the women's wear on the side with the tri-fold full-length mirror. A definite plus.

The second day she had called to see if she could sort the stock in the back room. *Just a little.* When I stopped by, I found the piles of boxes in the back room organized into neat, navigable rows, categorized, and clearly labeled.

She even found a missing box of cufflinks that represented nearly $5,000 worth of merchandise.

When she called the third day I answered with, "Do whatever you want, Kit. You're a genius."

I should have hired her two years ago. Walk-In Closet would probably be a nation-wide chain by now.

"Go ahead," I said. "I'm listening."

She ran through a quick accounting of the week's sales, the shipments that had come in, and the stock we needed to order. But when she finished her review, I sensed some hesitation. Like she hadn't really said everything she wanted to say.

"And that's it, I guess ..." she concluded.

"Is there something else?"

"Well, no," she said—I could almost hear her sucking on her lip. "Not really."

"Please, Kit. If there's a problem just tell me about it—"

"No, no," she interrupted. "It's nothing like that. It's just ..."

"Yes?"

She hesitated again, as if steeling her courage. "I think you should hire another sales associate."

"What?" I exclaimed. "You're quitting already? I thought you liked working—"

"No! Of course I'm not quitting," she hurried to reassure me. "I just think that if you hire another salesperson, so the shop can be open more hours, it would be worth the investment."

More than a little relieved, I considered her suggestion. At the moment, the shop was open Tuesday through Friday from ten until six and Saturday from ten until two. That way it hit the prize-hunting housewives, the just-off-from-work executives, and the weekend wanderers.

Granted, it was less than forty hours a week, but that was mainly because when the shop first opened I had maintained a part-time job until things took off. And when they did, I never bothered to change it.

"You're absolutely right. I'll take care of it as soon as I have time. Maybe early next week—"

"I can take care of it for you," she offered. "It's no problem, really. And I have a few friends at Parsons who might be interested in some part-time hours." Then, as if she felt she'd overstepped her bounds, added, "If that's okay with you, of course."

"Actually, it's a relief." Glancing at the piles of catalogs on my desk and thinking of the wardrobe I still had to pull together by Friday, I might not have had time until next March. "Kit, you're the best thing that ever happened to Walk-In Closet."

I could almost hear her beaming through the phone.

"And you're the best thing that's ever happened to—" She stopped short, like she was going to say something and then changed her mind. "Me. To me."

"Then it's a perfect arrangement."

I signed off, saying I'd be in tomorrow for the Saturday shift. Kit couldn't work *every* day of the week.

Chris popped his head back in my office as I hung up the phone. "Com'on Lange," he whined. "Let's go before the place is packed."

"Okay, okay," I relented.

Grabbing my purse, I gave one last longing glance at the mile-long *To Do* list before heading out the door.

"Finally." As I passed him, he reached out and pinched my waist. "Maybe you won't have to sit on my lap after all."

My cheeks burned.

If only that were a reward and not a punishment.

♥

"I USED to dress up my sister's dolls," Bryce explained in answer to a question about how he got involved in fashion. "She had the best-dressed Barbies in Flushing."

We—the entire cast, two cameramen, an electrician, a sound guy, and I—sat at a trio of tables pushed into one long surface in the back corner of the brewery. It was not lost on me that I was the only female in attendance.

From my seat at the head of the table, I could see everyone clearly. Chris and Bryce sat to my direct left and right, with Danial and Adam beyond them. Evan sat next to Danial—furthest from me without being drawn into the cluster of techies at the far end.

Emboldened by a strong Mojito—I'd been overwhelmingly relieved to discover they served more than beer—I watched Evan dubiously. Not that my gaydar was known for its reliability, but even expecting him to look gay he just ... didn't.

Dressed in a white button-down and khakis, he could pass for any of a dozen investments bankers in the brewery, just off work and throwing back a few to relax. He didn't have on eyeliner. Didn't add a lisp to every other word. Didn't even bat his eyes at the cute waiter who brought our drinks—whom Bryce made a production of flirting with.

My conviction deepened. Evan was not gay.

This was a scam. He was pulling one over on me, the cast and crew, and—if the show took off—all of America. This was about more than my embarrassing dating record. This was about justice.

I was the only one who knew the truth first hand and I couldn't let him get away with it. It was up to me to uncover evidence of his lies.

A woman in a miniskirt, ass barely concealed from view, walked by and—I swore—his gaze followed her across the room. No one else noticed. But I saw him checking her out.

Gotcha.

Now I had to prove it to the world.

"Whaddya say, Beth?"

At Chris's question, I tore my studious gaze away from Evan the liar. "I'm sorry. What?"

"I was saying maybe we could all wear matching sequined tux jackets, like Liberace."

"Oh. Well, I— I mean— Um—"

"It was a joke." Chris turned and looked at the rest of the cast. "We really need to lighten her up."

"We can start with highlights," Adam chimed in. "I'm dying to get my hands on those virgin locks."

"They're about the only virgin thing at this table." Bryce downed the remains of his scotch and soda before signaling the waiter for another. His eyes drifted to the far end of the table. "Or maybe not."

The sound guy responded by throwing an ice cube at Bryce, who in turn pulled open the first three buttons of his bright striped shirt and shouted, "Come on, baby. Do it again."

With a dismissive wave of his hand, the sound guy went back to his conversation about why wireless body mics were the greatest invention since celluloid.

I watched as Evan's face turned several shades of crimson. He abruptly pushed back from the table.

"Hey guys, sorry to cut it short," he explained as he shrugged into his leather jacket. "Just remembered something I gotta do. Catch you later."

Without further fanfare, he practically ran from the building.

My gaze narrowed. What was that all about?

They'd been joking around about my hair and a general lack of virginity and— Wait. That had to be it. The topic of sex had reminded him of our relationship and he'd had to bolt before they all found out he was really hetero.

"I have to go, too," I announced. Grabbing my purse, I quickly made my excuse. "Gotta check on the shop. Bye."

I was halfway back to the studio—and my waiting car— when Chris caught up with me.

"Hey, what was that all about?"

I tried to brush him off lightly. "I just have to go, alright. I'll see you Monday."

But he wasn't so easily deterred. "I know you don't have to

check on the shop," he continued as he fell in step beside me. "Kit went home half an hour ago."

"Right. Well. Still need to do, um, inventory."

"Bethany, what's going on?"

"Nothing, I just—" Stopping to look into his clear blue eyes I couldn't keep up the lie. But I couldn't tell him the truth, either. "I just have to go. Now. Okay?"

His gaze searched my face for a moment, as if weighing my plea. My skin heated under his scrutiny. What a time for my hormones to kick in; when I'm on the trail of a hetero pretending to be gay and fleeing from a gay guy for whom I'd drop my drawers in a heartbeat.

"Okay," he agreed, his face softening as if deciding to allow me my secrets.

"I'm sorry," I felt compelled to say as I started backward, covering the last few feet to my bright blue VW Beetle.

"No problem." He smiled brightly, though I could tell he still felt slighted. "Catch ya later."

Seconds later I was in my car and circling the area looking for Evan. I finally spotted him descending into the Carroll Street subway station. Diving my car to the curb, I threw it into park and hurried to follow him down the steps.

Reaching the platform level as he pushed through the turnstile, I whipped out my MetroCard, only realizing as the train pulled into the station that Evan was catching the Brooklyn bound F train. Away from his Manhattan apartment.

Head hung in thought—or, I hoped, shame—Evan stepped through the shiny silver doors and dropped into a plastic seat. Deciding not to risk being seen, I stepped on board the next car, watching him through the connecting doors.

The cars were half full of long-houred executives and

about-to-party twenty-somethings. At each stop, there were fewer execs and more partiers.

When the train pulled into the 15th Street/Prospect Park station, Evan rose. I followed him off the train, remaining a good twenty feet behind him at all times. At street level, he turned left and headed down the residential street.

Memory hit me in a flash. His mother lived in Park Slope. I watched him hurry up the steps of a white, clapboard house and open the front door. Even from half a block away I heard him call out, "Mom, I'm home."

Lord, I felt like a fool.

Certain I'd been tracking him to a secret tryst with his female love, logic had fallen by the wayside.

That didn't mean I was wrong though.

Evan Riley was *not* gay, and if I had to follow him home every night I would prove it. To myself, if no one else. I needed to know the truth. I couldn't pinpoint why it felt so critical, but I couldn't let him get away with the deception. I couldn't live with the doubt of forever wondering… what if I was wrong. I couldn't live with that fifth and fatal flaw on my dating history.

Slinking back into the subway, I only hoped I didn't make such a fool of myself every time.

Beep. I looked down at the turnstile card reader. Swiping my card through again, I got another *beep* in return. Great, I'd wasted the last of my MetroCard on a fruitless enterprise. What else could go wro—

That's when I felt the tug. A brief pull against my left shoulder. And *whoosh*, my purse was gone.

Before I could react, the little punk had hopped the turnstile and slipped through the closing doors of the train.

"Hey!" I shouted futilely at the departing train, pushing against the stubborn turnstile.

Shrinking back, I stared at the empty MetroCard in my hand, as if it was to blame. "Drat."

I started to throw it to the ground, but remembered that it might have something just under the two dollar fare left on the strip. It was all I had left. "Drat, drat."

"Miss," a static-y voice called across the station lobby. "Hey Miss, you need some help?"

Thank the Lord for the MTA.

"Yes," I declared, moving over to the dirt-stained window of the teller booth, a bright smile pasted on my face to hide the tears pooling beneath the surface. "That punk stole my purse."

The older man behind the counter smiled sympathetically. "This neighborhood is going downhill fast. Young lady can't even catch the subway without getting mugged." He picked up the telephone. "I'll call up to 7th Avenue. Most times they ditch the purse at the next stop."

Aldus, as his name tag read, chatted with the attendant at the next station for far longer than necessary in the given situation. But I kept myself from protesting since he was doing me a favor.

"Good news, Miss," he announced. "Jacqui has your purse. And the patrolman has your mugger."

I smiled gratefully, thanked Aldus, and headed up the steps to street level.

"Hold on," he called after me. "Where you going?"

"Oh, my MetroCard is empty," I explained. It wasn't too far to the next station. I could make it in my kitten-heeled mules. "I'll walk."

"Nonsense." Aldus waved me toward the gate used by

moms with strollers. "You get yourself on the train that's pulling into station in precisely forty-three seconds."

"Thank you, Aldus." I smiled as he buzzed me through, more relieved than I let on at not having to walk. "You're an angel. If there weren't bulletproof glass between us, I'd kiss you."

"If I weren't happily married, I'd let you."

By the time the train arrived, I had decided that next time I followed Evan I would have to be more organized. Implement some kind of strategy, a systematic surveillance that commenced every night when we left the studio. I would be in my car, ready, before he walked out the door. My cup holder would be full of coins for the parking meters. I would use every last ounce of my persistence and planning ability to catch him in the proverbial act.

No more spontaneity.

Spontaneous stalking just got me ticketed and mugged.

THREE HOURS, a trip to the police station, and six parking tickets later—thanks to leaving my car in the *No Parking Zone* in front of the subway entrance—I pulled into the garage around the corner from my building and lowered my head onto the steering wheel. Ten o'clock on a Friday night and I was worn out and looking forward to a long hot bath and the welcoming softness of my featherbed.

But all calming thoughts fled when I pushed open my apartment door and found every light on.

Eighteen years of Daddy's threats about owning stock in

the electric company had taught me to turn everything off before leaving each morning.

Setting my purse—thankfully complete with all the cash and credit cards I'd left the house with that morning—on the side table by the door, I pulled out my cell phone. I had just dialed 9-1 when I heard the twangy strains of bluegrass music filter through the apartment.

I'd never owned a bluegrass album in my life. What kind of thief brought his own music? The only person I even knew who listened to that hillbilly garbage was—

"Hey Bets. What's shakin'?"

"Randy!" I shrieked and dropped my phone. Heart pounding, I threw a stern glare at the lanky figure emerging from my bedroom. Marching across the apartment, I planted myself in front of him and shoved a finger at his chest. "What the hell are you doing here?"

"These Yanks teach you that language?" he threw back, equally reproachful.

We stared at each other for a ten count—each daring the other to blink—before I gave up and flung myself into his arms.

"Lord, I've missed you!"

"If it'll get you off my neck," he teased, faking disgust at my embrace, "then I'll say I missed you, too, sis."

He gave up the pretense and returned my hug. It had been three years since I last saw him. Three years since that Christmas when Daddy told me that if I wasn't coming home for good, I shouldn't come home at all. Three years that had changed this boy into a man.

Then again, three years with Daddy would age anyone. No wonder the boyish softness and the naivety had disappeared.

"Oh, shrimp, you've grown so much." This on top of every-thing else I'd been through pushed me over the edge. Through welling tears, I chastened, "But you haven't answered my question. What are you doing here? And how did you get in?"

"Your neighbor took pity on me waiting in your hall."

I needed to have a talk with Mrs. Franklin about the spare key I'd given her for emergencies. Letting in strangers found lurking around the hall did not qualify.

"Randy ..." I warned as I wiped at the tears spilling from my eyes.

His face cracked in a grin that reassured me he was still a boy inside. "I've run away from home."

"Lord, no," I cried, and I was sure my face fell, "Dad'll kill me."

FIVE

RANDY HAD NEVER BEEN AWAY from home for more than the duration of a spring break trip to Mazatlan. At twenty-four, it was high time, but running all the way to New York?

I was hesitant, to say the least.

"Have you told Mom and Daddy yet?" I handed him a tall glass of sweet tea and moved to sit beside him on the floral sofa.

"I left a note."

Swallowing a groan, I smacked him on the back of the head instead. "A note? You leave home for New York City without so much as an ounce of warning, and you leave a *note*?"

"What?" He blinked his wide, green eyes innocently. "Not good enough?"

If I hadn't been so happy to see him, I might have been more upset. I was about to relieve his concern, to assure him that everything would turn out okay, when my phone rang.

And I had the tiniest idea who it might be.

Gingerly holding it several inches from my ear I pressed the talk button.

"Hello?"

"My Gawd, Bethany," my mother screamed into the phone, "Randy's gone. Vanished without a trace."

Leave it to Mom to overreact.

"Mom, it's fine, he's—"

"We got home from the club and called him to dinner, but he never came."

"Mom, he's—"

"So your father went up to his room and he wasn't there."

"I know, Mom, he's—"

"Randall James Lange!" Daddy's booming voice echoed through the phone line.

I turned my best you're-in-so-much-trouble-you-won't-be-able-to-walk-for-a-week scowl on my angelic brother. Sounded like Daddy had found the note.

As if he weren't already mad enough at me.

"Is your brother with you?" he asked when he commandeered the phone.

"Yes, Daddy."

The sound of my whining, obliging voice turned my stomach. I took the phone and swung it repeatedly at my head, stopping a mere millimeter away each time. Why did I always become a simpering doormat around him? Maybe someday I would outgrow my instinctive reaction to metaphorically kneel before my father.

So far, on the one occasion I had ever stood up to him for what I really wanted he had practically disowned me.

"What is it, Franklin?" I heard Mom ask in the background.

"That no good son of yours up and flew to New York." The disgust in his tone was unmistakable. He drew out the end like it made his lip curl. New *Yaw*-ark.

Making eye contact with Randy, I clenched my fist and shook it at him. Why did he have to go and involve me in his bid for independence? I had enough problems of my own.

Mom's scream broke the silence.

I could almost picture her collapsing onto the settee and fanning herself with whatever she could find. If smelling salts had still been in vogue—she constantly lamented the disappearing art of "having the vapors"—she'd have had a little bottle in every pocket.

"My boy, my boy, oh my dear, sweet boy," she chanted.

"Put him on the phone," Daddy commanded.

It was not a request.

I held out the phone, shrugging helplessly at the accusatory look Randy gave me. I was not about to make this stand for him. This was his rebellion.

I was still suffering for mine.

Hey, maybe if Daddy were mad enough at Randy, I would be back in his good graces. That always worked with Gramma Rose. She never really liked any of us grandkids, she just hated some less than others at any given time. Every time cousin Daphne wound up pregnant I got some of great-Gram's jewelry for Christmas.

"Yeah, Dad," Randy said casually as he took up the phone.

He followed my example of holding the phone away from his ear—a good thing, too. Daddy could work up more decibels than Mom.

Since my presence was not required for that conversation, I slipped away to my room. Dad's tirade would probably last a long, long time. I still needed that long, long bath. Now was my best chance.

Pink terrycloth robe and matching slippers in hand, I

ducked through the living room—catching snippets of "No, I'm not coming home no matter what you say" and "I don't want your money, anyway"—and into the bathroom. A shrine to hospital quality tiles, the room's only redeeming feature was the bathtub. And, boy, what a feature it was.

The first time I walked into the apartment, I nearly turned around and walked right back out. It was tiny and filthy and wholly without a feeling of home. The only person I knew with a smaller space was Fiona, and she lived small by choice. But the real estate broker had been adamant, "You *must* see the bathroom." She resorted to taking me by the hand and dragging me in. At first glance, my opinion did not improve. Then I saw it. A beautiful, porcelain claw-foot bathtub. A genuine antique—not one of those fiberglass copies so popular today.

The kind of tub I could soak in, surrounded by bath salts and rose petals, and melt the day away in spacious style.

Needless to say, I was sold.

My first act of housekeeping was to re-glaze the tub. It was a major investment, but so worth the cost. That tub was my sanctuary. Hell, it was cheaper than therapy.

I set my robe and slippers on the commode and turned the vintage hot and cold spoked handles on full. When steam started to fill the room, I turned the hot down, dropped the plug, and poured in a dose of rose-scented salts. By the time they'd dissolved, I was lowering myself into the nearly-scalding water with a blissful sigh.

The only thing missing was a glass of wine, but I was not about to venture through the battle zone for anything.

"Hey, sis, you in there?" Randy pounded on the—thankfully locked—bathroom door.

Rather than answer, I took the pair of silk sachets from the chrome tub tray, dunked them in the bathwater, and pressed them over my closed eyes.

"Come on, Bets, I can hear you splashing."

Grrr. Randy knew better than to interrupt my bath.

"You know the rules," I said.

I heard him groan through the door, followed by the *thunk* as his forehead dropped against the wooden surface.

"I know, I know. Bath time is sacred. Thou shalt not disturb Bethany when she's in the bath. Thou shalt not stand outside the bathroom jiggling the door handle. Thou shalt not—" He paused, as if trying to remembering the third, and most important, bath commandment. "—no, I remember, Thou shalt forfeit thy bathroom time if the first two bath commandments are broken."

The rules were clear. Randy would go away. I released a deep breath and sank further into the bath, stopping when the water touched the tips of my earlobes.

"But aren't there exceptions for long-lost little brothers?" When he got no answer he continued, "I guess you don't want to know what Dad said to tell you."

My ears perked up. Drat! Randy knew I couldn't resist knowing what anyone said about me. And he would withhold every last detail. He was the only person I knew who could withstand Chinese water torture.

"Five minutes, okay?" I compromised. "Just give me five minutes to soak away the day from hell."

I could almost feel his grin through the door.

I hated being played almost as much as being mugged.

"HE OFFERED me *what* to come home?"

"A Porsche."

My eyes narrowed. "A $60,000 car. Just to come home for a week?"

"Well, you'd have to bring me with you."

That was a new low. A new tactic. Usually Daddy was a lot more passive with his manipulation. A hint of my mother's failing health. The empty receptionist's desk at his real estate office. Musing about redecorating my old room.

He probably turned it into a gallery of dead things—oops, I meant Hunting Trophies—a long time ago.

"Or," Randy continued, "as he put it, 'knock that darn fool notion clear out of his skull'."

What notion? I suddenly wondered if something more than escapism and a handy sofa-bed had prompted this trip to the city. "Why are you here, Randy?"

The instant his cheeks infused with red I understood.

"It's Laura Jane, isn't it?" Only talk of his on-again-off-again high school sweetheart could make my brother blush. "What's she done now?"

Randy plucked nervously at the gold fringe on a tufted, ivory throw pillow. Though I wanted to strangle the news out of him, I knew better than to rush him into anything. Though he might appear to act rashly, he never did anything without long and careful consideration.

"She left me, Bets," he finally admitted. "Really left me this time."

"Oh, honey," I soothed. Laura Jane had left Randy once a year for the last ten, and always—*always*—came back. "It won't last. She'll see what—"

"No." He met my gaze straight on, his mouth tight with

determination. "She's with another guy. Some flashy New York businessman with a private jet."

"But I'm sure—"

"She's wearing his ring, Bets."

Oh. Well, that was a little more serious. Southern girls did not wear the ring of a man they weren't planning on marrying.

Though I knew Randy was hurting, this was for the best. Laura Jane had tied his heart into more knots than my cousin Nicky—a career sailor—could unravel. He was the only boy in his high school with an ulcer. He gave up a full ride to Auburn to stay in Atlanta with her. And she repaid him by treating him like lowest kind of bass bait.

Not that I would ever say any of this to Randy.

Whenever I'd suggested that Laura Jane was a heartless bitch, he'd either walked out on me, punched a hole in my wall, or got drunk and wound up needing five-hundred dollars bail for an indecent exposure arrest. We never spoke of that night.

"So why New Y—" I began, even as the thought occurred to me. "She's here, isn't she?"

He dipped his head, hiding his expressive eyes. But I had my answer.

"You can't win her back, honey. She's made her choice."

"I know, I know. Really." He dove both hands through his shaggy blond hair. Clearly frustrated. "I just want to know."

"Know what?"

"Why. Why she left me. Why she left Georgia."

My heart ached for him. As big sister, I wanted to make all the pain go away. But some things can't be healed with a few soothing words.

I did know from personal experience that the quickest

route to recovery was occupation. Randy needed something to keep his mind off that witch Laura Jane. Idle hands were the devil's playthings and without something else to focus on he'd wind up with another ulcer.

He needed a hobby. Or a job.

And I had a good idea of where he could start.

"Well, while you're finding out," I said, hugging him close to my side, "how would you like to help out in the shop?"

His green eyes looked shocked and a little insulted. "In your boutique?"

I granted him a little male indignation. He was in emotional turmoil, after all. At least there was something other than despondency in his voice.

"It's not the end of the world." Maybe even the opposite. "You can earn your keep. This couch isn't free, you know."

He had every right to look skeptical. Because I had an idea that working in the shop might erase Laura Jane from his memory.

As I knew from personal experience, brown curls and a dimpled smile could be awfully distracting.

♥

"DON'T you think it's a little too ..." Danial fingered the charcoal silk tie I had just knotted around his neck, "... James Bond."

"Not James Bond," I explained. "Classic."

Danial was not the first to complain about the tie. But when I finally got all five cast members dressed for the publicity shoot, I had to admit they did look a little James Bond mixed with classic mobster. That was fine. Gave them a sleek, unified image for the first marketing campaign, which was due to start in less than two weeks.

While they posed in front of the camera, playfully hugging —and occasionally groping—each other, I smiled in satisfaction. One task off the list.

I glanced down at the clipboard and checked off the photo shoot. Now if I could pull the wardrobe together in time for the pilot shoot tomorrow, I'd be in terrific shape.

"Stop that, you tramp."

I looked up at Evan's exclaimed outrage. Bryce had grabbed him in a clinch-cover embrace, running his leg along Evan's thigh and stroking his chest beneath the suit jacket.

"C'mon, Bryce," Chris argued. "Leave the guy alone. The sooner we get this shoot done, the sooner we go home."

Evan managed to shove Bryce away, sending him tripping over Adam, who was squatting in front of the group, and tumbling to the floor. I saw Chris tense to intervene, but Bryce came up laughing and calling Evan a tease.

"A guy has to try," he said as he stood, brushing off the seat of his pants.

Adam slapped him on the butt for tripping over him.

Danial said, "We all know who the real tramp is here."

Chris looked relieved.

Evan looked annoyed. "Can we just get back to work?" he asked. "I don't know about you losers, but I have plans."

The guys "ooohed," slapping Evan on the back.

Bryce sang, "Evan's got a da-a-ate."

He shrugged them off and they finally got back to focusing on the shoot.

I, on the other hand, focused on Evan. Plans? What plans? But then, I had a pretty good idea. Plans of the female variety.

Deciding that I needed to finish up so I could be ready to leave when the guys were done, I quickly scanned my checklist and headed back to my office. I was just shoveling a stack of catalogs into my tote when Evan popped his head in.

"Got a minute?"

Um, ah, well, "Of course."

He slipped inside and closed the door behind him. Looking around the room uncomfortably, he finally took a seat on the couch, resting on the edge as if afraid to get too comfortable.

"Before this *thing*," he waved his hand in an all-encompassing gesture, "goes any further, do we need to have a talk?"

"About what?"

"About," his hand waved again, indicating the space between him and me, "*us.*"

About us. Right. There was no us anymore, and he was chicken enough to hide the fact there ever was. Well, I was not going to give him the satisfaction of a good, sit down, heart to heart. Not if that might alleviate—even the tiniest bit—his guilt for deceiving the producers, dismissing me, and being an all-around lying louse.

So rather than berate him as was my God-given right as a scorned woman, I tilted my head at a brainless angle, smiled brightly, and said, "What's to talk about?"

Evan sighed with relief. "You're great, Bethy."

He sprang off the couch and practically skipped out of the room. Must have been much lighter with all that weight lifted off his shoulders.

Little did he know.

I couldn't believe he'd called me Bethy, his pet name. He was the only one who'd ever called me that, and it grated. I cringed and fisted my hands so tight my French-manicured nails dug little crescents into my palms.

He might feel relieved right now, but he wouldn't when I made him pay. When I gathered incontrovertible evidence that he was a counterfeit queer.

He said he had plans tonight? Well, so did I.

Wherever he went, I went.

Whomever he met, I photographed.

I could see the front pages headlines already.

SIX

I WAS in my car waiting outside the studio when Evan walked out, hailed a passing taxi, and headed toward the Brooklyn-Battery Tunnel. This time I was prepared. Keeping my Beetle innocuously two cars behind the yellow cab, I settled into the chase.

Alright, it wasn't exactly a *chase* through the rush hour traffic, but I felt a bit like a spy.

When we emerged in Manhattan, the taxi headed up the West Side Highway, and I assumed they heading for Evan's East Village apartment. Looked like this was another stalking failure. First, he's going to meet his mom. Now, he was heading home.

But when the cab flew past the Christopher Street exit, even changed to a far lane, and sped beyond Evan's neighborhood, I rejoiced. I cheerfully followed them to the 42nd Street Times Square exit and the theater district.

The cab pulled up in front of Carmello's, a theater district institution since the birth of Broadway. While Evan paid the cabbie, I ducked down in case he looked my way. Peering over the dashboard, I watched him nod to the doorman and slip through the open door.

A parking garage on the other side of the street brightly announced vacancies, so I pulled in and handed my keys to the attendant. Before he drove away, I rummaged through my minuscule trunk and came up with a pink leaf print silk scarf my mother gave me for graduation and a pair of Jackie-O-worthy shades.

As my car zoomed off, I tied the scarf over my wavy blonde hair *a la* Grace Kelly and slipped the shades over my eyes.

When I approached the entrance, the doorman greeted me.

"Good evening, Madame. Welcome to Carmello's."

He ushered me in with surprising enthusiasm.

"Ah," the *maître d'* exclaimed in Italian-accented joy as I approached his podium, "welcome, welcome. A table for ...?"

"One," I answered, distracted by a search of the dining patrons.

The *maître d'* followed my gaze, offering, "You would like a specific table?"

My eyes alighted on Evan's heavily gelled brown hair at a table in a far corner. "Yes." I pointed to a booth near his table. "That one please."

"Of course, of course."

The *maître d'* clapped and two servers appeared at his side. He instructed one to fetch chilled mineral water and the other to bring a fresh bread basket. I trailed behind as he led the way to the booth, discreetly asking other patrons to nudge their chairs in as we passed.

I slipped into the closest bench, affording myself a direct

view of Evan's back. And the woman seated across the table from him.

A date! I could taste victory already.

"Do you require anything else?"

Dragging my attention from my quarry, I eyed the *maitre d'* suspiciously. He hovered over me, leaning in with an eager-to-please look on his face. What had I done to warrant such personal attention? Especially when attention was the last thing I wanted at the moment.

"Um, no, thank you," I declined graciously.

Still confused as the man bowed and hurried back to the entrance, I was grateful for the stellar service when a tall glass of sparkling water and a mouthwatering basket of bread appeared on my table almost immediately.

The servers nodded and stepped quietly away.

Shrugging off the odd behavior, I strained to hear the conversation between Evan and his date.

"What do you think I should do?" he asked.

The woman, mousy brown bobbed hair tucked behind her ears, looked like a bookworm. Or a librarian. With a soft voice to match—I couldn't hear a word she said.

Evan, however, came in loud and clear.

"I can't do that," he said. "It would ruin my career."

The librarian shook her head, then proceeded to explain at length why she apparently disagreed.

"You really think so?" Evan reached out and clasped her hand. "That's why I love you, baby."

Aha!

Caught straight-handed with his hand in the hetero jar!

What would I do next? Now that victory was mine I had to decide how to proceed. Confront him right now and watch his face fall when he realized his gig was over? Snap a picture with my phone and post it all over the studio?

I was in the middle of thinking up an even more torturous possibility when a waiter arrived to take my order. Distracted, I pointed to the first thing I saw—which turned out to be a *Prix Fixe* four-course meal.

Dinner: $75. Parking: $10. Victory: Priceless.

When I looked back up, the librarian had pulled out a briefcase and was setting several folders on the table between them. Hmmm, what kind of date brought work to the dinner table?

Since I was in for the long haul—four courses worth—I decided not to leap to any victorious conclusions. I captured a quick pic on my phone—one with the librarian smiling like a woman in love and Evan leaning suggestively towards her—and sat back to enjoy the meal. And the show.

Strangely enough, they spent most of dinner pouring over the librarian's folders.

Not exactly date-like behavior.

By the time my dessert—triple layer chocolate cherry torte—arrived, I was highly suspicious of their activities. Maybe I wasn't watching a *date*.

The *maître d'* appeared as the busboy cleared my dessert plate. I took the opportunity to ask, "Excuse me, but do you know the woman at that table?"

Following the direction of my subtle gesture, he turned back with a brilliant grin. "Ms. Portia Harker? But of course. She is a frequent customer."

"Oh," I answered vaguely. Was I supposed to know the name?

He took pity on my ignorance. "She is a literary agent.

Many celebrities use her to contract ghostwriters." Then, leaning down meaningfully, he whispered, "Would you like me to get her card for you?"

Um, ah, well. "No. Thank you."

With another polite bow, he excused himself.

At the same time, Evan and his companion pushed back from the table and rose to leave. They walked by my booth without a second glance, and I released my breath.

I turned to watch them leave. At the door, Evan held up Ms. Portia Harker's coat as she shrugged into it. Ah ha! Quickly digging through my purse for my phone, I turned back to snap another incriminating shot, only to see the trysting couple shaking hands.

That was awfully formal.

Then it hit me like a ton of red bricks: Agent. Evan was a rising celeb and she was his agent.

Lord, I felt like a fool. Again.

I sank back into the plush comfort of the booth, eyes closed and ready to wallow in my own foolish assumptions.

"Pardon me?"

I looked up to find a rumpled-looking old man holding out a piece of paper.

"Yes?"

"Woulda you asigna theese?"

What was he talking about? I could barely understand him through the heavily Italian-accented English. Clearly not a native speaker.

My confusion must have shown, because he repeated his request, slowly enunciating, "Would. You. Sign. Theese?"

"Oh," I replied, no less confused but at least comprehending. I looked down at the piece of paper and saw a clever drawing of Hollywood superstar Alexandria Crane.

The entire restaurant heard my gasp.

Looking around nervously, I noted that the entire staff and patronage was watching me—some tables were whispering about me, about my supposed identity.

Well, what did I expect coming to Carmello's, a shrine for New York stars? Especially dressed incognito. It was a tradition. Make it big, come here for dinner, and one of the resident artists would immortalize you. If you wanted to lay claim to being a genuine celebrity, you got your star on the Hollywood Walk of Fame and your face on the wall at Carmello's.

The red walls were covered in framed caricatures of celebrities, past and present, everyone from the Old Blue Eyes to Brangelina.

But, apparently, not Alexandria.

Glancing again at the sketch, I realized my mistake. Still sporting the starlet scarf and the celeb shades, I could easily be mistaken for a woman trying to avoid paparazzi and gawking fans. My disguise had worked all too well.

"Please?" the old man repeated.

Alright, I could react in one of three ways:

1. Tell the man he'd made a mistake, pay my bill, and slip away with my tail between my legs—with the scornful glares of the staff and patrons no doubt following me out the door.

2. Berate the staff for mistaking me for her—no offense to Ms. Crane, but she had a few years on me and it was not exactly flattering to be mistaken for a woman nearly twenty years my senior, no matter how beautiful she was.

3. Shamefully sign Alexandria's name, pay my bill, and slip away with my head held high until I reached the safety of my

car, where I could beat myself senseless on my steering wheel until the bliss of unconsciousness took me.

Looking into the beaming face of the artist—the joyful pride of his creation lighting him from within—and I knew the answer. I smiled in return and said, "Of course."

With a quick flourish, I scrawled an illegible rendition of Alexandria's name and added, "Thank you for making me feel like a star."

At least that was honest.

Desperate to escape the scene of my dishonor, I dug a $100 bill out of my wallet and laid it on the table. When the *maitre d'* refused, assuring me the meal was on the house, I folded the bill and pushed it into the artist's hand.

His face exploded with gratitude. I fled before he could thank me.

"Ms. Crane," a female voice called as I breezed past the doorman.

I turned to find Evan's agent waiting in lurk. She stepped forward, pulling a business card from the pocket of her black coat, and handed it to me.

"I'm Portia Harker, with Talent Corps. If you ever think of changing representation, please think of me."

Nodding, I pushed my sunglasses up my nose, turned, and ran to the garage.

If the attendants looked at me strangely while I waited, I didn't notice. All I could think of was getting home, slipping into my silk pajamas, and crawling into bed.

But as I sped away, I heard them say, "Hey, wasn't that—"
I floored the gas.

Actress Alexandria Crane Dines at New York Institution

"FUNNY," Chris mused after tossing the paper—open to the society page blurb—onto my desk, "I've always thought you looked a little like her."

Next to the blurb about how she had generously tipped the staff artist and graciously thanked the serving staff was a photo of Alexandria—*me*—fleeing the restaurant. Chris pointed at the photo and raised his eyebrows.

The headline might as well have read, Alexandria Crane Impersonator Institutionalized.

"Lord help me," I groaned.

Chris dropped into a chair. "Wanna talk about it?"

I eyed him suspiciously. "No."

How had he known it was me? Not even the gossip columnists, who lived by their knowledge of celebs and their secrets, had realized the error. After all, the only part of me visible was the lower half of my face. Hardly anything distinguishing.

"It was the mouth," he answered my unasked question. "Your lips curve more fully, like a cupid's bow."

"Oh." What could I say to that?

"Not to mention Alexandria is supposedly filming in Istanbul this week." He winked. "Kind of a long commute for Italian food. Rome would be closer."

Why me? Why did my every attempt turn into a disaster? Being mistaken for Alexandria was only the latest. Last time I'd wound up mugged. In my senior year of college, the one time I ventured out into the club scene with Fiona, we wound up at Center Stage the night of the legendary ATF raid.

Leaving my comfort zone seemed to have bad results.

Why, then, did I keep trying?

"It was all a big misunderstanding," I explained.

Chris laughed. "Your secret is my secret."

He smiled that warm, open smile that made my heart melt. Of all the men on the planet, why did my heart finally go all soft and gooey over a guy I could never have? My psychology must be off the charts. At least with married men or men with repressed sexuality there was a kernel of hope. A teeny-tiny seed. Getting palpitations over a man openly batting for the other team was an exercise in frustration.

And I was not about to wind up old, frustrated, and with a dozen cats for company. Furry things were not my friends.

Slapping my palms on the desk, I stood. "Ready to get to work?"

Chris frowned quizzically, maybe wondering what had set me off, before agreeing, "Whenever you are, boss."

"Good, because we have a pilot to shoot."

SEVEN

Episode 101

Straighten up and fly right.

THE GUINEA PIG for the first show was a commercial airline pilot named James. He was a tall, handsome man with a kind smile and bright white teeth. Trevor and Steven chose him for the pilot episode—not only because he was a pilot, very punny—because he wanted to propose to his girlfriend, a children's librarian named Sonja. A good emotional hook for the first episode.

Steven, as director, had given me the shooting schedule along with a few notes and suggestions for James's wardrobe. But the moment I saw James I knew the suggestions were wrong.

This man who spent his life in a boring uniform did not need a wardrobe of sleek black suits and dull oxford shirts. He needed clothes with color. With flair.

"Pour les Hommes," I declared as I extended my hand.

Pour les Hommes was an *avant-garde* label that put a wild twist on classic silhouettes. Button-down shirts in bold hibiscus florals and diagonal pinstripes. Casual pants in subtle plaids or covered in cargo pockets. Bright orange nylon quilted vests.

The kind of fashion statement only a guy like James could carry off. On anyone less grounded it would seem forced, but his classic good looks and ready smile could balance the outrageous clothes.

"Um," James looked around confused before shaking my hand, "James. Pleasure to meet you."

"I'm Bethany," I explained. "We're going to dress you in *Pour les Hommes*. Great clothes. You're going to love them."

He looked uncertain, but nodded and smiled. Kind of the way he might placate a crazy person. I shrugged and went to give Steven my suggestions.

An hour later, the filming crew was at Walk-In Closet along with Bryce, Chris, and Evan—Adam and Danial had stayed at James's apartment after the introduction shot to prepare for the next segment. The gang made a big production of James trying on the pieces I had pulled while Bryce sexually harassed him in the dressing area.

Apparently it was Bryce's trademark to manhandle other men.

Evan looked uncomfortable most of the time, only venturing into the shot when Steven barked an order. Every so often he would dart a glance toward the counter, where I was stationed to keep an eye on the filming.

I smiled as Chris gestured for James to turn so they could evaluate the brick red cargo pants and palm-frond-print short sleeve shirt he wore. Bryce lifted the shirt in the back—on the pretense of checking the fit of the pants—and squeezed the guys cheeks like he was trying for juice.

Chris laughed at Bryce's antics but admonished him to stay on task. His clear blue eyes sparkled, and it made me happy to see him having fun.

Randy had peeked out through the drape when we first arrived, eyed the film crew and the boisterous cast warily, and quickly decided that stacking boxes for Kit was safer than getting anywhere near the production.

Kit, returning to the counter after checking on Randy's progress, watched the antics with amusement lifting at the corners of her mouth.

"They're like kids in a candy shop," she commented as she leaned one hip against the counter.

"I guess if we got to play dress up with such a hunky guy, we'd be a little giddy, too."

My gaze drifted again to Chris, standing outside the dressing room. With those broad shoulders, muscled arms, and lean hips, he was a girl's dress-up dream. Or a guy's.

I sighed, drawing Kit's attention.

"Are you seeing anyone?" she asked, as if she'd read my thoughts.

"No, not since—" I looked sharply at Evan as he adjusted the alignment of James's belt at Steven's request. "—not for a few months."

Kit was silent for a long time, and I had a feeling she was working things out. I hadn't known her long, but already I knew that something was brewing when she was quiet for more than a few seconds.

Before Kit could voice her thoughts, Cassie ordered the crew to pack up and everything turned to chaos. Cameramen started packing their equipment into aluminum cases. Other crew members rolled up extension cords, took down lights, and collected microphones. Steven announced the location of the next segment—a chi-chi Tribeca furniture store where they would shoot Evan's main scene.

People started filing out the door, some headed for the show's big black Suburban that the cast drove from location to location, others heading for the crew van that followed them everywhere.

Cassie handed me a list of all the pieces Bryce and Steven had selected—pieces I needed to bring to James's apartment for the homecoming segment. All business when she was working, she was already hustling the cast outside before I even set the list on the counter.

Chris waved as Cassie shoved him—the last dawdler—out the door. For several long seconds I stared after them, my thoughts lost on the show, on misplaced lust, and on Evan.

Kit broke the silence. "Chris tells me Evan used to be your interior decorator." She paused. "Did he design the shop?"

There was something probing about her question.

"Yes," I answered guardedly.

"And your apartment?"

I inched back instinctively.

"Some," I hedged.

"The bedroom?"

It wasn't so much *what* she said as *how* she said it that caught my attention—drawing out *bedroom* like it was a naughty word. There was a sparkle of mischief and knowledge in her clear blue eyes. She didn't miss much.

"Yes," I finally answered. "The bedroom."

"I *see.*"

And I knew she did.

"It's been my general experience that men," she said, interrupting my rampant imagination, "are rodent droppings."

Randy, carrying an open box from the storeroom, dropped the box on the counter with a thud. There was something playful in his unyielding stance. He didn't say a word, but cocked his brows at Kit until she amended, "Blood relatives and present company excepted." She turned back to me. "Mostly."

Randy disappeared back into the storeroom.

"He's a hard worker, you know." She jerked her thumb toward the back room. "Too bad he's got his brain wrapped around that Southern skank."

"Don't I know it."

I got the feeling not much slipped past Kit Thompson. She'd only met Randy this morning but already knew him better than he knew himself. He might not like it, but she was probably going to make him forget Laura Jane. For good.

"I followed one to college, you know," she said. "All the way from California."

Startled by the change of subject, I stared at Kit.

"A man," she explained.

Oh. "What happened?"

"Dumped me the first week of school."

"Rodent droppings?"

"Definitely, but I graduated *Summa Cum Laude*. He transferred to a SUNY-Buffalo sophomore year."

"Ouch," I replied, shivering at even the thought of a Buffalo winter.

Kit smiled maniacally, "The fifty bucks I paid that Christopher Street gypsy to curse him really paid off."

"Remind me never to get on your bad side."

"Don't worry," she assured. "Bosses and my brother's friends are definitely exempt from my Voodoo."

"I'm much relieved. Now I just need to stay on *Chris's* good side."

"Not a problem." She moved around the counter and started to empty the box Randy had deposited. "He likes you. And he's hard to piss off."

IF I HADN'T SEEN the "Before" pictures of James's Riverside Drive apartment, I might have thought Evan did a decent job on redecorating. But the transformation from dark, dingy, dumping ground to airy, modern home was nothing short of a design miracle.

Gone were the dusty Venetian blinds and threadbare rug. No more white paint—peeling in several places to reveal a history of color palettes. Even the brown and gold plaid couch was nowhere in sight.

The calming pearly white walls, breezy window panels, lush oriental rug, and clean-lined sectional had turned the dungeon into a resort.

When I walked in to drop off the clothes from the shop, I nearly dropped my jaw.

"This is—" I struggled for the right word, not even caring that no one in particular was listening. "—amazing."

"Thank you."

I turned at the soft sound of Evan's voice. He was brushing some dust off his shirtsleeves—though it would take more scrubbing than brushing to get the splotches of paint off his cheeks and forearms—and greeted me with a broad smile.

Fighting the urge to scowl—because it's an advantage if your enemy doesn't realize he's your enemy—I tightened my cheeks into a strained smile.

"You're welcome," I managed through clenched teeth. "This place looks phenomenal."

"I'm glad you like it." There was sincere appreciation in his voice.

For a moment I was reminded of what I had liked—*liked*, just liked, never loved, Lord, I wasn't that foolish—about Evan. He was sweet and kind and humble about his brilliant talent. Where most men gloated about their abilities, he insisted there was nothing special about his designs. That he only rearranged what he saw, fixed things that didn't look right, and added a little paint and polish.

But clearly Trevor and Steven saw in him what I had always seen: genius.

My heart softened a tiny bit and I said, "You know I always loved your work."

"Bethany—" He hurried forward and took my free hand in both of his. "—thank you for being so understanding about—"

"It's nothing," I cut him off, not wanting to hear any simpering gratitudes for my magnanimous behavior. A moment of softness did not a forgiveness make. "I need to put these somewhere."

Holding the clothes out in front of me—a kind of shield protecting me from his fawning—I ventured deeper into the apartment and found a crew member to take the load, then turned to leave.

"Bethany," Cassie cried as she burst through the front door

with the energy of a Tesla coil, running smack into me, "you're not leaving before the Homecoming."

The way Cassie phrased it, it was not a question.

"Of course not," I replied, leaning in to whisper, "Just keep Evan away from me unless your makeup artist wants to cover up a black eye."

She smiled, "That bad, huh?"

"You have no idea."

"Fine," she declared with the authoritative tone that had earned her a position of power. "Evan, I need you to make sure the bedroom is ready for the fashion show. And clean that paint off your face. Crew, set up for the homecoming shot. The rest of the cast is waiting in the hall, and I don't know how long my threats will keep Bryce under control if I'm not there to follow through."

Everyone jumped at her orders. Evan scurried—yes, actually scurried—down the hall to the bedroom. The camera crew took their posts by the door. Cassie poked her head into the hall to yell at Bryce, "Stop groping the straight guy!"

I stayed safely out of the way. From the kitchen, I could see the front door, but I was out of the path of the stampede.

Then Cassie turned on the crew, ordered the nearest person to slate the scene, and started the cameras rolling. Steven—positioned by the monitor in the half bath—called "Action" over the headset. At his command, Cassie rapped sharply on the front door and seconds later, the cast was leading James in with a silk sash tied over his eyes.

"Ooh," Bryce cooed, "are you ready to see your brand new apartment?"

James grinned like the cat who caught the mouse, "Heck, yeah."

"This is cable," Danial assured him, "you can say hell."

Everyone laughed.

Chris, standing behind James, untied the blindfold.

"Holy smokes."

Bryce placed his arm sympathetically on James's shoulder. "My words exactly."

Everyone laughed again.

Cassie tapped me on the shoulder, nodding in the gawking straight guy's direction. "Kinda makes all the hassle worthwhile, no?"

James, wide-eyed and clearly in awe of Evan's artistic talent, struggled to take in all the sweeping changes. The paint, the rug, the windows, and the sectional. Re-polished hardwood flooring. Modern chrome-legged tables and tempered glass surfaces. It was a bachelor-hoping-to-be-a-groom's dream.

"Hey, Cass," I offered back. "Thanks for getting me on board with this mess."

"Anytime." She smiled as she took a moment to enjoy the fruits of her labor before clicking back to work. "Everyone to the bedroom for the fashion show."

The camera crew dutifully moved their set up and the cast followed after. I maneuvered around the remaining crew and headed for the door.

"Oh!" I exclaimed as I crashed into a curly-haired redhead in the hall. "Excuse me."

"No, no," she hurried to assure me, "it was all my fault."

"I guess neither of us were looking where we were going."

She smiled nervously, clearly still shaken up over our collision. A plastic grocery bag lay at her feet and I bent to pick it up. At my movement she dropped to her knees and snatched the bag up before I could grab it.

"Delivery," she explained. "For this apartment."

Discreet blue lettering indicated the delivery was from a gourmet grocery in the Village. "That must be for Chris," I reasoned. "He's inside."

"Chris," she agreed. "Yes."

"The kitchen's just inside on the left." I moved to the side and politely held the door for her.

Head down, she muttered a polite thank you and ducked through the door.

Relieved to be heading back to the shop to help Kit close up, I was stuck in gridlock at Columbus Circle before I remembered Chris telling me he had shopped at the West End Market for the show. What had the delivery girl been bringing?

"ARE you going to the final product shoot?" Kit asked.

We were cleaning up the last remnants of the whirlwind—also known as the *OSG* cast—that had swept through the shop, leaving piles overturned and hangers askew in its wake.

"I hadn't really thought about it," I said as I straightened a pile of cashmere v-necks. "Probably."

The final product shoot, according to Cassie, was where the cast got to watch James get ready for his big date. To see how much of their teaching he'd learned and could incorporate into his life. To see whether the makeover had succeeded.

Plus, they got to watch him propose.

"Gotta see the poor guy all gussied up and gushing his

heart out on national TV?" Randy teased as he collapsed the half dozen empty boxes—the remnants of restocking.

"He's going to propose tonight," Kit returned. "I think it's sweet that he wants to makeover his life for her."

Randy stomped down his last box. "More like he wants to impress her. To minimize the chance of rejection."

"When did you become such a cynic?" I asked.

If anything, Randy was the romantic of the family. Daddy was dictatorial. Mom was emotional. I was practical. Randy gave Valentines to every girl in his third-grade class, had four girlfriends at the same time in seventh grade, and vowed to marry his high school sweetheart. Would have, too, if she hadn't been a two-timing cow.

He was the last person I'd ever expected to hear mocking a man's attempt to romance and woo the woman he loved.

Maybe Laura Jane had done more than just break his heart.

Maybe she'd hardened it, too.

"That's not cynicism, Bets. It's realism."

With jerky movements, he stooped to grab the stack of boxes and stomped out the back. As I watched him disappear behind the drape, I wondered—with no little anger directed at the heartless witch who had dulled his shine—what had happened to my little brother.

"He—" I began, but shook my head in disbelief when I couldn't continue.

"Healing takes time," Kit sympathized. "His heart will mend."

"I hope you're right."

"If I'm not—" She nudged the hangers into an even spread before turning to face me. "—I'll tear the bitch's heart out myself."

She'd said it with a grin, but I had a feeling Kit Thompson was a woman who took care of her own. Violently, if necessary.

Thank the Lord she was on my side.

"So, you're going tonight," she said, returning to her original topic. "Chris wrangled me an invite. We can make a night of it—dinner and drinks after?"

"Sounds like a plan."

DESPITE RANDY'S CYNICISM, James's proposal went off without a hitch. His girlfriend, adorably nerdy with a frizzy hair and black-framed glasses, cried a waterfall and sobbed an overwhelmed, "Yes."

The cast, crew, and invited guests watched the night unfold from the show's "loft." It was actually a warmly decorated set with no ceiling and at least a dozen cameras.

The *OSG* gang watched on a big flat panel TV from the comfortable couches on the set. Everyone else watched on an off-set monitor. We all cheered as the happy couple embraced and James told his librarian how much he loved her.

As the picture on the flat panel TV faded to the show's logo, Trevor and Steven emerged from behind the set carrying bottles of champagne.

The catering staff, fast on their heels, hurried to pop the corks, fill the glasses, and pass them around.

Once we all had champagne Trevor called for our attention.

"You are all part of a show that will change television forever. To ending stereotypes and entertainment exile."

Trevor raised his glass in toast. "To the cast and crew. To a long, long run. And to a show well shot."

Almost everyone lifted their glasses and shouted in agreement.

Bryce scowled, adding, "Except for the crisis."

"What crisis?" Trevor asked, sounding concerned.

Cassie stepped in to explain. "Bryce lost his planner."

"I didn't lose it, someone stole it. And it isn't just a planner, it's my life."

"Why would anyone want to steal your life? The only people at the site were cast and crew—we already know your life in agonizing intimate detail." Cassie rolled her eyes. "I guarantee no one wants to know more. If you have secrets, keep 'em."

"I don't care what you think, someone stole my planner from James's apartment."

Cassie shrugged at Bryce's determination.

"Good job, everyone," she congratulated. "Now, let's get this mess cleaned up so we can party."

EIGHT

"EVAN," I slurred, two hours and twice as many Mojitos later, "is a louse."

Kit, across from me in the cramped booth, smiled, nodded, and signaled the aging waitress for another cup of coffee. The woman—fifty if she was a day—waddled over on her thick-soled shoes and poured more murky thickness into my cup.

"Drink up," Kit ordered, "or you'll be sorry in the morning."

Wary of the heavy, diner-issue mug, I lifted the pungent brew and took a sip. The caffeine shot straight to my brain.

"Good Lord, is there any water in this?"

"Not much."

The coffee jolted me from my rum-induced haze. I looked around at the dingy diner, walls covered in peeling blue wallpaper in a pattern someone must have once thought contributed to the atmosphere. The scarred, melamine tabletops looked vintage 1962. The red naugahyde upholstery might have been replaced in 1970.

"What are we doing here?" I asked, incredulous.

The whole thing seemed light-years from any New York restaurant—if I could call it that—I'd ever visited.

It reminded me of a typical mobile home diner parked in perpetuity on a vacant lot just outside the city limits of a small, southern town.

It reminded me of home.

"Sobering you up," Kit explained. "If you go to bed with all that rum and sugar in your gut, you'll be emptying your stomach all day tomorrow."

As if in agreement, my stomach churned.

I quickly downed another mouthful of coffee sludge.

"Finish that cup." Kit withdrew her wallet and laid a five on the table. "We've got an apartment to stake out."

The sludge went down the wrong pipe and I choked on the bitter taste.

"St-stake out?" I asked around coughs.

"Evan's not going to stake himself out."

Images of Evan, staked out in the desert and left to the vultures and the scorpions, made me smile. I indulged in the delicious revenge fantasy until reality intruded.

Fractured memories played in my mind like overexposed home movies. Kit questioning me about my history with Evan. Me spilling every last, sordid—alright, not so sordid—detail. Dear Lord. I smothered a groan. Rum should be outlawed.

Um, ah, well. "Kit, I—"

"Hurry up," she interrupted. "Everyone stuck around the party after we left, but he's probably headed home by now."

Purse in hand, she slid out of the booth and marched across the diner. When she reached the door and realized I wasn't in step behind her, she threw me an impatient look and motioned me into action.

What could I say? Kit welcomed no argument.

I downed the last of the sludge. She'd done a pretty good job of digging out my secrets. If anyone could make Evan confess, it was Kit.

♥

"WHICH FLOOR IS HIS?" Kit asked as she—untainted by the single bottle of East River Ale she had imbibed at the Red Hook party—pulled my Beetle into to the curb across from Evan's building.

I gazed up at the four-story brick building—a historic, Greek Revival row house dating back nearly two-hundred years—a building I hadn't laid eyes on in nearly a year.

A building I had once dreamed of moving into.

I even spent a few afternoons in the city archives, researching the building's history. Turned out it was a wedding gift from one of the city's early mayors to his son and new daughter-in-law.

In retrospect, I might have been a tad too eager about a potential future with Evan.

"Third floor," I replied. "On the front."

She plunked the car into park and turned off the engine. Turning in the driver's seat to face me, she asked, "Now what?"

"Now what?" I parroted. "This was your idea."

"Hardly. This is your stalking."

"I'm not—" *stalking Evan*, I started to say. But, if you looked at it in a certain light—bright, glaring daylight perhaps—my actions could, if considered with rational detachment, be considered stalking-*esque*. Thankfully it was dark as night and rationality was nowhere in sight. "I'm not stalking him. I'm just ... curious."

"Curious," Kit snorted.

"Yes, curious. I might have followed him, you know, once." Or twice, if I wanted to be anal about the details. "To see who he was meeting—."

"You don't have to explain to me. I know all about rodent droppings, remember. You deserve to know the truth and the louse deserves whatever he gets."

Put that way it sounded almost logical. Like I had a right to shadow Evan's every move until I uncovered his deception and made him pay for throwing our relationship away and making a fraud of himself.

Kit clearly excelled at rationalizing extreme behavior—

"Shoot." She ducked and pulled my head down after her.

The sudden movement sent my brain, still slightly muddled by alcohol, swimming. My mind buzzed, even as I tried to figure out what was going on.

"Kit, what are you—"

"Shhh!" she admonished. Then, in a fervent whisper, explain, "Evan's coming up the sidewalk."

"Is he alone?" I lifted my head to see.

Kit tugged me right back down. "Stay out of sight."

In the quiet of the car, I listened to my breath whoosh in and out as we waited. Evan's street—one block from St. Mark's Church in the Bowery, one of the oldest parishes in the city—was silent in the early morning hours, a stark contrast to the bustling activity that brought it to life during the day. This was a neighborhood you could raise a family in—and the thought made my heart ache.

With every failed relationship, my dreams of a family and a

future slipped a little further away. At thirty-two, I could only see them faintly in the distance as they threatened to drop below the horizon forever.

This was why I needed to stay far away from alcohol—it made me melancholy.

Footsteps echoed on the sidewalk.

I held my breath—and heard Kit suck in hers—as the footfalls approached. Evan's muffled voice reached my ears.

"You know I love you," he was saying. "I tell you every day."

Who was he with? When I tried to sneak a peek, turning my head and peering up through the driver's side window, Kit —hunched across the center console to avoid the steering wheel—smacked my thigh.

"Head down," she whispered.

Lord, she should have been an army general. No soldier would dare disobey her orders.

"I wish we could be together, too," Evan continued. "But that's not possible right now. We both made this choice to put the job first. For now."

Sounded like he was talking on his cell.

"I'm almost home." He was right next to the car. "I'll call you tomorrow, sweetheart."

Sweetheart?

"Miss you." His voice grew fainter as he moved beyond the car. "My bed is empty without you."

Silence, except for the sound of his steps as he crossed the street. Waiting to give him a chance to get into the building and for Kit to give the all clear—I was woman enough to admit she frightened me—I pondered the eavesdropped conversation. Clearly he had been talking to a lover. A lover he couldn't, given current circumstances, see right now.

That louse!

Evan had a secret girlfriend.

"He is *so* busted," I whispered.

Kit looked at me like I was crazy.

Maybe I was.

"WANT TO STAY OVER?" I asked as Kit pulled into my parking garage. "Randy's on the sofa, but my bed's real big."

"No thanks. My place is only a few blocks away."

She cut the ignition and dropped the keys in my lap.

"Really," I insisted, "you shouldn't walk home alone this late at night."

"I'll be fine."

Kit was definitely the kind of woman who didn't ask for assistance on anything. She handled it all and then some without a stitch of help.

But even if it's unnecessary, sometimes a little help is nice.

"At least let Randy walk you home," I offered.

"No, I'm fine—"

"I insist."

She met my gaze with those intense blue eyes and clearly saw my determination. Shrugging, she relented. SoHo was not a neighborhood to go wandering alone at night.

Randy, who had been waiting up for my return, started in as soon as we walked in the door.

"Where in hell have you been?"

I tensed. My first instinct was to retort, "Where do you get off?" But I was in no mood to start an argument. Ignoring his outburst, I shrugged my purse off my shoulder and set it on the hall table.

"I've been waiting up for hours!" he continued. "You could have at least called!"

Sounded just like Daddy, mad at me for breaking curfew back in high school.

Randy was more like our father than he cared to admit—leaping in without thinking when he got the least bit worried. But I was willing to forgive him that if he stopped now and cut his losses. My silence should have clued him in to my displeasure.

It didn't.

"I was worried sick!"

He came at me, finger pointing and voice rising.

"I called the police and the hospitals and—"

"Randy! Enough!" I interrupted when the thin veneer of my patience cracked. Swallowing my anger, I concentrated on sounding calm—though I was only mildly successful—as I said, "Kit needs to go home. Would you please escort her."

It was not a request. Kit wasn't the only one who could issue orders.

Clearly shocked by my outburst, he snapped his mouth shut and grabbed his coat in silence. He had learned long ago that when my patience snapped it was time to get out of the way.

Like the time he had put his pet garter snake in my bathroom sink every morning for a week. The last time, I'd screamed my head off, carried the snake at arm's length back to Randy's room, and threw it on his bed before punching him in the face—Daddy had taught me how to throw a mean jab.

He'd had to explain to everyone at school how his sister had given him a black eye.

Now he knew better.

"My pleasure," he assured Kit.

As soon as the door shut behind them I peeled off my ballet flats and flung one at the wall. I'd been on my own in New York since I was eighteen. The last thing I needed was a chaperone keeping track of my every move and chastising me for not checking in.

I'd left my father in Georgia and didn't need another one.

"Bethany?" Randy's voice came muffled through the door. "Are you alright?"

I flung the other shoe at the door.

"She's fine," I heard him say. "Let's go."

That was the problem with Southern men. They might be chivalrous, but they could also be overprotective.

With a sigh, I unbuttoned my cardigan and padded barefoot into my room. Naked in seconds, I slipped into the silk pajamas neatly folded beneath my pillow. Ahhh, the softness of silk was almost as relaxing as a hot bath, even if it didn't soothe sore muscles.

I promised my aching body—sore from a long day and even longer night—a hot bath first thing in the morning. Setting my overprotective brother straight was the only thing between me and my soft, sateen sheets.

When Randy burst in fifteen minutes later he looked ready to pick up his lecture where he'd left off. I was waiting for him in the kitchen.

"Don't even think about it, baby boy," I shouted before he had a chance to speak.

Though it galled him to be called a baby, he was younger

by nearly eight years. It would do him good to keep that in mind.

"You take a seat on this barstool and listen."

I waited until he complied. He slunk over to the breakfast counter like a guilty little boy. Which he was.

"Don't think for a second that you can come into my life, into my apartment, and take charge like some big, strong man. I've managed quite admirably on my own. I don't need your protection or your censure. Either you realize I am a grown, fully capable woman, or you find another couch."

Head hung, he ran a hand over his dirty blonde hair. He was silent for several long seconds, the only sound in the room the even rasp of his breath.

"Lord, Bets," he said finally, his voice pained. "I'm just like him, aren't I?"

His torment deflated my fury.

"No, honey," I assured him. "You're nothing like Daddy. You care so much that sometimes it clouds your better judgment."

And in matters other than family relations, I added silently. He took the same caring, protective approach with Laura Jane.

"I just— I worried, and I couldn't help it, and—"

"I know. And it's okay to worry. Hell," I said, "I'd be hurt if you didn't. But you need to respect me enough to know I can take care of myself."

"I do, honestly. You're a big city career woman and I am so proud of you. I know you can manage without my interference. But you'll always be my sister." He shook his head, as if trying to reconcile the contradiction. "And the city is a scary place."

His eyes got a faraway look and I could tell he was no

longer thinking about my independence. He was thinking about another woman close to his heart. Another woman living in the danger of the city.

Laura Jane was never far from his mind. I could see her in the shadows that darkened his bright eyes when he thought no one was looking. She haunted him, and he needed to get her out of his system.

Pulling him into a hug, I asked, "Have you seen her?"

His entire body stiffened in my arms.

"Yes," he bit out.

Whoa! There was a lot of anger in that one word. It didn't take woman's intuition to guess that meeting hadn't gone well.

He pulled away, busying himself with hanging his coat on the rack in the hall. I lowered onto the stool, watching his jerky movements and certain he was not going to say more.

He finally spoke without turning, still facing the wall. "I should have dumped her a long time ago."

I started to agree, but decided to hold my tongue.

When he turned toward me, his youthful face was hard as stone. "Aren't you going to say, 'I told you so'?"

There was so much pain in those words. More pain than my baby brother should ever know.

Tears leaped to my eyes.

I blinked them away and shook my head.

"Well, you should." Then, in an instant, his façade crumbled, his face fell, and wetness streaked his cheeks.

I watched helplessly as my own tears ran.

"Do you know what she said?" he asked, pained. "She said I was a useless hillbilly with no future. She said she'd found herself a real man who could take care of her and buy her expensive things. How—" His voice cracked. "—how could she say those things? Sh-she loves me."

When I couldn't bear it any longer, I moved to comfort him.

Just that fast his demeanor changed. Jaw clenched, he brusquely wiped at his tears and held me off. Without another word, he stalked to the bathroom and locked the door behind him.

I released a wrenching sob since there wasn't anything else I could do. My baby brother was hurting and I couldn't do a thing about it.

All I could do was hope that this pain would help him heal.

Healing by fire.

RANDY WAS GONE when I woke up the next morning. I called Walk-In Closet and Kit assured me he was there and physically healthy. Maybe a good night's sleep had eased his pain.

My pain, on the other hand, was only beginning.

Despite Kit's caffeinated efforts, my head throbbed with every subtle movement. All I wanted to do was down a pair of aspirin, crawl under my covers, and spend the day in the oblivion of sleep.

The phone rang before I folded back the duvet.

Running through the apartment to find my cell before voicemail picked up—cursing the pain that accompanied every pounding step—I finally found it beneath a couch cushion.

"Hello?"

"Morning, sugar."

The deep male voice on the other end of my phone haunted my fantasies, invaded my dreams.

"Chris?"

"You got plans?"

I looked longingly back at my bedroom door, imagining the fluffy softness of my bed and the bliss of a lazy Saturday of lounging.

"No," I said sadly, because the prospect of spending time with Chris—unavailable though he may have been—was a thousand times better than spending the day alone. "No plans."

"How would you like to go aisle shopping?"

"Aisle shopping?" I asked as I headed for my closet.

"Like window shopping," he explained, "but at grocery stores. I need to scout out some markets for the next episode."

"Sounds like fun."

Flipping quickly through the rack of florals, toiles, and paisleys in my closet, I realized what I was doing and quickly chastised myself. What kind of head-case dressed to impress a man she could never even hope to attract?

Maybe I needed more therapy than I thought.

"Good," he said, and I could hear the smile in his voice. "Because I'm standing outside your apartment."

My therapy needs forgotten, I rushed over to the window overlooking Broome Street three stories down. There, on the busy sidewalk buzzing with people, stood Chris, cell phone in hand. Staring back at me.

He looked heartstoppingly attractive in a crisp blue camp shirt, black leather blazer, and clean cut khakis. Straight from the pages of *GQ*. I could so easily imagine unbuttoning that preppy shirt, peeling it off to reveal the muscular chest I knew was there—

Stupid, stupid, stupid. Stupid irrational fantasies. *Stick to reality, Bethany.* I briefly beat myself over the head with the phone before saying, "I'll buzz you in."

By the time Chris stepped off the elevator, I had given myself a serious talking to about the pitfalls of lusting after a man who wasn't interested in my gender. I was even almost convinced that my attraction was an overblown fantasy—no one could possibly live up to the image of Chris I had planted in my mind.

But then he walked off the elevator and I was hit full force with a desire to bear his children.

Lord, but he was the most attractive man I'd ever seen, and he was within reaching distance. He was smiling—a broad, welcoming smile that popped a pair of dimples into the smooth planes of his cheeks—and that made his clear blue eyes sparkle like the Hope Diamond.

Up close I could see how well his clothes fit, hugging every muscular inch with just the right amount of give. His brown curls looked finger-combed, like he had rolled out of bed, raked his hands through his hair, and headed out the door.

Unfortunately, my brain stuck on the image of Chris rolling out of bed—or, more accurately, Chris *in* bed.

Le sigh.

I managed to smile, despite my lusty fog, and opened my arms in a welcoming hug.

"Sexy threads," he said as I released him, "but maybe a little casual for grocery shopping."

"Hey"—I smacked him for his insolence—"these happen to be imported. You're never underdressed in 100% silk."

He lifted his hand to my shoulder and slowly—torturously—trailed his fingertips along the pale pink silk, tracing over my bicep, the sensitive inside of my elbow, and down my forearm until silk gave way to skin. My breathing quickened into little pants. My blood throbbed as my heart beat a pace to match hoofbeats on Derby day. Every nerve in my arm tingled.

"Silk." His gaze focused on the spot where his fingers met my wrist. "So soft."

Every sense cried out for him, and I leaned in. With my whole body. My lips parted in breathless anticipation of a fantasy realized.

Then I made the mistake of sighing, "Chris."

As soon as I spoke, his eyes darted to mine.

He blinked twice.

He looked shocked.

Then embarrassed.

Hell.

NINE

"THE PAJAMAS," Chris blurted as he backed away, his hand clutched against his chest and his eyes blinking furiously. "Soft. Silk." Blink, blink. "Fabric."

I nodded.

He blinked.

"I should, um, change," I stammered.

Drat. I never stammered.

Not out loud, anyway.

He blinked.

Chris didn't seem ready to speak anytime soon, and I needed to get out of my pajamas as quickly as possible—wait, I didn't mean that how it sounded. I needed to change into something less, um, suggestive as quickly as possible. Either way, I turned tail and hurried to my room. And closed the door sharply behind me.

Don't be even stupider—er, more stupid?—I told myself as I pulled on a knee-length, denim pencil skirt. Chris was gay. Gay. With a capital G and a cable show.

I was misinterpreting, overreacting to the situation. My

modesty was ridiculous. If I strutted around wearing nothing but heels and pearls, Chris wouldn't bat an eye. He couldn't possibly care what went on behind my bedroom door. Not while I changed. Not the rest of the time, either.

Not that anything noteworthy had happened in my bedroom in several long, long months.

"*Grrr.*" Frustration consumed me.

What was I thinking, getting involved with a gay reality show? With my dating track record, it was a recipe for institutionalization. I must have been paying for the sins of past lives. I must have been a very, very bad person.

"*Grrr!*"

"Um, Bethany?" Chris asked hesitantly. "Is everything alright?"

I had to stifle another growl. "Yes," I bit out as I tugged my pearl-buttoned, winter white cardigan over my head. "Just fine."

"I—" He paused—and, I could imagine, blinked. "Were you growling?"

He'd heard that?

"Will you think I'm certifiable if I say yes?"

The briefest hesitation before, "Of course not."

But his hesitation said, *Hell, yeah.*

"Then no," I said. "I wasn't growling."

"Oh, okay then." He sounded amused, and I was relieved.

Setting a pair of low-heeled, camel-colored slingbacks on the floor, I stepped into the shoes and secured Great Gram's watch around my wrist below my charm bracelet.

Pulling the door open, I opened my mouth to call out, "Ready to go."

But Chris was standing in the doorway and I crashed right

into him. His hands came up to steady me, grabbing me just below my shoulders and holding me firmly upright and several inches away. Thankfully, the soft layer of cashmere insulated better than whisper-light silk.

There was no sign of the shock that had rendered him speechless minutes earlier. His friendly self was back with a bright smile and shining eyes.

"Great." His gaze dropped to my feet. "Can you walk in those?"

"In these?" I twisted one foot to the side to examine the modest inch-and-a-half heel. "These are child's play. I'm Southern, honey. I've worn heels since before I could stand."

"Okay then, let's go."

"I just have to grab—" My phone started ringing before I finished.

Following the sound to my bedroom—where I'd dropped it when I saw Chris out the window—I checked the caller ID. *Evan?* Why was he calling me?

And why hadn't I deleted his number from my phone?

Um, ah, well. "Hello?"

"Bethy, it's Evan."

Duh. "Yes, Evan?"

Even when we'd been dating for months, he still felt the need to identify himself. That should have been my first clue that the relationship was doomed.

"Do you remember the name of that Italian place we went to on our first date?" he asked.

"I'm sorry, what?"

"You know, that little underground place with the candles dripping down over the Chianti bottles."

Had our rocky history suddenly evaporated? Was I

supposed to forget the fact that he'd crushed my heart and was perpetrating a grievous fraud on the American public? Were we magically best friends again?

"Evan, I—"

"Do you still have your cork?" he asked, his voice laden with remembrance. "I have mine."

His reminiscence triggered a flood of memory. Of a romantic night full of promise and fantasy. We'd popped the cork on a Pinot Noir and sipped the night away. By the time they kicked us out at two a.m. we had finished a second bottle. As mementos of our first date, we'd each taken one of the corks.

"No," I lied. "I shoved it down the disposal."

"Oh."

Evan grew quiet.

And I felt a little ashamed of my cold response.

Until I remembered that he'd broken my heart.

"Noli's." I opened my nightstand drawer and closed my fingers around the cork. "On Mott Street."

"Thanks," he said quietly.

It was only the sharp memory of his betrayal and his secret girlfriend that kept me from relenting.

"Sure." With a click, I ended the call. Turning to Chris, smiling bright, I asked, "Ready?"

He shook off a confused frown. "Yep. Let's go shopping."

♥

"YOUR HUSBAND, HE COOK?"

The ancient Chinese woman eyed me with much speculation, as if I was a failure of a woman if my man had to do the cooking.

"He's not my husband," I explained.

"Your boyfriend, he cook?"

I smiled patiently. "He's not my boyfriend, either."

Her sparse brows lifted skeptically.

Leaning in, I whispered, "He's gay."

Eyes wide, she stared openly a Chris as he examined a shelf of canned goods—the labels were in Chinese, but the pictures looked like spiky sea urchins.

The entire shop looked like it had been transplanted directly from downtown Shanghai. Heavy incense clung in the air. Bundles of dried herbs and flowers hung from the ceiling. Strings of Feng Shui-ing mirrors and the bodies of smoked poultry filled the storefront window. I chose to stay on the other side of the tiny store, next to a pen of chickens so fluffy they looked like pompoms in the making, and told myself they were being sold as pets.

One snowy white hen tried to leap into pecking distance, intent on the charm bracelet dangling from my wrist. I nicknamed her Chicken—cleverness was not my strong suit.

The woman shook her head. "No gay. No gay."

She was obviously attracted to shiny jewelry. The chicken, not the old woman.

"Yes," I replied. "He is."

"Stupid girl." With a huff, she threw her hands up in surrender and stomped away, muttering to herself in a stream of unflattering-sounding Chinese.

Lord, how I wished she was right.

Even after three hours of traipsing across Manhattan and back, hunting for obscure ethnic groceries and gourmet food markets, Chris looked as yummy as a Peach Cobbler with vanilla ice cream and extra cinnamon. Neither of us mentioned my little pajama-induced indiscretion, though I swore I could still feel his tingling touch on my wrist.

I jumped as Chicken flung herself at the cage wall, grazing my wrist in her determination. I jerked my hand out of reach. I was not about to lose a lifetime of charms to a fashion-obsessed chicken.

Chris turned to me, cans in hand. Seeing my hands empty, he asked, "You're not getting anything?"

"Oh no," I assured him. "I'm all stocked up on eye of newt and tongue of bat."

His face lit up. "They have newt eyes? Where?"

My face fell. Maybe Chris was emotionally unbalanced. Or maybe he was into the occult. Or—

"I'm kidding, Bethany. Kidding."

Um, ah, well. "I knew that."

Chris laughed, and his untroubled joy warmed over me. Then I was laughing too, at myself, at him, at the ironic nature of life.

"You're a nutty gal, Bethany Lange." Chris wiped at the tears laughter had squeezed from his eyes. "Nuttier than a fruitcake."

"You're pretty fruity, yourself," I teased back.

He froze and stared at me. I realized what I'd said, shocked at my unintended pun. I was ready to apologize until Chris doubled over, laughing.

The Chinese woman glared at us and shook her head.

Was she giving us the evil eye?

I had a silly feeling that, as soon as we left, she would do some Chinese Voodoo cleansing ritual. Probably with choking incense fumes, ancient mystic chanting, and the sacrifice of an innocent—

The woman's small brown eyes darted to the cage. Following her gaze, I saw Chicken leaping with tireless energy, desperate to reach my charms. Chicken shook her head, blowing the silky feathers out of her face for a second, and stared at me with intent black eyes. Pleading. Begging.

I looked from Chicken to the woman.

Back to Chicken.

Back to the woman.

A picture of Chicken, her little throat sliced and a flood of red coating her beautiful white feathers, popped into my head.

Without thinking, I turned and lifted Chicken from the pen, ignoring Chris's bewildered look as I announced, "I'm taking the chicken."

Chris paid for his pickled garlic, dried seaweed, and canned abalone—ew. I shelled out nearly eighty dollars for my four-pound chicken. Apparently this was an imported chicken and the price included airfare from China.

"What are you going to do with her?" Chris asked.

I looked down at Chicken. "I don't know."

The chicken lay content in the brown paper bag the woman had given me. Compared to the other way she might have been leaving the store—in butcher paper—maybe she realized this was a better way to go.

Or maybe she thought that if she went home with me she'd have a chance to get hold of my charms.

Then again, she was just a chicken. Maybe she didn't know any better.

As I shifted my purse to get a better hold on the bag, Chicken stood up, flapped her wings in a startled attempt to fly away. Of course the bag was too small for her wingspan and she just ended up smacking her wings against the paper, making me almost drop her.

Chris held the door open for me. "Then why'd you buy her?"

For a second I debated whether I should tell him the real reason—he already thought I was a total nutcase. But I didn't have another reason. I mentally smacked myself upside the head, trying to remember that it didn't matter what Chris thought of me. We would only ever be friends.

Friends didn't need to be reassured of each other's sanity. Shared lunacy only strengthened a friendship.

As we walked out of the store I started to tell him about what I had seen—er, imagined. One of the dozens of mirrors spinning in the front window caught my eye as I walked past. In it, I saw the reflection of the Chinese woman.

She smiled like someone for whom things had worked out exactly as planned.

Looking down at Chicken, I wondered what the New York City Health Code had to say about chickens living in apartments.

"IS THAT DINNER?" Randy flopped onto the sofa, eyeing the cage in the corner of the room.

After separating from Chris, I had gone to a big pet store on the way home and—shockingly enough—they had a complete line of chicken supplies. At least the clerk had claimed they were chicken supplies ... they might have been for really big parrots or something.

Chicken now clucked and pecked contentedly in a roomy cage with a floor of shredded newspaper that she seemed intent on clawing into a big pile in the corner.

Kit, close on Randy's heels, approached the cage.

"Looks kinda scrawny." She poked her finger between the wire before I could warn her. With a yelp, she jumped back as Chicken pecked.

"That," I explained, "is Chicken. My new pet… chicken."

"A pet chicken?" Randy watched me, eyes wide and jaw dropped. "You freaked out when I brought home an ant farm in third grade."

He was wise not to mention the garter snakes.

At the kitchen counter, I dipped the stainless steel scoop into the bag of pellets and carefully poured the sweet smelling feed into the ceramic bowl inside the cage. A few pellets spilled out onto shredded newspaper, but Chicken quickly dug them out. "Yes, well, I didn't have a choice. She was about to be sacrificed."

Head tilted and brows scrunched, Randy stared at me like I'd dyed my hair purple. Then, as if deciding I was far too convoluted to decipher, he shook his head and reached for the remote.

Kit turned to me. "Ready for tonight?"

"For what?" I watched Chicken approach the bowl slowly, hesitantly. She pecked at the food, testing it. She must have found it satisfactory because she stepped right up and dove in.

"The stakeout."

My head snapped up and I darted a glance Randy's direction. What had Kit told him?

"Don't worry, Sis," Randy assured me as he flipped

through the few channels of my basic cable. "I'm all for you outing the bastard."

I wasn't sure having Randy's full-fledged support was such a good thing.

He looked at me. That mischievous grin spelled trouble.

"Or would that be inning?" His blue eyes looked me over once. "Shouldn't you be dressed in black?"

I grabbed the nearest object—a book on chicken-rearing—and flung it at his head. Drat, I'd always had terrible aim.

"I don't own black."

Randy shrugged, picked the book up off the floor, and set it on the coffee table. The sounds of SportsCenter came on the television and his attention on me evaporated.

"Men."

"Don't I know it," Kit agreed. "Now, shouldn't you get ready?"

"What's to get ready? I don't even know what we're doing."

"We're staking your guy out."

"He's not my guy."

"Fine." She waved a dismissive hand at me. "We're staking your *ex*-guy out."

"I don't think so."

Kit stepped toward me, her jaw set and determination blazing in her eyes.

I backed away. "Listen, Kit. Last night was a mistake."

She continued her advance.

"I was drunk."

By moving to the right, she maneuvered me in the opposite direction.

"Vulnerable."

I glanced at the front door, but Kit moved lightning fast to block my path. She must have played sports in high school. Maybe basketball. Or soccer. Those were quick reflexes.

"We can't do that again."

"We can," Kit said, advancing faster. "And we will."

"No, we—"

As I spoke, Kit herded me into my bedroom, closing the door behind us.

"Bethany. This is your chance—a chance for all women everywhere—to get irrefutable proof that your ex is a two-faced, cheating, deceiving louse. He deserves to be inned for the sake of all humanity. Don't let him profit from any more of his lies. He cheated you once; don't let him cheat you again."

Something dark and desperate shone in her eyes. Something that told me she took Evan's betrayal as something deeply personal. And as I watched her watch me—hope mingling with her despair—I knew I had to do whatever it took to prove the truth. For Kit. For me. For any woman who had been or was about to be deceived. I had to stop the lies, if only in this one instance.

"You're right, Kit," I agreed, laying my hands on her shoulders. "Let's do this."

Her face lit up. "Great!"

I headed for my closet to change out of the cardigan and pencil skirt I'd worn out with Chris. Kit followed, peering over my shoulder as I searched the stack of shelves on the left for the one pair of jeans I owned.

"You really don't have any black," she commented, a touch of awe in her tone.

"I'm not in mourning," I explained.

"I didn't think anyone could live in New York and not have a wardrobe of black, black, and more black."

Aha! I found the jeans. The soft denim brought back memories of home and my teenage days working at Calbert's Restaurant—an appallingly hillbilly establishment where they threw—*actually threw!*—fresh rolls across the room to the customers. I could almost smell the fried okra and sorghum molasses. My body shuddered involuntarily.

Those were the days before Daddy moved us to Atlanta.

Those were memories best forgotten.

"I am almost certain"—I returned my attention to Kit, distracting myself from the memories—"there is nothing in the Manhattan water that turns clothes black."

"I know," she said, still gawking at my mostly-pastel wardrobe, "but I just thought—well—jeez, Bethany, you are an anomaly."

"Thank you." I selected a crisp white t-shirt from the stack and headed behind the Chinese screen in the corner to change. "I think."

"I mean," Kit said, "I'm not a Goth or anything—"

I slid down my zipper and shrugged out of my dress.

"—I don't even wear black often, really—"

Stepping into the jeans, I pulled them up over my hips. They still hugged my curves like they were made for me.

"—it makes my hair look blah—"

The t-shirt smoothed down my hair as I tugged it into place.

"—but I still have tons of black," she finished.

I emerged from behind the screen, tousling my hair back into shape. My bare toes curled into the plush oriental carpet that covered most of the room as I crossed to the full-length mirror on the closet door.

Kit joined me, staring blatantly at my reflection.

"Holy crap! Bethany—" She smacked my shoulder, nearly sending me tumbling. "—you're a sexpot. Why don't you dress like this all the time?"

"Like what?"

"Casual. Basic." Her hands fluttered up and down in an encompassing gesture. "Hot."

I shrugged, but turned to evaluate myself in the mirror anyway. Casual had never been my style. Even in high school I'd leaned more towards formal. Classy. Ladylike. Senior year I was voted "Most Likely to be First Lady" because I wore a pink pillbox hat to the College Fair.

The casual girl in the mirror was unfamiliar. The simple cotton t-shirt clung to her, stretching across the smooth roundness of her chest and skimming over the flat plane of her belly. Soft blue denim, frayed at the hems from countless washings, fit loosely from her waist to her knees before flaring into a subtle-but-sexy bootcut—I'd never gone in for the skinny line. Her hair, a blend of caramel, honey, and golden tones, hung past her shoulders in carefree, bed-rumpled waves. Somehow completing the picture and making it all the sexier were her bare feet, cotton candy pink polished toes wiggling under the unaccustomed scrutiny.

Lord, I *was* hot.

Getting into the full swing of casual style, I dug around my closet for my sole pair of sneakers. They were remnants of my early days in the apartment when I'd spent most of my free time painting, plastering, and tiling—not activities suited to pumps. Buried beneath a pile of extra blankets—even after nearly fifteen years I was still not accustomed to Northern winters—the sneakers looked practically new. Still as bright white as the day I'd bought them, the only signs of use were smudges of dirt on the insoles and one dot of mint green paint, *a la* my kitchen.

As I laced them up I remembered how much fun I'd had refinishing the apartment. Implementing Evan's designs. It had been a long time since I'd worked with my hands. Suddenly I felt the need to get dirty.

Maybe I could take up pottery.

Squaaaaawk!

"*Aaack!*"

The screeching cry of human and poultry echoed through my closed door. Oh dear Lord.

"We'd better go save Randy from the chicken," I said, knotting my laces into quick bows and heading for the door.

"Don't you mean save the chicken from Randy?" Kit asked.

I faced her as I reached the door. "You would think, wouldn't you?"

"You know," Kit mused as I turned to leave, "if you keep looking this good, you might tempt Evan into dropping the pretense yourself."

She smiled as she said it, so I knew it was a joke. But as she pushed past me to rescue man and fowl from each other the idea settled in and wouldn't leave.

Hmmm. If nothing else worked, that just might—

"Get that feathered monster—*aaack!*"

"Bethany," Kit shouted, "you might want to—"

"I'm coming," I said. But the thought of tempting Evan back into the closet just wouldn't go away.

TEN

KIT HELD up a six-pack of Fuzzy Navel wine coolers. "I brought the reinforcements."

"Can't," I said, motioning to the steering wheel in front of me. "I'm driving."

Not to mention the fact that, although I was inspired to my act of womanly duty, I was hesitant to have a repeat of last night's drunken confessions. The car seemed like the easiest excuse.

Besides, my stalking enterprises hadn't turned out real well when I was sober. I could only imagine what would happen if I tried it drunk.

The wine coolers did look really refreshing, though.

Never deterred, Kit leaned across the console, plucked the keys from the ignition, and tossed them in the back seat.

"I'll won't let you drive drunk."

I started to reach back to find them, but she stopped me.

"Come on, let's have a little fun with this." She handed me a bottle. "We might be here all night."

Suddenly I was very thirsty.

Twisting off the cap, I admitted she was right. We could be here, parked in my Beetle across the street from Evan's for a long time. The six percent alcohol content would make the time fly by faster.

It only took one swig to erase my nervous energy.

Kit smiled. "Good?"

"Oh yeah." Another swig. "We used to down these by the case in high school."

"Really?" She pulled out another bottle before setting the six-pack on the floor. "You don't strike me as the type who partied in high school."

I shrugged. "Not much else to do back home."

She twisted off the lid and took a sip. "I thought you were from Atlanta."

We were. Now. Back then we lived in a tiny burg in the Florida panhandle—an area not named Floribama without reason. Cypress Springs was the size of a kettle of grits and about as exciting. Hot and humid in winter. Hotter and more humid in summer. About the only things to do were get drunk, get pregnant, or get arrested. I chose option A.

The truth was, I told people I was from Atlanta. Not that I was ashamed of my rural roots, but—okay, I was ashamed. And I wasn't some movie heroine, about to return home and find happiness with that backwater dot on a map after fifteen years of city life.

My parents lived in Atlanta. I spent my senior year in Atlanta and graduated from prestigious Woodward Academy. Unless someone tracked down my grammar school records, my life began in the Horizon City.

After all my less-than-fond reminiscing, Kit was chugging

the last of her wine cooler and seemed to have forgotten her question.

Good. I hated lying to friends.

An hour later it was dark and the six-pack was gone.

We had pushed back both the seats to give us as much room as possible and had so far observed Evan scratching his head, talking on the phone—probably to the secret girlfriend—and taking off his shirt.

When he appeared, bare-chested, in the window, Kit asked, "How long did you two date?"

I cringed.

No, that wasn't fair. It hadn't been a bad relationship; up until the end it was actually the best I'd had. The end, however, was definitely cringe-worthy. "Almost a year and a half."

She let out a low whistle.

"You're telling me."

A year and a half of my life wasted on a louse. There were better men out there—good men—there had to be. Why couldn't I find them?

Chris's blue eyes popped to mind.

Aaargh! Bad Bethany, bad, bad, bad. Unavailability poster boy. Let me rephrase that: There had to be good, *straight* men out there.

Chris's image wouldn't go away.

I pressed my fingertips to my temples, hoping to massage away those errant, erroneous thoughts.

"Drat." It didn't work.

"What's wrong?"

Kit lolled her head back and forth against the headrest, eyes closed and blissfully unhaunted by disturbing images of blue eyes and dark hair and dimpled smiles and broad shoulders and muscular chests—

"Heaven help me," I groaned, and hung my head in my hands.

Lolling to face me, Kit opened her eyes. "Tell me."

I looked at her—far from sober and so willing to help, to listen—and I cracked. "Can I tell you something in the strictest confidence?"

"Of course."

"Even stricter than the bonds of family?"

"*Yes,*" she said, clearly exasperated.

She had even less patience when she was drunk.

Leaning back in the seat, I dropped my head back and stared up through my moonroof—the clouds above peach-tinted by the city lights—convincing myself that confession was good for the soul.

"I kind of—" I faltered and tried again. "I can't stop—" Nope, not that time either.

From the corner of my eye I saw that I had Kit's rapt attention.

Swallowing my pride, I clamped my eyes shut and confessed, "I've got the hots for your brother."

Silence filled the car.

Not even the sound of breathing—because I, of course, was holding my breath. Consumed by curiosity, I pried my eyes open. Kit had her lips pressed together so tightly little white lines radiated out in every direction. Her eyes, wide as saucers and full of surprise, glistened with a sheen of tears.

What was going on? I tilted my head to the side—as if the altered angle would give me a better perspective on what she was thinking.

Then, in a sudden and gusty burst, she exploded in a flurry of gasping laughter.

"Priceless," she managed between laughs. "Absolutely priceless."

Well, what kind of reaction did I expect? I had just confessed to a growing obsession with a gay man. It was pretty funny, in a sad-pathetic-and-delusional kind of way. My laughter joined hers as I faced a realistic look at the situation.

"What kind of fool," I asked, "who has dated five guys who later came out gay, falls for one she knows is gay up front?"

Kit sobered—a little. "Irony's a bitch."

My laughter died on a sigh.

I needed less irony in my life. More certainty.

"What we need," Kit cheered, voice slightly slurred and sing-song-y, "is more wine cooler."

"And food," I agreed. "Chinese."

When I started to reach back for the keys, Kit stopped me. She pulled out her phone. "I'll take care of it."

I shrugged. Kit dialed.

"Hey," she said when someone answered, "I want a delivery from Hop Sing's."

She must have been ordering from a delivery cooperative—the kind that delivers for a group of restaurants.

My eyes drifted back up to Evan's window. The lights in the living room were out, but I could see the flickering glow of the television. I could imagine Evan laying on his maroon velvet couch, relaxed against the *fleur-de-lis* print throw pillows with gold piping. How many nights had I laid against his chest on that couch eating *Mia Famiglia* Sicilian pizza while we watched reality TV?

"Do you miss him?" Kit asked as she pocketed her phone.

Did I?

I missed having someone to share with; the closeness.

I missed having someone warming the other side of my bed.

I missed having a regular Friday night date.

But no—I shook my head—I didn't miss Evan in my life.

"I miss the relationship," I explained.

"We can do something about that." She smiled, then turned no nonsense. "Let's stop this pity party. This is a girls night out, and we're here to have fun."

"I thought we were here to prove Evan was a louse."

"Exactly." She flung open the car door and stepped out. Ducking down to glare at me when I didn't move to follow, she said, "Don't make me drag you out of the car. We have just enough time before the food gets here."

She straightened and turned away, slamming the door as she spun. I climbed out of the car. By the time I dug the keys out of the back seat she was already across the street. Clicking the door locks with a reassuring honk, I hurried to follow.

As she pressed every call button on the intercom panel, I wondered what she was up to. Then some unsuspecting stranger buzzed us in and I followed her into the lobby.

She made a beeline for the bank of mailboxes.

"Which one?"

"Wha—"

"Which mailbox is his?" She swept a hand impatiently at the boxes.

"3B," I offered hesitantly.

Before I could blink, Kit pulled a bobby pin from her pocket and attacked the lock on box 3B.

I didn't bother asking why she had a bobby pin in her pocket, because I had a feeling the answer would only alarm me.

"What are you doing?" I asked in a rushed whisper. Peering over her shoulder as she worked, I watched as she bent and twisted the metal pin in the lock.

"Sneaking a peek at your boy's mail," she answered casually.

"He's not my boy," I argued.

"Fine," she said. "Your *ex*-boy's mail."

As if this were just another daily enterprise.

"Tampering with the mail is a federal offense."

"I'm not tampering," she argued. "I'm just looking."

"I doubt the FBI will see the distinction."

I had visions of Kit and me, under the bare bulb of an interrogation room, trying to explain the difference between tampering and looking. They all ended with sunglassed smirks and handcuffs.

I shuddered.

To distract myself, I glanced through the pile of catalogs on the shelf below the boxes. Everyone in the building dumped their unwanted Pottery Barns and Restoration Hardwares on that shelf. It was a treasure trove of commonplace and obscure catalogs, and I used to love sifting through the stacks.

At the distant sound of a buzzer, I paused in my perusal to glance at the front door. Through the glass panel I could see a swarthy delivery man holding a pizza box and a paper bag.

I leaned casually against the shelf, resting my hand on a Victoria's Secret catalog, in an attempt to not look like a crazed stalker breaking into someone's mailbox.

"Ah-ha!" Kit exclaimed. One final twist of her wrist and the little bronze door swung open. "Damn."

The box was empty.

"He must have picked up his mail already," I commented needlessly.

Kit threw me a *duh* look.

"Hey," she said, glancing at my hand where it rested on a red-lace-clad supermodel, "nice bra."

She pulled it out from under my hand and lifted it to get a better look.

"You know, I noticed you don't stock any push-up bras at the shop," she continued, "Maybe you should." She lowered the catalog to look at me. "A lot of those middle-aged housewives want to enhance what they've got and it might boost sales."

I barely heard what she said. Grabbing her wrist, I lifted the catalog back to eye level.

"What?" she asked, trying to peer around the slick pages.

With a twist, I turned her forearm so she could see—and read—the back cover of the catalog.

"I don't—"

"Look!" I pushed the catalog closer.

"I still don't— Ohhh!" She pulled the catalog out of the way and met my gaze, eyes blazing. "Someone's been reading racy catalogs."

There, in the lower right corner of the back cover, was Evan's name and address. What would a gay guy want with a lingerie catalog?

"Naughty, naughty boy," I said.

Kit's wicked grin would have made the devil proud.

I had one to match.

"Let's call this"—She tucked the catalog into her back pocket.—"Exhibit A."

Footsteps echoed down the stairwell at the far end of the lobby. Probably whoever had ordered the pizza. Through the window, the delivery man moved and I could clearly read the *Mia Famiglia* on his t-shirt.

Evan's favorite pizza place.

"We need to get out of here."

I grabbed Kit by the arm and ran for the door. The delivery man watched in mild amusement as we hurried past, bursting out onto the street and making a mad dash for the car. I beeped the car locks as we approached. We had just pulled the doors shut around us when the front door opened. Evan stood in the doorway, door propped open against his shoulder as he paid for the food.

My heart was pounding at the thrill of our success and my breath whooshed in and out, but we watched in silence as Evan took the food and returned inside.

"That was close," I said when he was out of sight.

"That was nothing," Kit returned. "I got caught in my ex's dorm room going through his dirty laundry."

Awed by her nerve, I asked, "So this isn't your first stalking?"

"No." She laughed as if the idea were ridiculous.

That was, I supposed, a reassuring thought.

Not just because that meant Kit was a serious asset to this enterprise, but because it meant that I was not the only woman in history reduced to hunting her ex like escaping prey. Suddenly I felt a lot less ashamed.

"I thought I was being obsessive," I said.

"A little fixation is natural. In the great grand scheme of

things," she explained, "you are just the latest link in a long, long chain of women intent on revenge."

"Really?"

"Oh yeah." She motioned me closer. "I had a friend who wrote her name in nail polish on the hood of her ex-fiance's '64 Mustang. And another who mailed a tape of her ex in a *ménage a trois* to his Southern Baptist parents."

"Wow."

That made the incident at Carmello's look like prank call.

"Then, of course, there's the urban legend of the woman who Bobbitted her husband and mailed his piece to his mistress."

"Good Lord!" I gasped. "There is no way that's true—"

Knock, knock, knock.

"*Aaack!*"

We both jumped at the knock on my window. Huddling away from the door, all I could see was the paper bag with a menu covered in Chinese characters stapled to the top. Kit recovered first. She reached across me and lowered the window.

"It's about time," she admonished.

Still startled by the sudden intrusion of the delivery, I hung back. I nearly fainted when the blue eyes of my fantasies bent down to peer into the car.

Smiling, Chris asked, "Now what are nice girls like you doing out here on the streets?"

ELEVEN

"JESUS CHRIST," Kit shouted. "You scared us, you bastard."

"Hey, you called me." He pulled my door open and held out the delivery bag. "Be nice if you want your food."

Kit leaned across me, snatching the bag from her brother's hand. She threw him a twisted look before adding, "Did you bring the beverages."

"Ah-ah-ah." He shook a finger at her. "I didn't hear the magic words."

I looked at Kit, still leaning across me to reach Chris. She rolled her eyes.

"Alright," she relented. "Get in."

Then Kit pushed me out of the car. Oh, not like fully out and onto the ground, but hard enough to propel me to standing on the sidewalk. And into Chris's arms.

"Evening, chicken lady."

"Ha, ha." I scowled and stepped aside, but my ire faded as soon as he flashed his dimpled smile.

His clear blue eyes scanned my body and I was suddenly acutely aware of my casual appearance. If he were straight, I'd have said his gaze lingered where the t-shirt hugged my breasts and the jeans skimmed my hips. But, since he wasn't, I knew he was just evaluating my outfit in a purely objective sort of way.

Somehow, that made me more nervous.

When his eyes returned to mine, they were smiling.

"Nice threads, sugar," he said. "Laid back looks good on you." He started for the car, but stopped. "Then again, every-thing looks good on you."

I couldn't help grinning. Like I'd been eagerly awaiting his approval.

Still, a compliment was a compliment, no matter the source.

He stepped toward the car as Kit tugged the lever to release the seat, sending it snapping forward. Chris ducked down swiftly, easing into the cramped back seat with the ease of an athlete. I found myself watching the way his muscles rippled beneath his plain black t-shirt as he reached forward to push the seat back into position.

If he was uncomfortable in the tiny space, he didn't let on. His grin never faltered.

I slid back into my seat, jerking the door shut behind me.

"So what's the occasion?" Chris asked as he handed forward another six-pack of Fuzzy Navels.

"We're undertaking a stalking," Kit explained.

She took the six-pack, handed me a bottle and offered one to Chris.

He declined. "I think one of us should stay sober."

Kit shrugged, as if it didn't matter one way or another. I twisted off the cap and threw back a good gulp.

Chris, leaning forward between the seats, asked, "Who are we stalking?"

I cringed.

But before I could say anything, Kit blurted, "Evan."

Tact did not appear to be in her everyday vocabulary.

"Evan?" he repeated. "From-the-show-Evan?"

I groaned and closed my eyes.

Kit elaborated. "Bethany used to date him."

"Curiouser and curiouser," Chris mused. "I take it that was *before* he came out of the closet."

"Yes—"

"Actually," I explained, "he's not gay."

Kit dug out the cartons from the bag, handing me my spicy vegetable lo mein and a pair of chopsticks. I rested my bottle between my knees and dug into the food like a starving model.

I could feel Chris's eyes on me. "You're kidding."

"Yeah," Kit continued as she sniffed her carton of cashew chicken. "Who'd ever imagine a guy pretending to be gay just to be on some dumb TV show?"

She said it with such an odd tone, I turned to look at her. She and Chris were glaring at each other with an intensity capable only between siblings. When she saw me watching them, she cocked her brows and ended the stare-down, turning her attention to her food.

Chris turned and looked at me.

He met my confused look with a searching intensity. Like he was trying to figure out what I was thinking. If only I knew. The Fuzzy Navels were taking their toll on my mental faculties.

"Why stalk him?" he asked.

"To prove he's straight," I admitted. Might as well spill the whole story. "To prove he's a lying louse."

"To whom?"

I hadn't really considered that. "To myself, I guess."

"But you already believe it," he countered.

"Then to the world," I quipped, feeling defensive. "I want it on the CNN news crawler. *Evan Riley is Straight* speeding across the bottom of my TV."

He held my gaze for a long moment. He held it so long that it turned into a staring contest. Neither of us was going to look away. Nothing was going to—

Kit tugged on my sleeve. "I think he's gone to bed."

She pointed up at Evan's window.

I leaned down, peering through the passenger window. His window was pitch black. Not even the flickering glow of the television interrupted the darkness.

"Some stalkers we are," I mused. "So boring even our quarry fell asleep."

"At least we got Exhibit A," she countered.

Chris leaned up from the back seat. "What's Exhibit A?"

Kit and I just looked at each other and laughed.

♥

"JUST LISTEN FOR A SECOND, LAURA JANE."

The first thing I heard when I let myself into my apartment after Chris drove us home was Randy pleading into the phone. The plaintive sadness in his voice tightened around my heart like a vise.

I wasn't proud of my actions, but I closed the door silently and stood in the front hall. Listening.

"I just want to talk. You never—"

Leaning against the door, I listened to the rhythm of my breathing as Randy waited for Laura Jane to finish speaking. I could almost hear her deceptively honeyed voice cutting his heart to pieces.

"—but if you would just give me another chance—"

Thump.

The sound of Randy pounding a fist on the kitchen counter echoed through the apartment. Clearly Laura Jane was not up for giving him another chance. I started to leave my eaves-dropping position to be by his side, to comfort him.

But his voice stopped me.

"Please, Laura Jane. I'll give you anything you want." His voice caught as he finished, "I promise I can change."

My cheeks flamed. Between the two of them, Randy was not the one who needed to change. He was a sweet, devoted, and loving boyfriend. A loyal boyfriend, even when she didn't deserve his loyalty.

She was the cheater. The manipulator. The one in need of a personality makeover.

If I ever got my hands on that conniving bi—

"Fine." He sounded completely dejected. "I understand."

Seconds later I heard the phone click off.

"Damnit!"

Deciding it was better if he didn't know I'd been listening, I opened the door and slipped back into the hall. The last thing I wanted was to add embarrassment to his heartache. Keys in hand, I jangled them loudly as I stabbed at the lock, intention-ally missing several times before connecting. I twisted the lock and opened the door.

"See you later Mrs. Franklin," I shouted down the empty

hall. I wanted to make sure Randy had time to compose himself.

He appeared in the doorway to the kitchen, a bright smile on his face and no sign of the despondency I'd heard just moments ago.

"Welcome home, Bets." He forced his smile wider. "Have fun tonight?"

There was a tension in his voice—a combination of Laura Jane's dismissal and, I was sure, keeping from interrogating me about my nocturnal activities. He was trying. Any huff I might have mustered deflated in the wake of Randy's pleading conversation. He didn't need me on his case.

He needed a friend more than a sibling.

"A blast," I replied with a forced grin of my own. "Had dinner with Kit and Chris in the East Village."

Not entirely a lie. We had eaten dinner. And we had been in the East Village. I just left out the part about stalking my ex from my car across the street.

"That's nice. I think I'll turn in." He glanced at the couch. "Kit ran me ragged today."

"Oh. Okay."

I watched helplessly as he trudged to the living room, pulled out the sleeper sofa, and pulled back the covers. He crawled under, wearing sweatpants and an Auburn t-shirt.

It was like I was back in middle school, on those nights when Randy used to come into my room when he had a nightmare. He would pull the covers up to his chin and lie motionless, waiting until he thought I was asleep to relax and roll into my arms where he would snuggle all night. By morning, he was always gone.

But this time hurt more.

This time I wouldn't be there when he rolled over.

Shutting off the lights, I stepped out of my sneakers and padded quietly down the hall to my room. Before I closed the door, I glanced back at the motionless figure on the sofa.

I wouldn't be there to caress his back when he shuddered in his sleep. It was a hard feat telling myself he was no longer that frightened little boy. I'd left him on his own to face becoming an adult, to face Daddy's rules and regulations without me as a buffer. He'd been dealing with his own problems for years without me.

If I expected him to let me live my life without his supervision, I had to grant him the same independence.

Still, it was hard to let go.

I lifted my fingertips to my lips and blew him a kiss.

"Sleep well, baby brother," I whispered as I closed the bedroom door.

With the jumbled memories of Chris and Evan and Kit and lo mein bouncing around my wine cooler-fogged brain, I hoped I would find the same peaceful sleep.

TWELVE

Episode 102

Ray in the Morning.

MONDAY WE STARTED SETTING up for the next episode: radio deejay Ray whose fashion sense seemed heavily rooted somewhere between Magnum P.I. and Miami Vice. A whole lotta Hawaiian shirts and short white shorts and not enough tan to pull off the tropical look.

Not enough hair, either.

Thankfully grooming was not my responsibility.

"What do you think for our boy?" Bryce asked as he sashayed into my office and plopped dramatically onto the couch.

I shuffled the pictures of Ray around on my desk, pulling out one taken of the slightly balding, slightly plump man surrounded by three round-faced children with his same warm brown eyes. Happy children. Happy father.

He just needed a little maturity in his wardrobe.

"Well," I mused over the photo. "He came to us because his

radio station is changing their lineup from heavy metal to golden oldies. His clothes need to reflect that change."

"Sweetheart, he's on radio," Bryce teased. "No one's going to see his clothes."

"I know, but what's on the outside will affect how he feels on the inside. If he's dressed like a grownup, he's more likely to act like a grownup. That will come across to his listeners."

"What's your plan?"

"I'm thinking preppy meets professional. A little Southampton and a little Wall Street. A little bit of the classic Fifties for a man in his fifties."

Bryce stifled an over-exaggerated yawn. "Bo-ring."

I crossed my arms over my chest and turned my best you-think-you-can-do-better look on him. "What would you recommend?"

"Right idea," he explained. "Wrong execution. Lose the professional, keep some preppy, add some business casual. Khakis. V-neck sweaters. Sport shirts. And—" He stood up and swung his arms wide, a triumphant grin on his face. "—cowboy boots."

"Cowboy boots?" I repeated.

Ray was a deejay, not a cowboy.

"Come on—" Bryce sauntered over and perched one hip on my desk. "—picture it. The preppy-casual-business outfit, maybe gray khakis and a periwinkle polo shirt. Neat. Clean. Typical. But—" He leaned across my desk, meeting me nose-to-nose. "—add black cowboy boots."

As he described the outfit I pictured it on Ray. The youthful fun of the polo shirt. The classical functionality of the khakis. The attitude of the cowboy boots.

Bryce was right. They were exactly what Ray needed.

No wonder he was the fashion guru.

"Okay," I conceded. "Cowboy boots."

"You know what that means?" Bryce waggled his dark blonde eyebrows.

Um, ah, well. "No."

Hand pressed to his chest, he uttered reverently, "We're going shopping in the Village."

Chris appeared in my doorway. "Did I hear someone say the Village?"

"Yeah," Bryce replied. "You need cowboy boots too?"

"No." Chris looked puzzled, like he didn't quite get the Greenwich Village-cowboy boots connection. "Nameko mushrooms."

Bryce shrugged, as if it made no difference to him, and said, "I'm going to grab my blazer." He sauntered to the door, sliding past—or, more accurately, along—Chris as he exited. "I'll meet you two out front in five."

Chris, still looking confused, glanced my way. "Why do I feel like I've just been molested?"

"Bryce has that effect on people." I grinned as I grabbed my cardigan off the back of my chair. "So what do you need Nameko mushrooms for?"

"I'm going to teach DJ Ray how to make traditional *miso* soup," he explained as he crossed behind my desk, took the cardigan, and held it up for me to slip into. "There's a little Japanese grocery on Charles Street that should have an excellent stock."

I smiled in gratitude for his gentlemanly gesture—as if I hadn't already faced enough evidence of his sexual preference—and led the way out of the building. Really, what straight man helped a woman into her sweater anymore?

We walked in a companionable silence. Side by side, with no pressure to make small talk or appear intelligent. Maybe this had been—past tense, because my days of falling for gay men were *over*—why I was attracted to all those unavailable men. If I knew from the start it would never work out, the pressure to impress was off.

Why couldn't I find that with an *available* man?

"Daydreaming, sugar?"

"Yes, of a sort."

Chris put his arm around me and pulled me to his side. "Well, spend your dreams on something that puts a smile on your face, not a scowl."

I looked up into his clear blue eyes and I knew what fantasy would put a smile on my face. But in the end, it would wind up just another heartache.

"Hey," he chastised, giving my shoulder a squeeze, "that was supposed to cheer you up, not bring you down."

"I know." Shaking off self-pitying thoughts I concentrated on the shopping adventure. "And it did. Promise."

"Good." He released my shoulder as we passed through the front doors and out onto the sidewalk. "Now maybe you can explain the connection between the Village and cowboy boots."

Bryce, shrugging into his corduroy blazer, burst through the doors right behind us. "And you call yourself a gay man," he teased Chris. "Every queer knows the best boots in the city are at Anthony's."

Chris and I looked at each other, actually managing to hold a straight face for a good ten seconds before bursting out in laughter.

Bryce clucked. "Now, if you two lovebirds are ready to go ..."

My laughter abruptly stopped.

Was my uncontrollable attraction to Chris obvious to everyone? Lord, I hoped it wasn't obvious to *him*. I wasn't sure who would be more embarrassed by the revelation.

I looked up. Chris was watching me, his smile softening as if he could my thoughts.

I took that back. I knew exactly who would be more embarrassed: me. Definitely me. I would be mortified.

I shook my head and, desperate to launch some genuine conversation and divert myself and others from my impending mortification, asked Bryce, "Did you ever find your planner?"

Bryce, a man I had been certain was incapable of blushing, actually pinked at the cheeks.

"Actually," he muttered, "I found it in my apartment later. I just ..." He shook his head and scowled. "I know I had it at the shoot, so how did it get back home?"

"Timebuilders error," I offered.

Both men looked at me like I had escaped from a mental ward. As we headed to my car for the trip into Manhattan, I explained my mother's theory of missing things.

"Mom always told us that every second of time was constructed by the Timebuilders. They work 24-7, seconds ahead of the current time to construct the next second and the next and the next." We approached my car and I unlocked it with the remote.

"That's a lot of seconds and a lot of details to keep track of. Sometimes they forget to build something into a second—or more. Then, when they finally remember, they put it back in somewhere you wouldn't have looked in the first place. So, when something goes missing and turns up somewhere it shouldn't have been, it's a Timebuilders error."

I glanced at my shopping companions before opening the driver's door. Bryce looked confused, a deep scowl wrinkling his brow right between his eyes. Chris looked amused, a soft smile turning up the corners of his full, sexy mouth.

Darn it! Stop staring at his mouth, no matter how full and sexy and kissable—

No!

"Let's go," I ordered. "I don't want to get caught in rush hour."

I yanked open the door, noting as I dropped into the car that, at eleven o'clock in the morning, rush hour was a long ways off.

Mom also said it was never too early to plan ahead.

♥

"HOW ABOUT THESE?" Bryce asked as he held up a pair of turquoise and magenta cowboy boots decorated with rhinestones and rosette stitching.

Not precisely mature straight guy wear.

Surely Anthony's had some less outrageous styles.

"I think Ray needs less turn it up and more tone it down." Browsing through pair after pair of cowboy boots—Chris had taken one look at the miles of stock and run back out the door, saying he would get the mushrooms he needed and then meet us out front—I pulled out a pair of black ones. "Black goes with everything."

Bryce snapped his fingers, bringing an eager young salesman in his wake as he came to take a closer look.

"Details, Wyatt," he demanded.

"B-black lizard," the nervous Wyatt answered. He didn't take his eyes off Bryce, even as he recited the major bullet points. "Black Teju lizard foot. 13-inch full height. Cushion comfort insole. Black welt stitch."

Bryce took the right boot, holding it up for closer inspection. He inhaled deeply, like he was testing the scent of the leather. "More."

Wyatt's eyes grew wide—in what looked like fear—but he continued. "Hand rolled. Hand-pegged steel shanks—"

"Comfort?"

"Like walking on a cloud—"

"Lifespan?"

"With the proper care?" Wyatt asked, then answered desperately, "Forever."

Bryce scrutinized both the boots and Wyatt, his green eyes squinting first at one then the other. I watched, feeling like I was seeing a master at work. Of course, with his work history —dotted with the likes of Colette Couture, Bradford's, and Ferrero—he was a master. He probably knew more about men's fashion than almost anyone.

With one last squint to evaluate Wyatt's own choice in footwear—a pair of cream-colored alligator boots that matched his cream colored jeans and the fringe on his denim shirt— Bryce smiled and grabbed the left boot from my grasp.

"We'll take 'em," he announced, shoving them into Wyatt's chest.

Boots in hand, Wyatt raced to the register.

Bryce turned to me, eyes bright with excitement. "And

now," he said, "it's my turn." His eyes scanned the store. "So many boots, so little—" Gaze frozen over my left shoulder, his face fell. He backed up two steps, then muttered, "I've seen enough boots to last me a lifetime. I'll be out front."

He spun away and hurried out of the shop.

One second he was keen on boot shopping for himself, the next he was out of the store. I turned to my left, wondering what could have set him off like that.

All I saw was a young woman with curly red hair checking out a pair of pink ladies boots.

Though I was, of course, appalled by her choice in footwear, I didn't see anything disturbing enough to send Bryce racing out of the store.

The woman looked up, her bright brown gaze pinning me to the spot. A scorching fury filled her eyes. And it was directed at me. There was something vaguely familiar about her, but I certainly didn't know her. And certainly not well enough to earn that kind of scorn.

Who did she think I was—

"Three-forty-seven ninety-nine," Wyatt announced from the register.

Dragging myself away from her penetrating stare, I pulled the show credit card out of my wallet and handed it over. By the time I had signed the receipt and taken the shopping bag from Wyatt—who informed me that he had scribbled his number on an Anthony's business card and could I please see that Bryce got it—the shop was empty.

The curly-haired redhead with some serious anger issues was gone.

BRYCE AND CHRIS were sitting on a green bench in the small park across the street from Anthony's.

"Let me take that," Chris offered as I approached.

He jumped up and took the plastic bag from me, even as I tried to protest that it wasn't too heavy. Holding it out of my reach, he clamped a hand on my shoulder to keep me from taking it back.

"I have a treat for us," he announced.

I gave up grabbing for the bag.

"Ooh, does it come in chocolate and vanilla?" Bryce cooed.

"Neither." Chris turned and headed up Bleeker Street. "Follow me."

With a nervous glance at the Anthony's storefront, Bryce hurried after Chris, staying to the far side. Though I had my own transportation and could leave them to their own devices, the flash of mischief I had seen in Chris's eyes compelled me to follow.

The buildings in this part of the Village—west of Seventh Avenue—were taller and slightly newer than the quaint streets of three- and four-story rowhouses typically associated with the neighborhood. But still, the streets were narrow and the buildings were predominantly brick. Massively different than the wide streets and cast iron facades in SoHo. It felt like an entirely different city.

We turned left on 10th and stopped in the middle of the block in front of a red brick building. There was a small hand-painted sign in the basement window that read, MADAME RUFONI GYPSY FORTUNETELLER.

This struck me as odd since most fortunetellers advertised with glaring neon signs and flashing lights. Maybe she was a discount palm-reader.

"Oh no," I argued as Chris descended the stone steps to the black door with a big brass knocker. "I am *not* getting my fortune told."

"Why not?" Chris argued. "It'll be fun."

"Scared, Bethany?" Bryce taunted.

"No, of course not. I just—"

"No arguments," Chris countered as he tapped the brass knocker three times. "I've already paid."

"—don't like having strangers in my business."

The black door swung open with a noisy creak.

A little, dark-skinned woman with age-earned wrinkles and sharp black eyes peered out at the trio who had dared to knock on her door.

I couldn't have pictured a more stereotypical fortuneteller. She was dressed in deep reds and purples, from the paisley print scarf tied over her long gray hair to her voluminous dress that hung about her in a mass of folds and ruffles. Gold hoop earrings dripping with jingling gold charms, stacks of gold bracelets on each wrist, and chain after gleaming gold chain draped around her neck.

As her penetrating black gaze took in each of us in turn, I felt like my body was stripped away and she looked directly into my soul.

I started to shake off the crazy notion, but then she started laughing. As if she could read my silly thoughts and my even sillier dismissal of her insight.

"Come," she urged in a crackling voice heavily accented by some eastern European language. "You will find what you seek inside."

Leaving the door wide open, she turned and shuffled into the darkened room.

"I don't think this is such a good idea ..."

My argument fell on deaf ears. Or rather deaf backs, as Chris and Bryce disappeared into the darkness after the old gypsy woman.

No way was I going in there. It was dark and creepy and it smelled like—I took a deep breath, surprised to find myself relaxing as I did—it smelled like magnolias. I couldn't resist magnolias. With a sigh, I stepped into the gloom, closing out the light of day by pulling the door behind me.

As my eyes adjusted to the dark room I felt a presence at my side. I was about to scream when Chris shushed me.

"Bryce volunteered to go first," he whispered.

"What a surprise," I whispered back.

I heard—and felt—him chuckle.

Mystical and eerie music filled the room. Like New Age with a Buddhist twist.

The hushed fervor of Madame Rufoni's voice rumbled beneath the tinkling music. Bryce laughed out loud before pushing back from the draped table in the corner.

"I hope so, Madame R," he murmured as he walked away. "I'd be lost without her."

There was a melancholy tenor to his voice, a dramatic change from the usually over-the-top, over-exaggerated Bryce. Without another word, he opened the front door and climbed out of sight. Chris and I looked at each other and shrugged.

"You." Madame Rufoni pointed a red-lacquered fingernail at Chris. "Next."

With a wink, Chris took his place across from the gypsy.

While he got his reading I occupied myself by surveying the room. The only illumination came from a pair of wall sconces just inside the front door and another pair on either side of a beaded-curtained doorway leading to a back room. Simple, abstract paintings of near-, middle-, and far-eastern mystical symbols hung on the walls. And other than the table and chairs in the corner, the only furniture in the room was a glass display case in the front window.

Though the window was heavily draped, blocking out all daylight, the flickering candlelight illuminated the contents with a magical glow.

Tarot cards, crystal balls, relatives of the Ouija board, and dozens of little stones carved with various ancient symbols filled the case.

If I bought into mysticism, I would have felt like a kid in a candy store.

"Your turn," Chris whispered in my ear.

I jumped at his sudden appearance and was about to thoroughly chastise him for sneaking up on me yet again when Madame Rufoni called out, "I tell the fortunes of believers and skeptics alike."

I spun around.

Okay. She had guessed from my body language that I didn't believe.

That's how fortunetellers performed, right? They were fluent in the art of body language. Nothing mystical about that at all.

I approached the table cautiously, trying to curtail any other blatant body language. Madame Rufoni motioned me to hurry up, urging me to take my seat and give her my hand. When she curled her wrinkled fingers around my wrist and yanked my palm closer, I felt a shock shoot up my arm.

"Not all that is magic is in the mind," she cautioned.

I tried to pull away, but her grip tightened.

Maybe she had an electrode or something in her palm. Something that sent a tiny shock of electricity on contact.

She smiled, her teeth bright against the dark tan of her skin. Then she dropped her head and focused on my palm. Her aged finger traced the lines and she hummed softly to herself.

"Very determined," she mused. "Obstinate even. You think you can solve everyone's problems."

Hey! I thought fortunetellers were supposed to tell flattering tales, give positive readings so their clients would come back for more.

"I tell only the truth as I see it." Madame Rufoni turned my palm into the candlelight and squinted down at the area beneath my index and middle fingers. "You give your heart too easily. I see several heartaches that have not healed."

Leaning across the table I looked down at my hand, wondering how she had seen that in my palm.

"But they will," she decreed. "Solve one and all will heal."

Now that was hitting too close to home. I whipped my head around to glare at Chris. He must have told her about Evan and my romantic past. Although, I reasoned, he didn't know more than I had told him and I hadn't told him a lot.

"Your boyfriend did not talk of you."

Aha! My attention shot back to Madame Rufoni. "He is not my boyfriend."

Caught in a mistake. Let's see her twist her way out of that one.

"No. But he soon will be."

"Not likely," I countered. "He's gay."

Madame Rufoni let out a short burst of laughter. The sound seemed foreign to her and she quickly recovered her composure.

"He," she asserted, her heavy accent coloring each word, "is not gay."

What was it with ancient foreign women believing Chris wasn't gay? I mean, I didn't have the best history with determining a man's orientation, but even I could see he swung for the home team.

No matter how much I wished it weren't true.

I started to argue, but Madame Rufoni waved me off.

"There is something important you must learn," she advised, folding my fingers to my palm and pushing my hand away. "You can make no one truly happy but yourself. And if you spend all your time trying to solve the problems of others, you will never solve your own."

Now she was going too far. "I do not try to—"

"Do not argue!" Madame Rufoni surged to her feet and towered over me. "If you wish to find happiness—peace—you must heed my warning."

Staring up into her wizened, wrinkled face I felt myself compelled to listen.

Her face softened and she leaned down across the table to whisper, "The one you love will love you back." Her gaze flickered over my shoulder to Chris and back to me. "If you let him."

"But—"

Before I could respond, she turned with a swirl of her skirts and disappeared behind the beaded curtain.

Stunned, I rose and walked towards the door.

"What did she say?" Chris asked.

"I—" I looked back over my shoulder. "—I don't—"

"No," he interrupted before I could answer, "don't tell me. I think Madame Rufoni's fortunes are only for intended ears."

I wondered what fortune she had told Chris.

Glancing up at Chris, his clear blue eyes intent on me and full of mischief, my heart thudded in my chest. He was so close and so handsome and so—

Drat you, Madame Rufoni.

She just made my efforts to keep my lust in check a million times harder.

All the same, I grabbed a business card off the front display case on our way out the door. I had a feeling I might want a one-on-one with Madame Rufoni again someday.

THIRTEEN

"IS YOUR BROTHER THERE?"

I held my phone away from my ear and stared at the screen. No *Hi Bethany.* No *How are you?* Just *Is your brother there?*

Love you, too, Daddy.

No matter how many times he gave me the cold shoulder, blew me off because he had better things to do or I wasn't doing what he wanted, I always held out that tiny piece of hope. The unfounded hope that someday he would realize just how much I loved him, how much his dismissal hurt, and he would actually talk to me. Show an interest in my life. Believe in my choices and trust that I would get where I wanted to go —or be ready to catch me if I didn't.

See me as more than a disappointment and a receptionist.

It hurt so much that I lashed out.

"Here," I threw the receiver at Randy's lifeless form, slumped on my couch. "Pops wants to talk to you."

I could hear Daddy screaming all the way from Atlanta.

He hated when I called him Pops. Or Daddy-o. Or, even

worse, Frankie. He came from the strict Southern school of showing proper respect to elders. Not that he had ever shown such respect to *his* father. No, he just took the insurance settlement from Grandad's accident, turned it into a multi-mil corporation, uprooted the family to Atlanta, and disavowed all knowledge of our less-than-elite history.

Funny thing was, most of Atlanta's upper crust seemed content not to delve deeper than the plush depths of Daddy's wallet. As long as he paid his country club dues on time, who cared that our mail was forwarded from Cypress Springs?

"No, Dad," I heard Randy explain, "I'm not coming home."

I started to tell him he didn't need to explain anything, that his life was his own and no one else had the right to tell him how to live it, but then I realized that I was doing just that. I didn't have the right to run his life any more than Daddy did.

The compulsion to intervene was almost too strong to overcome. Rather than stick around to fight the impulse, I decided to find release elsewhere.

Grabbing my purse, I mouthed to Randy that I was going out and bolted for the door.

I headed for the one place that could make even the most persistent inclination fade into the background.

Jubilation Day Spa.

I called my aesthetician—number three on my favorites list after my stylist and my manicurist—on the way and pleaded for an appointment.

"I am in desperate need of your magical seaweed wrap," I begged as I practically ran the three blocks from my building to the spa. "As soon as possible."

"For you, Bethany? Always."

Beauty treatments were as necessary as food and shelter.

No matter how tight the bank account got, I always found the funds for regular trips to the spa. Not only were facials and massages excellent for tension relief, but in my business appearance was paramount. I needed to look like the woman my customers wanted to be.

Weeks where my nails went unpolished showed a noticeable drop in revenue. Like every businesswoman knows; you have to spend money to make money.

"Delphine—" I tugged open the bright aqua front door of Jubilation. "—you are an angel."

She was standing behind the counter when I silenced my phone. There was something soothing, reassuring about an attractive, well-coifed European woman in a white lab coat. I could already feel my anxiety melting away.

Holding a white terrycloth robe and matching slippers, Delphine led the way to the locker room.

"Jeremy absolutely loved the cufflinks you suggested." She set the robe and slippers on the gray, ultra-suede sectional before turning a beaming face to me. "He proposed the next day!"

She held up her perfectly manicured left hand, wiggling the fingers as I inspected the massive stone on her ring finger.

"Congratulations!"

I pulled her into an enthusiastic hug, trying to tamp down the feeling that their marriage wouldn't last six months. Granted, Jeremy had stood a little too close and spent a little too much time drooling over my cleavage at the spa's annual Christmas party last year. But who was I to judge?

Delphine *was* French. Maybe she was more open-minded than most American women.

So I just hugged her and put on my congratulations face,

secretly hoping that she didn't quit her day job when she married the millionaire real estate developer. I didn't think anyone else could wrap me in seaweed the way she did.

"You get changed." She waved her left hand at the robe and slippers. "I will be back to fetch you shortly."

With a sigh that let loose all the tension of a day spent following Bryce around the Village—and a lifetime of dealing with Daddy—I started unbuttoning my cardigan and fantasizing about the feel of fluffy terrycloth against my skin.

That was when my vibrated.

"I'm just going to ignore that," I said to myself and proceeded to shove my purse into the nearest locker.

A quick zip and my mint green gabardine skirt dropped over my hips and to the floor.

My phone buzzed again.

I started humming *That Old Black Magic*.

Seconds later I was out of my white lace underthings and shrugging into the robe and stepping into the slippers. I had just set my neatly folded clothes on the locker shelf and was turning the key in the lock when my phone buzzed a third time.

Hand frozen, I debated the merits of ignoring the persistent caller for the bliss of an uninterrupted hour of pampering.

But ...

What if there was a family emergency?

Or an accident on the set?

Or a problem with Chicken?

Shoulders drooped in resignation, I returned the key and rushed to dig my phone out before it went to voicemail.

"H-hello," I panted, catching it midway through the fourth ring.

"Bethany," Cassie said, "we have a crisis."

"What?" Keeping the phone to my ear, I pulled the pile of clothes back out, ready to get dressed and rush to the studio. "What's the matter?"

I heard Cassie's exasperated sigh and set the clothes back on the shelf. Years and years of phone conversations had taught me how to read Cassie's voice like a picture book.

"Danial," she explained in exaggerated panic, "absolutely refuses to wear the shoes you selected for Episode Ray."

Muffled—but clearly agitated—conversation interrupted her melodrama. I could picture Cassie holding the receiver against her chest and rolling her eyes at Danial's argument.

She hadn't gotten to be Production Manager without learning how to manage a crisis. Real or not.

"He *says*," she emphasized, "that they—" Major sigh. "—make him look—" Groan. "—fat."

Stifling a giggle, I told her, "Tell him they didn't make Gage Richards look fat when he wore them to the People's Voice Awards, but I'll be happy to find replacements if that's what he wants."

While Cassie relayed my message, Delphine returned. She frowned at my being on the phone—maybe because of spa's cell-free policy, or maybe because she sensed that dealing with work would negate some of the calming effects of the treatment—then led the way down the back hall to her treatment room.

"You are a genius, Bethany Lange," Cassie cried when she came back on the line. "He just skipped out of my office. I bet he tells the rest of the cast that he's wearing Gage Richard's shoes tomorrow."

"Glad to be of help."

We reached the treatment room and Delphine gestured me onto the massage table before quietly slipping out into the hall to give me time to get under the sheet. The room surrounded me with the cleansing scent of eucalyptus oil and the calming sound of ocean surf.

"If that's all you needed,"—I shrugged out of the robe and hung it on the valet hook next to the door—"I'm in the middle of something right now—"

"Actually," Cassie interrupted, "there is something else."

Oh no. That was Serious Cassie speaking.

I pulled back the crisp white sheet and lifted myself onto the table. "Okay." I wiggled into place and pulled the sheet up to my chest. "What's really wrong?"

"I hate to ask you this, and if you don't want to then say so and we'll find another solution, but it would be really great if you did and—"

"Cassie," I cut in. It was so unlike her to dance around an issue—dance right on top of it was more the norm—that my anxiety grew just listening to her. "Ask me. We'll take it from there."

Delphine knocked softly on the louvered door before reentering the room. Another frown at my still being on the phone. I shrugged apologetically.

"Right. Here's the deal."

Now this was the real Cassie.

"Ray in the Morning has three kids."

"Yes," I replied. "I saw the picture."

Delphine mixed up a big bowl of dark green goo at the corner sink, stirring it into an even consistency before setting it aside and grabbing a shiny silver packet off the shelf. She turned to me, unfolding the packet into a full-size foil sheet—

like one of those emergency, heat-retaining blankets they give you for camping. Not that I'd ever been camping, but I'd heard the tales.

"They live in a co-op with a *No Mammal* policy and have never had a pet. And I thought it would be a really nice gesture if we got them one." Cassie cleared her throat nervously. "A pet, I mean."

"Yes, I know what you mean." But what did getting Ray's kids a pet have to do with me? I was the fashion consultant.

With a gentle touch, Delphine rolled me to one side and slid the emergency blanket under me.

"And, I mean, since they can't have a mammal or anything, and it's such short notice since we're shooting tomorrow—"

Delphine moved to my other side and rolled me the opposite way, pulling the blanket across the table before urging me back down. Now I was lying on an emergency blanket, ready for my reviving seaweed treatment, and more than a little exasperated by Cassie's evasiveness.

"For Christ's sake, Cassie. Just spit it out."

I heard her take a deep breath before she blurted, "Could-we-give-them-your-chicken?"

I was speechless for a good thirty seconds. I could almost hear Cassie holding that deep breath. Delphine started slathering the green goo onto my calves, lifting each leg to get the back side.

Give up Chicken? She had only been in my life a few days, but already she was a part of my family. I had never known a pet could become so important so quickly.

But I had to consider whether a life with me was the best life for her. I was gone so much—I was almost always at the shop or the studio or hunting down the perfect piece for one or the other. She was a social chicken—she'd had several chicken friends in the cage at the Chinese grocery—and deserved more loving attention than I could give her.

I pictured those three smiling faces in Ray's picture. Three kids—two boys and a girl—who would dote on her and treat her like the queen she was.

Her life would be better there. As her owner, it was my responsibility to make sure she had the best home possible.

That home was with Ray's family.

The last of my tension oozed away. "I'd be honored to give them Chicken."

Even Delphine—massaging palmfuls of goo onto my thighs— probably heard her sigh of relief through the phone.

Eyes closed, I relaxed fully into the softness of the table. And ignored the chilly emergency blanket.

"I just didn't know if you'd grown attached to her or if you had other plans for her—not to imply that just because you're Southern you'd fry a chicken as soon as look at one, but how was I to know. I mean—"

"Cassie," I interrupted, "if that was all you needed ..."

"Oh, yes. You were in the middle of something. Right. Well, then, I'll come by tomorrow to get the chicken and—"

"Goodbye, Cassie."

I ended the call.

Wallowing in bliss, I was only vaguely aware of Delphine's hands leaving my body and the phone disappearing from my hand. By the time she had covered every last inch of my flesh in goo and wrapped me in the emergency blanket, I had nearly forgotten what a phone was.

Hell, I'd nearly forgotten who I was.

WHEN I GOT HOME I found Chris on the couch next to my still lifeless brother—clearly not spurred to action by Daddy's phone call. My heart fluttered a little at the sight of the two boys I cared most about in the world sitting together.

Then, with a thwack, my brain reminded my heart that my little brother was no longer a boy. Neither was Chris.

Then, with an even bigger thwack, my heart pointed out to my brain what I had just thought about caring about Chris and between the two thwacks I nearly faintly.

Before I could succumb to that peaceful end, Chris looked up from the TV and flashed me that boyish smile and both heart and brain fluttered so intensely I had to hold myself up with the help of the front door.

Thankfully his attention returned to what sounded like football—or baseball or basketball or cockroach racing, they all sounded the same to me—before I had to collapse in a fluttering mass on the floor. Though I wished my brain would have a conversation with my heart about this unacceptable lusting—even though recent flutterings indicated more than mere lust might be involved—I had a feeling my brain had deserted me and was siding with my heart on this matter.

So, with every last ounce of physical stability I could muster, I walked into the living room, set my purse on an end table, and poured myself into the nearest chair.

"Kit's on her way over," Chris announced.

"Good God why?" Randy whined, his gaze riveted, undeterred, on the television—rugby, who'd have thought?

Ignoring my brother—was it my fault he couldn't match

Kit barb for barb?—I asked Chris a little more breathlessly than intended, "Are you coming with tonight?"

Kit was coming over for the latest night of stalking, but I didn't know if Chris's provisions delivery service had been a one-time deal or if he was joining our team.

Clear blue eyes speared me to the spot. When I could stand again I'd have to make sure his gaze hadn't pierced the upholstery.

"Do you want me to come?" His voice was a low whisper.

Um, ah, well. "Sure." Had that sounded as calm as I hoped? "If you want to. Three's company, right?"

"I thought three was a crowd?" Randy asked as he jumped up from the couch and headed for the kitchen. Rugby was on a commercial break and his bowl of pretzels apparently needed a refill.

"Depends on the three," Chris countered.

"With your sister," Randy complained, "*one* is a crowd."

I laughed nervously, only because both boys laughed and it might look a little suspicious if I didn't. As if I were sitting there fantasizing about spending the evening in close quarters with Chris and what if Kit were to cancel and we went out alone, just the two of us, and—

A burst of blaring melody—vaguely familiar—echoed through the apartment, originating from an area near my door. That was not the same chime I'd heard the last time my doorbell rang.

Glaring at Randy, who had turned a little red at the ears, I demanded, "What the hell was that?!"

Randy, eyes again glued to the screen—it looked like both teams were huddled into a big giant mess while the referee threw the ball into the middle—answered nonchalantly, "Kit, I would imagine."

"Not *who*," I clarified. "*What*?"

"What do you mean, sis?"

I turned my glare on Chris. Maybe he knew something about this.

"Don't look at me." He shrugged his broad shoulders helplessly. "I have no idea what's going on."

While I continued to glare, that horrible tune sounded off again. Chris, clearly sensing that I was not going to move again until I got an answer from Randy, bounded to the door and let his sister in.

"Was that horrible racket your doorbell?" she asked as she entered.

"That's what I'm trying to find out."

Kit made herself at home, hitching up onto a stool at the breakfast bar. "You know, it sounded like that car from *The Dukes of Hazzard*. The one with the horn that—"

"Randall James Lange!" I bellowed. "Did my doorbell just play the first line of 'Dixie'?"

His whole face flushed red, but he still didn't dare look at me. He had replaced my charming *ding dong* with the horn from the General Lee. And he knew I would be furious.

"Maybe," he answered sheepishly.

I took a deep, fury-settling breath.

"Kit, Chris and I are going out for the evening." I snatched up my purse and stomped to the front door, not waiting to see if Kit and Chris were on my tail. "I am going to ring the doorbell when we get back and either I hear a normal chime or your butt had better be back in Dixie."

Flinging open the door, I turned back to conclude, "Or you'll wish it was!"

Kit and Chris barely made it into the hall before I hauled off and slammed the door.

Randy was lucky I'd been Jubilation-ed or he'd be roadkill already.

"Okay," I exclaimed as I marched onto the elevator and punched the first-floor button and pretended not to notice how Kit and Chris huddled in the corner of the elevator, as far out of reach as possible. "Let's go stalk us a straight guy."

FOURTEEN

"YOU NEED A MICROWAVE IN YOUR CAR," Kit suggested as she climbed back inside. "I'm not walking three blocks for popcorn every night."

She, Chris, and I sat in my Beetle, watching "Evan's Boring Life." In what was fast becoming a nightly ritual, he hadn't done anything more interesting than watch TV.

When she had left for the movie theatre around the block—because what goes better with *real* reality TV than movie theatre popcorn?—I'd climbed into the back seat with Chris. Not only did it feel a little weird to sit separately in the same car, but sadly I just wanted to be closer to him.

I knew this meant accepting the ridiculous attraction I'd been trying to fight. But fighting it wasn't working and maybe if I wallowed in it for a while it would work its way out of my system.

Because that *always* cleared up a crush.

Lord, who was I kidding? I wanted to have his children, and getting closer to him was only going to make it worse.

"Shoot!" Kit exclaimed from the passenger seat. "I forgot the Twizzlers."

Without another word, she jumped out of the car and headed back down the street in the direction of the movie theatre.

"Your sister is a little bizarre," I commented.

"You have no idea." Chris dipped his hand into the bucket of popcorn in my lap. "I have a lifetime of psychological scars."

"Poor Chrissy," I cooed, leaning into his shoulder and batting my eyelashes up at him. "Did his wittle sister make him cry?"

With a mischievous grin, he pinched my arm. "I bet Randy has horror stories to tell."

"Absolutely not." I wiggled away from his pinching fingers, nearly dumping the popcorn when he snuck in a poke at my ribs. "I was the perfect big sister."

He lunged for the popcorn, snatching it out of my hands and digging in for a big handful. Which he raised, aimed, and tossed in my face.

"Hey!" I cried, wiping at the greasy butter—if you can call that orange mush they melt all over the popcorn butter—on my face. Laughing, I said, "That was uncalled for."

"Aw ..." Chris set the popcorn on the floorboard and grabbed a tissue from the driver's seat pocket. "Come back here."

Wrapping an arm around my shoulders, he tugged me back against his side. I went willingly. As he dabbed at the greasy splotches on my cheek and forehead I stared up into those clear blue eyes, shadowed by a fringe of dark lashes that would make a supermodel jealous.

He watched me watching him.

Those clear blue eyes connected with mine—a much darker, less entrancing blue than his, I knew. His hand froze, the tissue hovering just above my left temple.

I couldn't catch my breath and started inhaling faster to get more oxygen. I was in one of those movie moments when the female lead and her romantic interest find themselves inches apart and each starts to lean in. Micro-millimeter by micro-millimeter.

And then someone always pulls away at the last second.

His magnetic eyes drew me closer—or was that him leaning in?

Any second he was going to realize what he was doing and jerk away. Just like that morning he fondled my pajamas.

Only he didn't stop. Didn't jerk away.

He continued his slow-motion descent.

I closed my eyes, knowing I couldn't bear to see the look of shame in his eyes when he—

His lips touched mine, a gentle sweeping contact that barely brushed against that sensitive skin and sent shimmering sparks along my nerves on a direct path to the sensitive regions of my body.

My fears and scruples abandoned me, allowing me the unconscionable freedom to sink into the kiss like a warm bath. With my back pressed against the car wall and his fingers hovering above my temple, our lips were the only point of contact. But that was more than enough.

I wished I could say that birds sang, bells rang, and stars burst, but the honest truth was I couldn't think of anything besides the feel of his mouth on mine. And that was more than my poor brain could handle.

I wasn't sure what brought me out of the trance. Was it him tilting his head to deepen the kiss? Or me lifting my palms to his warm chest? Or the resurrection of my misplaced morals?

Whatever the cause, suddenly I was pushing him away.

"Chris, you can't do this," I heard myself say, panting. "You can't abandon who you are just because we have a connection—"

"Bethany, please—"

"—I mean, it's only friendship. That's all it can ever be. I won't be the one who makes you question your identity—"

"Bethany—"

"—and if you're just looking to experiment, well I don't want that either, because—"

"Bethany!" Chris shouted, finally grabbing my attention.

He looked a little out of breath and a little exasperated.

"I'm sorry," he said. He pulled me into a hug—a tightly, friendly hug. "I shouldn't have done that. I know you're not— I know I shouldn't— I just—"

"It's okay." I returned his hug, squeezing my arms around his waist. We were both embarrassed and confused. "Really. I'm sorry, too. I shouldn't have let it—"

Chris leaned back.

"Let's both agree to be sorry." He wiped the last of the butter grease off my temple with the tissue still clutched in his right hand. "Let's forget about it."

He said this with a forced smile, but I knew the sentiment was genuine. I returned an only-slightly-forced smile of my own. Then I lifted his arm over my shoulder and snuggled into his side.

Friendship went beyond the bounds of embarrassment and confusion.

"Forget what?" I asked with forced lightness.

That was the great thing about having gay men for friends: physical comfort without the emotional strings. Barring the occasional lip-locking lapse of judgment, of course.

No wonder I'd been drawn to them time and again and again and again.

"Aren't you cute as two peas in a pod?" Kit hopped into the front seat, a mega-size drink—sure to be root beer—and a jumbo pack of Twizzlers in her hands. "I take it you told her," she said to her brother.

"Told me what?"

"Kit," he said, warning in his tone, "stop sticking your nose in places it might get bitten off."

"Told me what?" I repeated.

Chris looked at me and blinked. "That I ... uh ..."

"That he ... uh ..." Kit tried to help out when it looked like Chris wasn't going to find the words. "He bought a toy for your chicken."

"Oh," I said. "That's ... nice."

Somehow that seemed a little trivial for the emotion it had summoned in Chris's response. Kind of anti-climactic.

But still, it was a sweet gesture.

"Thank you."

Chris blushed. "Yeah, well, it's just a little ball with a bell in the middle that she can peck at or something." His attention riveted on the popcorn, he added. "Maybe it'll get her mind off your charm bracelet."

"That's sweet. I'm sure she'll love it. Really," I assured him. "But I'm giving Chicken away. Ray's kids have never had a pet and Cassie thought they might like her."

"Great," Chris said with overt enthusiasm. "I mean, not

great that you're getting rid of Chicken, but great that the kids are getting a pet and all. We can send the toy with her."

"Cassie's coming to pick her up while I'm working at the shop tomorrow, so if you can bring it by in the morning then we can send it with her."

This felt like one of those awkward conversations, like we were talking around a subject that no one wanted to mention. Only I didn't have to avoid it; I had no idea what the subject was. Unless it was the kiss. Darn, I hoped that didn't make us awkward around each other all the time. That would be, um, awkward.

Clearly I'd lost my ability for coherent thought.

"All this sugary sweetness is making me sick," Kit interjected from the front seat. "You two need to get a room."

At that, Chris's face erupted in red flames.

I was sure mine did, too.

"Kit," Chris growled in a commanding voice. "Shut up."

My sentiments exactly.

Keeping the embarrassment in check was hard enough without her input.

"Hey," she said, her unconcerned attention on the brownstone across the street, "did you guys even notice whether Evan left?"

I shot up and, practically pressing my nose against the glass of the little back window, looked up to find Evan's apartment window dark.

"Drat," I whispered, not wanting Kit to hear my admission of defeat.

Failure number— Aw, heck, I'd lost count.

Still, she heard me. "Next time, keep your eyes on the window," she reprimanded, "and off each other."

Determined not to blush this time, I turned to Chris and asked—in an even quieter whisper, "She does know you're gay, right?"

He glared at her seat, as if he could burn through the light gray upholstery and her dark brown hair, right into her skull. "Sometimes I wonder."

I WAS IN THE STOREROOM, searching for a box of cloisonné cuff links, when I heard the doorbell jingle.

Kit was working out front, so I didn't worry about rushing to the door. I had just located the box and was going for the stepladder when I heard the ruckus.

"Jesus, Mary, and Joseph!" a male voice roared, followed by a loud bang and some very animated squawking. Then Kit screamed.

At a dead run, I burst through the drape.

Kit stood by the front counter—next to Chicken's empty cage and looking unharmed—hands pressed to her cheeks in horror.

Fred the mailman stood just inside the front door, furiously fanning his face, a small canister clutched in one hand.

Chicken was on the floor in front of Fred squawking her brains out and flapping around on the floor uncontrollably.

"What the heck is going on?" I demanded.

"H-h-he," Kit stammered breathlessly, "he *maced* Chicken!"

"What!?" I turned on Fred. "You did *what*!?"

"Sweet Jesus," he cried, grinding his fist into one eye socket, "I got mace in my eye. Oooh, Lord it burns!"

As if that would gain my sympathy. "You deserve it, you sonofawitch. You maced a helpless chicken."

A helpless chicken who was currently somersaulting across the floor. I rushed to her side, diving to catch her before she somersaulted into a rack of feathered pashminas—the irony was not lost on me.

Since everyone else in the room seemed to be in shock, I took charge. "Kit"—I grabbed Chicken with both arms, hauling her against my chest to settle her.—"call the animal hospital to find out what we can do to help her."

"What about me?" Fred cried.

I was tempted to let him suffer. After all, he had only brought this on himself. But my Southern rearing got in the way of the sweet taste of revenge. I could not leave a man to writhe in pain, no matter how much pleasure the thought gave me.

"I'll get a wet cloth for you," I offered. Then, because I did have my priorities straight, added, "*after* I get Chicken settled into her cage."

Fred, not knowing he was skating on the very thin ice of Southern generosity, complained, "This wouldn't have happened if that thing had been in its cage in the first place. She—" He waved his hand in what he probably thought was Kit's general direction. "—let the monster loose and it attacked me."

"I didn't let her out," Kit said, holding a finger to keep her place in the phone book, "I was trying to put her away. But you just waltzed in here without giving me a chance to lock the door. If you weren't so impatient—"

"She's a chicken," I explained—I motioned for Kit to make

the call—quite proud of my reasonable tone considering the situation, "not a monster. What harm can a chicken do?"

Kit threw him a good glare before turning her attention to dialing the animal hospital.

"Listen lady." Now Fred waved a finger at me. "I've been attacked by dogs, cats, snakes, rabbits, gerbils, rats, mice, everything. And let me tell you, *every* animal is a *wild* animal. They can all do harm."

A *gerbil*? Clearly humans were not the only mammals Fred had communication issues with.

That was no excuse for his extreme reaction.

Or his rude behavior.

I saw red. And if Kit hadn't gotten through to the hospital at that moment, I would have let Chicken loose so he could see just how wild she was.

While I set Chicken back in her cage I eavesdropped on Kit's phone call.

"So we should wipe off her face with a wet towel, trying to rinse out the eyes," she repeated back. Then threw a glare at Fred. "Just the same as we'd do for a human."

At that news I headed to the restroom to grab two wet towels, making sure Chicken's was wetter than Fred's. See, I could eke my own little revenge fantasy.

When I returned, I threw a towel at Fred and ministered to Chicken. Kit was still on the phone.

"You mean this isn't the first case of chicken-macing you've had?" She listened for a moment. "Fourteen cases this year? God, people are weird," she exclaimed.

Chicken tucked firmly beneath my left arm, I gently cleaned her face with the towel. The cool water must have felt good because she sat calmly while I squeezed a few drops into each eye.

"Well yes I realize I called for that very problem—" Kit protested. "No I don't think I'm better than everyone—" Kit looked exasperated. "Fine! Thank you for your help."

She slammed the phone down. "Some people are so freaking touchy!"

I grinned. Kit had a knack for antagonizing just about everyone in Manhattan. If she had the chance, she'd probably manage a good chunk of the world population, as well.

In my arms Chicken had calmed down. I'd gotten as much of the pepper spray out of her eyes as I could, but I knew the irritation would linger for days. I set her back in her cage and turned my last remaining ire on Fred.

He was dabbing at his eyes one last time before wadding up the towel and dropping it on the floor.

That was the last straw.

"Excuse me," I drawled in my best Southern belle, "but it is *not* polite to leave the remains of someone's hospitality in a heap on their floor." I braced my hands on my hips. "Please pick that up."

"Lady, your chicken attacked me," he argued. "Hospitality ain't got nothin' to do with it."

Kneeling to the floor, he began gathering the loose mail that had scattered from his mailbag. And completely ignored both me and the towel that was leaving a big wet spot on my hardwood floor.

Calm as could be—shaking with fury on the inside—I walked towards him, my peep-toes clapping against the floor with each step.

He didn't even have the courtesy to look up when a lady approached.

"You, sir," I said in my best prideful, offended voice, "are rude, discourteous, and—" I stomped my foot onto the last pile of mail as he reached for it. His fingers narrowly missed becoming stiletto pancakes. "—you will apologize to me and to Chicken."

He started to protest, but I continued. "Or I will sue you, the postal service, and the federal government for false accusations and cruelty to animals."

His gaze traveled from the tip of my shoe, up my bare leg, over my gray tiny-plaid skirt, skimming my ivory satin blouse, and finally to my face.

"Lady," he said, grim-faced, "take your foot off that mail before I have *you* arrested for tampering with government property and felony mail fraud." He jerked at the pile, surprised when it released so quickly—I hadn't really been putting my weight into it. "That's a federal offense, you know."

I sighed. Fred was not meant to have conversation—maybe that was why he stuck to single word responses most of the time. The more words he said, the more he sounded like a jerk.

"Alright, Fred. I apologize for—" I tried not to sigh. "—interfering with your postal duty. If you will apologize for macing a defenseless chicken, I will pick up the towel and we will come out even."

Lord, that felt like a negotiation with a two-year-old. Only toddlers were more rational.

His shoulders stiffened, and for a moment I thought he was going to argue. But he finally released his breath and said, "I'm sorry I maced your chicken, okay?"

As far as apologies went it was pretty weak. For Fred, however, it was a serious surrender. He was probably suffering apoplectic shock at having strung together so many words in one conversation.

There had been complete sentences involved.

Rather than worsen the shock, I silently let him stuff the last of the mail into his bag and walk to the door. I was allowing him a graceful exit.

It wasn't my fault he tried to leave without delivering our mail. His hand was on the door when he realized.

Mouth set in a grim line, he turned, marched back to the counter, slapped the mail down on the glass surface, and stomped back to the door.

He passed Chris on his way out.

"Hey," Chris said in greeting, "what's up with your mailman?"

Beside me, Kit erupted in fits of laughter.

"If I told you," I said, shaking my head, "you wouldn't believe me."

FIFTEEN

CHICKEN WAS a resounding success with Ray's kids. I watched the final product shoot on the monitor at the loft set as Chris—selected because he had a personal history with Chicken, *not* because he knew how to make a killer Chicken *Parmigiana*—unveiled the shiny cage in the corner of the eldest boy's bedroom.

The three blinding smiles were enough to melt the coldest heart.

Something deep inside, near my ticking biological clock, twitched. I had always dreamed of having boys. A pair or trio of rough and tumble little men with dirt smudges and guilty looks on their faces.

But it was the little girl who tugged at my soul. A little round-faced five-year-old with blond pigtails that bounced as she clapped for Chicken.

When her brothers let her name their new pet—she chose the name Bubbles because a neighbor's fish had that name—I almost cried. Randy had never been that sweet to me.

Of course I had been the older child.

When I had children, I hoped I had a boy first—an older brother who would worship and protect his baby sister.

Now I snorted at the thought. That was a dream that would never come true if I kept lusting after guys with no interest in my reproductive parts.

Even if they did kiss me every once in a while.

Chris and I had an unspoken agreement not to mention that night. If only I could stop myself from *thinking* about it. My stupid heart practically exploded every time he caught me looking at him. One of these days it was going to give out altogether and put me out of my—and everyone else's—misery.

The final product shoot went on, showing Ray—dressed in one of Bryce's outfits and wearing the cowboy boots— preparing the *miso* soup recipe Chris had taught him. There were moments when we thought he might burn down the whole building in the process.

Then the babysitter Cassie had hired showed up and Ray took his wife, Darla, out for a romantic evening. Orchestra seats for *La Traviata* at the Met. Chocolate-laden dessert at Fortunata. Moonlit carriage ride through Central Park.

The monitor faded to the *OSG* logo and I sighed.

What a perfect show.

"Hey," Chris whispered, sending my heart into convulsions by sneaking up behind me when the viewing wrapped up and Steven was handing out champagne, "I overheard Evan say he was going out tonight."

I didn't risk turning around until my heart had resumed a reasonable pulse. "Oh?" I kept my eyes forward, pretending to watch Evan across the room as he spoke to Bryce. "Where?"

"Don't know." I could practically hear the smile in his voice. "But that never stopped you before."

I let out a nervous little laugh. Chris was standing too close. The heat of his chest, just millimeters from my back, sent my body into alternating shivers and sweats.

"I, uh—" I struggled to say the words. "—don't have my car."

"That's okay." He closed the distance to whisper against my ear, "We can follow him on foot."

I nearly passed out right there.

Darn it, Bethany! He was only being conspiratorial. Secretive. The man was *not* trying to send you into a frenzy.

I took a deep, shuddering breath and released it in a slow, steady exhale. I could do this. I could put the lustful fantasies of Chris out of my mind. And I could do it without therapy.

Facing him, I smiled—half nervous smile, half genuinely-happy-to-be-with-you-smile—and said, "Sounds like a plan."

He looked relieved, like he had sensed the tension battling inside me.

If he only knew.

♥

"WE'RE AT *GEOFFREY'S*," Chris told Kit over the phone. "It's on Pearl Street between Pine and Cedar.

He hung up the phone and looked at me.

"She's on her way?" I assumed.

"Be here in about ten minutes."

Geoffrey's was on the ground floor of a building that had been standing since it's address had read New Amsterdam. It was dark and dingy with only two small windows on the front façade and a handful of wall sconces for illumination. But, if you got past the fact that it smelled like stale beer and that dropping a dime on the floor meant it disappeared into the layer of dirt, it had a kind of comfortable character.

A neighborhood bar that had long since outlived its neighborhood.

Now it was full of Wall Street bankers fresh off work and looking to let off steam by throwing back a few. There was a "No Necktie" policy, so most of the men had their ties tucked into their jacket pockets. The rest had them around their heads or wrists, or waists—it wasn't a necktie if it wasn't around your neck, I guessed.

Several of the women—probably needing even more release because they had put up with the men all day—had shed their jackets, revealing slinky camisoles and silky shells. A different image of power women.

There was only one thing I didn't understand.

"What is Evan doing in a bar like this?" Chris asked, voicing my question.

After trekking all the way from Brooklyn, Evan had approached the bar, climbed onto a stool, and ordered a drink. He didn't speak to anyone. Didn't look around like he was searching or waiting for someone. Just sat there, looking out of place in his beige denim shirt and blue jeans with an embroidered pattern running the length of the outside seams, and swirled the swizzle stick in his glass.

Several men occupied the other stools, sipping drinks and staring at the TV above the bar—tuned to Bloomberg financial news. All looked like the after-work business type.

The one to Evan's right caught my attention. When he turned to order another drink I saw his tie folded and neatly sticking out of his jacket pocket like a silk handkerchief. With his wavy black hair and swarthy looks—reminding me of the actor who played Tony in the West Side Story movie—he was almost the most attractive man in the place.

Second only to Chris.

What struck me most about this after-work hangout was that everyone seemed straight-laced. And I wasn't just talking about the laces on their shiny oxfords.

I got a little excited at the prospect of success. Maybe this was the night. Maybe tonight he was meeting his secret girl-friend, thinking no one from the show would be caught dead in a place like this.

"Is this even a gay bar?" I asked.

"How should I know?"

I looked at Chris. Was he losing his mind? "Because you're gay," I explained when he looked blank. "Shouldn't you be able to tell?"

He shrugged.

I thought that was an innate ability, like some evolutionary development to help scout out an appropriate mate. Not that my own ability had proved successful in the past, but I had to figure I was in the minority. Otherwise there would be a lot more miserable, lonely people out there with a history of dating the wrong gender.

Then again, maybe there were.

While I continued to stare at Chris across the cramped corner booth we'd snuck into while Evan's attention was on his drink, Chris watched Evan. From his side of the booth he had a clear view of the bar. If I wanted to see Evan I'd have to crane my neck out around the end of the booth.

"Maybe he's here to pick up chicks," I offered.

"In *that* outfit?" Chris threw me an exasperated look. "Any woman he picked up would have an Adam's apple."

"You never know," I said, defending my opinion. "There's no accounting for taste."

"Bethany," Chris began, his attention fully on me, "Evan is gay. Nothing can change that. The sooner you accept—"

"No. He's not gay. He's just—" He couldn't be. He just couldn't, because my romantic history didn't have room for another gay guy. Because four was bad enough—four was a bad movie-of-the-week—but five? Five would mean I needed counseling.

Besides, all the signs were there: he got Victoria's Secret catalogs, he has a secret someone he can't see right now, he ogled that woman in Red Hook Brewery, he—

I gasped. "I've got it!"

Chris eyed me warily. "Got what?"

"I know how to catch him." Snatching up my purse, I pulled a twenty out of my wallet. "I have a plan."

The fear did not leave Chris's face. In fact, he looked more worried. "Bethany—"

"I'll be right back."

I slid out of the booth and headed for a group of women in the far corner of the room, certain victory was close at hand.

When I got back to the booth Kit had arrived and taken my seat. Which was fine by me. I squeezed in next to Chris, eager to watch events unfold.

"What did you do?" Chris asked.

I just grinned.

"Bethany ..." His voice was a growled warning.

"What's your problem, big brother?" Kit demanded in my defense.

"She's got some scheme cooked up." He waved a hand at

me, as if she didn't know who he was talking about. "Thinks she's going to prove Evan is straight once and for all."

"It's just a little—" I searched for the right word. "—experiment."

"No fair," Kit whined. "I can't see him from here."

Chris, grumbling next to me, said, "Don't worry, I'm sure you'll get a play-by-play."

"Shhh!" I hushed the squabbling siblings as my hired gun approached her target. "She's making her move."

The woman, Marcy, was a day trader who probably didn't need the cash, but welcomed the challenge. Dressed in an above-the-knee black pencil skirt and a silver silk camisole that swayed low over her full C-cups, she showed more flesh than fabric.

When she reached the bar, Marcy lifted one strappy stiletto onto the bar rail, throwing her body into a seductive pose. At first Evan appeared not to notice. What hot-blooded man didn't notice a sexy woman sidle up next to him at a bar?

I started to worry maybe Evan *was* gay.

Then Marcy leaned in to ask for a light, thrusting her breasts into view, and suddenly Evan was interested.

Score!

He tore a match from a book he grabbed off the bar and flicked it against the striker strip. Leaning in to reach the flame, Marcy grinned seductively as she lit her cigarette.

Evan smiled back—a goofy grin.

They started chatting, I could tell, but from across the bar I couldn't even read their lips, let alone hear what they said. Marcy ran a palm over his chest as she spoke. I was almost giddy with the thrill of success.

Then she leaned in and whispered something against his ear.

He nodded, and when she turned and walked away, hips swinging—Evan watching every sexy sashay—I knew I had won. She was going back to her girlfriends to collect her things.

"Oh my God," I whispered. "She's going to take him home."

Purse in hand, Marcy walked back to the bar, crossing past our booth on the way.

"Oh no," I cried and ducked down, but it was too late. "Darn, he saw me."

Evan blushed, a guilty flush coloring his cheeks, then looked around the bar like he'd been caught with something forbidden. Or some*one* forbidden. Looking relieved that there was no one within two stools of him—it was getting late and the crowd had started to thin—Evan pointed at me and waved when Marcy returned to the bar. She looked at me, apologetic. After handing Evan a business card, she stopped by on the way back to her table.

"Sorry, girl," she apologized. "I tried."

"No problem," I grumbled, disappointed by the failure.

She tried to hand me back the twenty, but I waved her off. Even if she'd failed, she'd earned it. As she sashayed away—a little less swish in her step—Evan left the bar and came to our table.

"Hey you guys," he said as he walked up. "Got room for one more?"

Um, ah, well.

"Sure," Kit answered before I could decide what I was

going to say. She slid further into the booth, making room for Evan next to her.

Was she crazy? How were we supposed to get evidence on Evan when he's sitting with us?

It couldn't have gotten worse, I supposed. He'd already seen us. He wouldn't have slipped up again if he knew we were there. Besides, maybe we could get some useful information from him.

"So," I began, leaning over the table conversationally, "what brings you to—" I checked the flickering neon sign hanging in one of the front windows. "—*Geoffrey's?*"

"Oh." Evan looked taken aback. "I, uh, come here—" He glanced at the bar. "—all the time. Just for, uh—" He looked around the room. "—fun."

Hmmm, evasive and guilt-ridden. Interesting.

"Are you meeting someone?" Kit prodded.

Leave it to Kit to get right to the heart of the matter. I knew she was useful for more than organizing inventory.

"N-no," he stammered. "I mean, um, no."

"Secret rendezvous?" Chris scowled, leaning across the table to ask meaningfully, "Secret *boy*friend?"

"I have to go!" Evan jumped up. "To my mother's. Dinner. Forgot. She'll worry."

With that cryptic—and disjointed—excuse, Evan fled the building without looking back.

"Well, that was interesting," Kit announced as the door slammed shut. "I guess now I can go get a drink. You two want something?"

Lord, did I. "I could use a Mojito."

A lesser woman would be deterred by the string of failures I seemed destined to face. But I wasn't going to give up. Just because my every effort wound up thwarted didn't mean success was impossible. Swing at enough balls and eventually I'd have to connect. Right?

"Grab me whatever's on tap." Chris pulled out his billfold and handed Kit a credit card. "Start a tab."

"We were so close." I massaged my temples, trying to rub away the dull ache that settled behind my eyes. Being undeterred took a toll on my sanity. "If he hadn't seen me I'd have my proof right now."

Chris opened his mouth like he wanted to say something, but snapped it shut when Kit returned.

"He'll bring the drinks over." She slid back into the booth, tucking a strand of dark brown hair behind her ear. "Randy's on his way."

"He is?" I asked with wonder, distracted from my failure.

Since he set foot in New York City he hadn't been anywhere but my apartment, the shop, and a one-time-only trip to grocery store to see for himself that they didn't have grits in stock. He was practically a recluse.

How had Kit talked him into venturing out?

"Shoot," Kit said. "I figured if the stalking is blown we might as well have a party." She grinned as the bartender—a good looking thirty-ish with an open smile—set our drinks on the table. "Besides, no one has to drive home tonight."

Amen to that. We only had to stay sober enough to find our way to the subway station.

"How did you convince him to come?" I asked.

"I threatened to call his ex." She downed half her rum and Coke in one gulp. "He knew I was serious."

I looked at Chris, who took a satisfying sip of his beer. My stalking might have been ruined, but that didn't mean the night was over. I plucked the straw out of my Mojito, flicked the clinging rum droplets at Chris, and lifted the glass to my lips. Really, did life get any better than good friends and a stiff drink?

Well, maybe a good drink and a stiff—

"This round's on the woman in silver." The bartender jerked his head toward Marcy as he set three fresh drinks on the table. "You guys look ready for more."

Kit batted her eyes at him, her pink-tinted, heart-shaped face beaming up at him like a schoolgirl. "Don't let the well dry out," she ordered sweetly—not a term I *ever* expected to use in describing Kit.

The bartender blushed but winked at Kit before returning to the bar.

By the time Randy arrived, we were on round four.

♥

THE NEXT MORNING, Kit rolled over in her sleep and smacked me in the nose. I bolted upright. It took me several fuzzy seconds to remember that she had crashed in my bed last night rather than walk home at three a.m. totally plastered.

Chris, I remembered, was sharing the couch with Randy.

At least then the dreams made sense. Dreams of Randy getting over Laura Jane once and for all and having a go with Kit. Dreams of Chris realizing he wasn't gay after all and having a go with me. Lord, those were the worst kind of dreams to wake up from. Dreams that you wanted to come true but knew never would.

"Yeck," Kit yawned. "What time is it?"

I peeked at the antique clock on my nightstand. "Twelve-thirty."

The last time I slept that late— No, wait, I never slept that late.

"What *day* is it?" she asked, stretching her arms—still sporting the pacific blue sweater she'd been wearing last night—from beneath the covers.

What was *I* wearing?

"Sunday," I replied, lifting the covers to find that I, too, was still wearing the latte colored, easily wrinkled blouse from the night before. "I think."

Testing my legs, I wiggled them around beneath the blankets, not really surprised to find they were bare. A quick glance around the room and I found my camel colored skirt draped over the back of my vanity chair.

The last time I went to bed without getting undressed— No, wait, I never went to bed without changing into sleepwear.

"I don't suppose the boys got up early and made us breakfast." Kit sat up, looked around the room, thought better of it, and collapsed back into the pillows.

"Not likely."

My eyes felt sticky, like I— Oh no. I reached up and swiped a finger across my eyelid. The tip came away a smear of black.

"Holy hell."

I'd even gone to bed without washing my face. I didn't have to think about it to *know* that I'd never done that before. My mother would never have allowed the thought to even enter my mind.

"Glad to know you have a few good curses in you," Kit muttered sleepily.

As she drifted back into dreamland, I tossed back the covers and climbed out of bed. Quickly gathering a fresh change of clothes—a pair of dove gray yoga pants and a thistle turtleneck—I was so not physically capable of wearing real clothes today—I clutched the pile to my chest and ducked out of my room.

I was two steps from the bathroom when I spotted Chris in the kitchen. Standing in front of the stove cooking something —Kit must have trained him well—he wore nothing but light blue boxers. The same color as his eyes.

Chris's naked chest was the last thing I needed to see. Oh I definitely *wanted* to see it, but in the grand scheme of things it did more harm than good.

Sure I'd seen him barely clad in fittings, but that was BTK —before the kiss.

I shivered at the memory. Then shivered again and realized I was standing there gaping, wearing nothing but a wrinkled blouse and a lacy thong.

Swiveling faster than you can say, "I see London, I see France," I had my hand on the bathroom door when Chris called out, "Morning, sugar."

I froze, hand on the doorknob, my practically-bare butt sticking out there for God and everyone to see.

Only not everyone saw it. Just Chris.

"Morning Chris," I managed, thankful he couldn't see my face, then burst into the bathroom before my blush reached the cheeks he *could* see.

I barely recognized the raccoon in the mirror. Black scoops beneath my eyes made me look more than my thirty-two years —and a bit like an NFL player. Sleeping on my stomach had earned me three sheet stripes on my left cheek.

A quick scrub with my tingly cleanser erased the coon eyes. Hopefully the tingling would stimulate enough blood flow to take care of my racing stripes, too.

When I emerged from the bathroom twenty minutes later—face still striped—I felt like a new woman. Hungover, but refreshed.

Chris was setting plates out on my antique pedestal dining table. "Feel better?"

"Loads."

I got out four cloth napkins and some silverware to help lay out the table. Chris stopped me before I could begin.

"Let me," he offered, his fingers brushing over mine as he took the place settings. "I'm a full-service chef."

"I won't argue with service."

"Coffee, tea, or—" He winked at me. "—juice?"

"Tea sounds divine."

Settling into a rush-seated Napolean chair, I relaxed while Chris prepared my cup of tea.

As I watched him bustling around in the kitchen, in his element, I wondered about him. About his life. About his past before he landed the show.

He was a phenomenal chef—I had gotten to taste test the dishes he selected for the show—and he had a seemingly infinite knowledge of anything related to food and wine. He should be running a five-star restaurant or writing a column for *Fine Food* magazine or hosting his own cooking show on The Gourmet Channel.

"How did you wind up on *One Straight Guy*?" I asked.

He shrugged those big, beautiful shoulders. "Luck."

"Good or bad?"

"Both," he stated so seriously that I wondered.

He set the steeping cup of tea in front of me, and I inhaled the dreamy aroma of Darjeeling. I closed my eyes and focused on the relaxing scent, certain Chris wasn't going to say anymore.

"I was out of work," he finally said, his back to me as he prepared something on the counter. "The last three restaurants I'd worked at all folded in under a month. My bank account was non-existent. I was weeks away from not being able to pay my rent on my tiny Lower East Side studio that's the size of your kitchen. I got another gig at a high concept diner, but the restaurant industry was flagging and I was afraid it wouldn't last."

Picking up a tray of what looked like crescent rolls, he carried them over to the oven and slid them inside.

"I couldn't leave Kit." He set the timer on the oven. "I know she's a grown woman and she tells me almost daily that she doesn't need me to protect her, but I'm her big brother. With our parents gone, she doesn't have anyone else to look out for her. I have to be here."

A sentiment I could relate to. Older siblings must never outgrow the sense of responsibility for the younger. I would probably be trying to fix Randy's life long after we'd both entered nursing homes.

"A friend showed me the audition notice." Pouring himself a cup of coffee, he rested a lean hip on the counter in an ultra-sexy relaxed pose.

I was so past trying to suppress my lust.

"At first I thought it was crazy. Me?" He gestured to his chest. "On TV?" He took a long sip of coffee before continuing. "The diner folded before it even opened its doors and I thought, 'Maybe TV is more reliable than food.' So I went to the audition, made my famous pineapple pancakes, and the rest—" He shrugged and lifted his coffee mug in a helpless gesture. "—is history."

It was reassuring when good things happened to good people. Chris persevered in the chef-eat-chef city for the sake of family, and he wound up a TV star.

"Oh Chris," I sighed as I stirred a spoonful of sugar into my tea. "Why did you have to be gay?"

He sprayed a mouthful of coffee over my white tile floor. "What!?"

If I couldn't overcome my obsession, I might as well embrace it all the way. Holding it inside would only make it fester. Better to confess the foolishness and move on. Chris would probably find it hilarious.

"You're sweet and sexy and funny." I set my spoon gently on the saucer. "The perfect guy."

Chris wasn't laughing. No, he was staring at me intently, like I had said the most offensive, insulting thing in history. Maybe I had. Maybe gay men didn't like to be lusted after by straight women.

I was about to apologize when Kit emerged from the bedroom.

"Do I smell breakfast, big brother?"

She looked like a rag doll. Wavy hair mussed and sticking out in every direction. Yesterday's sweater and jeans slept-in wrinkled. Cheeks tinted apple red. A fragile, innocent rag doll.

No wonder Chris felt so strongly about protecting her.

Shuffling over to the oven in her bare feet, she inched the door open and took a deep whiff. "Pineapple pancakes?"

"What else?" Chris replied.

She let the door close with a snap. "Wahoo!"

"Keep down the racket," Randy grumbled from the couch.

"Your brother's still in bed?" she asked.

"Yeah." I looked at the pile of bedding on the couch, rising and falling with the pattern of Randy's breathing. "He sleeps a lot lately."

"I know," she said. "He's going through Stage Four."

"Stage Four?"

"The Five Stages of Grief," she explained. "Stage Four: Depression."

"Depression?" That couldn't be good.

She looked at me, her clear blue eyes warm with sympathy. "That's a good thing. That means he's almost through." She pulled out the chair next to me and laid a hand over mine as she sat. "He's almost over her."

Eyeing the bedding warily, I hoped she was right. It had been too long since I'd seen him happy. And once I secured his happiness I'd be free to worry about my own.

SIXTEEN

Episode 103

Lost in Cyberspace.

BRYCE CAME FLYING into my office Monday afternoon, tossed a file folder on my desk, and collapsed on the couch.

"Have you seen this guy?"

"What guy?" I asked, picking up the stack of catalog pages that the flying file folder had knocked to the floor.

"The next straight guy. Lyle." He pointed wildly at the folder. "Look."

Knowing he wouldn't leave until I did, I flipped open the folder. And nearly dropped it.

"What is this guy?" I pressed my nose closer to the picture for a better look—this must have been some kind of camera trick. "A hobbit?"

Lyle looked short, stocky, and like he hadn't seen the better end of a brush since puberty. The picture was one of those taken by a computer webcam. In the background I could see vast amounts of computer equipment, wiring, tools—a mad hacker's dream workshop.

"Let me guess." I lifted the picture to read the bio stapled into the back of the folder. "He's a computer geek."

"Drop the computer, sweetheart," Bryce cried. "He's pure geek."

Scanning the bio I saw that Lyle was actually five-nine—not the five-two he looked in the picture. He ran a computer consulting business out of his one-bedroom apartment and rarely needed to leave home for anything but groceries—frozen dinners and Red Bull—and technology fairs.

This one definitely needed a world of help more than Ray and James. This was going to be *One Straight Guy at a Time*'s greatest test. If we could turn Lyle's life around, we could help anybody.

"Okay, Bryce," I said, setting the folder aside and mentally rolling up my shirtsleeves, "what do we do first?"

"I don't even know where to begin."

"Well, considering his grooming habits,"—or complete lack thereof—"maybe we should collaborate with Danial."

"Did I hear my name being taken in vain?" Danial popped into my doorway, his spiky hair paired with a tight black button-up shirt only buttoned halfway and tight black jeans.

"Christ, have you seen Lyle?" Bryce gasped.

"The straight guy?" Danial joined Bryce on the couch. "He's a nightmare. Did you see that beard? I'm going to need hedge clippers."

"You?" Bryce cried. "Unless there's a body hiding under that army jacket, I'm going to need industrial strength shoulder pads."

While I couldn't argue with their assessments, overreacting

wasn't going to get us anywhere. As the lone voice of reason, I interceded.

"Let's start with the basics. What's his big event?"

Danial made a face. "He's meeting his online girlfriend for the first time."

Why was I not surprised?

"Do we have a picture of her?" I asked.

"She," Bryce drawled, "is gorgeous. Tall. Blonde. Fashionable."

I frowned. "Then what's she doing meeting guys online?"

"She's a catalog model," Danial explained. "She travels all the time and doesn't get the chance to meet guys that aren't in the industry."

"Well, that's something." I tried to sound hopeful. "Has she seen him?"

Bryce pressed a palm to his forehead. "She saw the same picture we have."

My jaw flopped open.

"And she still wants to meet him?"

I didn't mean to sound as shocked as I did. I didn't think of myself as a particularly superficial person, but I had a hard time seeing the attraction in Lyle the super-geek.

"Different strokes for different folks," Danial remarked.

I took it as a sign of Bryce's great distress that he didn't make a single suggestive comment about stroking.

This was more serious than I thought. If we were going to transform Lyle we needed more data.

We weren't really supposed to see the straight guy before the day of the show, but... "Maybe we can get a better look at Lyle before we start planning."

Bryce and Danial exchanged excited looks.

"Sweetheart," Bryce said. "I love how your devious mind works."

WE WERE STANDING outside Lyle's apartment building, trying to decide how to get a look at a man who never left his apartment, when my cell rang.

My caller ID flashed "Mom."

Dreading a confrontation about Randy, I flipped open the phone and said, "Hi, Mom."

"Your father's in the hospital."

I dropped the phone.

Scrambling to my knees, I scraped three nails across the concrete picking it up. "What? What happened? Is he okay? Is it serious?"

"T-the doctors say he's in s-stable condition." The very fact that she stuttered showed how rattled she was. Mom never tripped over her speech. "He had a m-mild heart attack."

"Heart attack?" I gasped.

My whole body started shaking. Bryce and Danial, overhearing my panicked conversation, each wrapped a reassuring arm around my shoulders.

"A mild one. He's resting now," she explained, her voice growing calmer. "They gave him some medication to dissolve the blood clot. He won't need surgery."

I sagged with relief, thankful that Bryce and Danial held me up when my knees would have given out.

"Okay, I'll just throw a few things in a bag and go right to the airport and find a flight when I get there. I should be in Atlanta before—"

"Your father doesn't want you to come."

"—dinner." My mind froze. "He what?"

"Honey, your father didn't even want me to tell you."

I couldn't breathe. My own father didn't want me to know he'd nearly died? Didn't want me by his hospital bed? Didn't want me period. I'd known this for a long time, but I always thought—

A sob escaped. I'd always thought that underneath it all he still loved me—even though I'd stayed in New York.

"You know how proud he is," Mom explained, trying to soothe my inconsolable pain in true mother fashion. "He doesn't want his children to know he's just a man. With all the fragility that entails."

She could say whatever she wanted. I knew the truth.

"Right. Sure. Whatever." I wiped at the tears. "Let me know if things get worse. He can't keep me away from his own funeral."

Not giving Mom a chance to respond, I ended the call. Nothing like having a family crisis in the middle of a workday.

I took a few fortifying breaths. While trying to decide if the call was a blessing or a curse, I realized that if Daddy'd had his way she wouldn't have called me at all. Had she thought to call Randy, too?

I tried my apartment and his cell phone, but both rang through to voicemail. Either he was out or sleeping.

Still shaking, I carefully slipped my phone into the little pocket in the lining of my purse. There was nothing I could do from hundreds of miles away. And no one wanted me closer.

My eyes tingled again, but I shook them off. I had a job to do and darned if I wasn't going to get it done.

"Okay." I straightened my shoulders, shrugging off Bryce and Danial's supportive arms. "I'm ready."

"Sweetheart, are you—"

"If you need a moment, we can—"

"No."

I knew they were concerned without having to look at their faces. But I didn't have time for a pity party. I'd come to grips with Daddy's law a long time ago. This was just the latest amendment. No amount of pity would help.

Leaving them wondering on the sidewalk, I marched up the steps, bending to pick up an abandoned New York Times on my way. They caught up with me as I waited for the elevator.

"What's the plan?" Danial asked, thankfully leaving my family crisis behind.

"You two," I said as I punched the button for the tenth floor, "need to stay out of sight. He might recognize you."

Bryce looked pleased at the prospect of being a recognizable celebrity. "And you?"

"Me?" I dug around in my purse for a pen and a stray receipt with a blank back. "I'm going to meet Lyle face-to-face."

When the doors opened on the tenth floor, I sent Bryce and Danial down the hall and around the corner. I clutched the newspaper across my left arm like a clipboard, holding the receipt against it with my fingers, and knocked on Lyle's door.

The smell of high school cafeteria wafted out even before he opened the door.

"Good afternoon, sir," I greeted, trying not to stare at the disastrous mess behind him. Evan had a lot of work ahead of him. "I'm from the New York Times and we're offering a complimentary copy to non-subscribers in return for answering a few lifestyle questions." I poised my pen over the receipt. "First, where do you shop for clothes?"

Lyle looked confused, but answered, "Z-mart."

I heard a big thud from down the hall. I had a feeling Bryce had passed out in horror. In his world, Z-mart was a four-letter word.

♥

BRYCE'S LIVING room was bigger than my apartment.

Lord, his *bathroom* was bigger than my apartment.

Life as a fashion queen must pay very well.

The three of us—he, Danial, and I—were crowded around his dining table going over my notes on Lyle.

As it turned out, Lyle had a lot of potential. He carried his less-than-average height well. Without the army jacket, he had broad shoulders, and the punk rock T-shirt was just tight enough to suggest he had decent muscles.

But his eyes were the key.

A pale, pale aqua blue rimmed with charcoal, they glowed from behind the bushy beard and overgrown eyebrows. Once he shaved and groomed they would sparkle like nothing else. Even disguised as they were I'd had a hard time looking away from them to evaluate the rest of him.

"He needs to be in blues and greens that make his eyes pop even more," I said as I referred to my notes, a crowded jumble of letters that covered the receipt.

"But you swear he has shoulders," Bryce demanded.

"Yes," I sighed, reassuring him for the fifth time.

This time he actually relaxed. "That will make everything easier."

As if shoulders were the linchpin in any good makeover.

"First," Danial mused as he studied the snapshot I'd covertly captured with my phone, "I need to get that hair under control. Shorter, but not cropped too close. I can't tell if he has a strong enough mouth and jawline to go clean-shaven, maybe—" He pressed his nose to the phone. "—maybe just a little scruff to give him some texture."

"I have a feeling," I said, envisioning Lyle without the bushy beard and hair, "this guy is going to look like a Hollywood heartthrob when we're done."

"Then all we need are—" Bryce held up his hand and started ticking things off on his fingers. "—classic tees, button-down shirts, sports jackets, well-fitting jeans, and the perfect sunglasses."

I wrote each item down. On a clean receipt.

If I ever got audited I'd be in trouble.

"This is going to be a coup." Danial handed back my phone. "If we can turn Lyle the Yeti into a movie star, we can save any guy from the dark depths of straightness."

I was just relieved to see Bryce relaxed. He'd looked like an aneurysm waiting to happen when he flew into my office earlier today. Now he looked like he'd spent eight hours in a mud bath.

I checked my watch.

"Good Lord, it's after six."

"How long have we been here?" Danial asked.

"I'm not sure," I replied, trying to think back to when we'd decided to head to Bryce's place instead of back to the studio because it was closer. "A few hours, at least. Maybe four?"

"Damn, I have a date in an hour." Danial pushed back from the table. "My friend—boyfriend—has an exhibit opening tonight at White Wall. You're both invited. Evan and Adam will be there, too."

Bryce lifted his head out of his relaxed stupor. "What medium?"

"Photography." Danial beamed. "I'm in the exhibit."

"Are you clothed?"

Ah, the old Bryce was back.

"You'll have to come to the exhibit to find out," Danial teased with a wink.

"I've got to run, too." I gathered my notes and lifted my purse onto my shoulder. Thoughts of my phone conversation with Mom resurfaced in the lull and I needed to talk to Randy in case she hadn't called him.

I'd tried his cell several times throughout the afternoon, but always got his voicemail. I hoped he wasn't dodging my calls.

We said our goodbyes, leaving Bryce and his perverted thoughts behind.

"Let Chris know about the opening," Danial said to me as we closed the door.

"I don't know if I'll see—"

"Damn," he said, grabbing his wrist when we reached the elevator. "I forgot my watch. I'm always taking it off and leaving it places." He backed away. "I'll catch up with you later."

"If I don't make it tonight," I said, "tell your boyfriend good luck on the exhibit."

Danial nodded and smiled as the elevator arrived, then disappeared back into Bryce's apartment.

My phone had no signal in the elevator, but as I crossed the lobby I tried to call Randy again. And again got his voicemail. Where was that boy?

Maybe he was asleep.

I stepped out into the sunshine—a gorgeous cloudless day—trying not to think about Daddy lying in the hospital all alone. Not that Mom would leave his side for any longer than was absolutely necessary. In their entire marriage, they'd never been separated for more than the space of a few hours—

"*Ooof!*" I ran smack into a woman standing in front of Bryce's building. "I'm so sorry, I wasn't looking where—"

"No problem," the woman bit out.

I smiled sheepishly, but she didn't notice. Her attention was on the upper stories of the building, her head lifted so she could see past the brim of the baseball cap covering her curly red hair.

Feeling like an idiot, I started to walk away. But something about her tickled a memory.

Red curly hair. Red curly—

Aha! The woman from the boot store. The one who had glared at me so furiously and sent Bryce fleeing for the street.

How odd.

I turned back, not sure what I planned to do. She was gone. That was some coincidence, her showing up in front of Bryce's apartment. And I didn't believe in coincidence.

WHEN RANDY WASN'T SITTING in front of the TV when I got home I was worried. That was how I'd found him every day for the last couple weeks. Zoned out with a bowl of pretzels and three channels of ESPN.

"Randy," I called as I set my things on the kitchen counter, "are you here?"

A muffled voice called from the bathroom, "In here."

The door was open. *Ew.* I thought he'd stopped that when he hit puberty.

Convinced I didn't need to hear—or see—that, I headed to the fridge to get a glass of sweet tea.

"Hey Bets," he called again, "do you have any baking soda or Borax?"

Baking soda? Borax?

The only thing I knew they were good for was odor removal.

"Aw, Randy," I whined, imagining why he would need to remove odors in my bathroom, "you didn't miss the bowl, did you?"

I grabbed the open box of baking soda from the fridge and the Borax from a high and rarely accessed cupboard and braced myself for the sight in the bathroom. Which wasn't what I expected.

Randy was on his knees scrubbing at the faint rust stain around the drain of the bathtub.

"You're cleaning?" I asked in disbelief.

He took the Borax from my hand. "I do know how."

"But—" I couldn't quite bring myself to say, "You've been a complete blob for two weeks and the last thing I expected to see when I got home this afternoon was you cleaning my bathtub."

"I've been sitting around on my butt long enough," he said, responding to the comment I hadn't voiced. "Might as well make myself useful since I'm not paying rent."

He sprinkled some Borax around the drain, drizzled lemon

juice—which he had stolen from my fridge—over the white powder, and rubbed the compound into the enamel with a rag. Seconds later he turned on the water, rinsing away the paste. Bright white enamel shined in its place.

I'd scrubbed at the stain endlessly, and had never accomplished more than ruining my nails.

"Wow, that really worked."

Wiping off the rest of the tub, he replied, "I have skills, you know."

A quick glance around the bathroom told me just how useful. The entire room sparkled. For that matter—I poked my head out the door—so did the kitchen. And the hardwood floors looked fresh-polished.

"Did you clean the entire apartment?"

"Yep." He stood, wiped his hands on his jeans, and gathered up his cleaning supplies. "Had some free time and excess energy."

There was a hint of sadness in his eyes. Probably thanks to Laura Jane, but it reminded me about Mom's phone call.

"Randy," I said quietly, "I have to tell you something."

"About Dad?" he guessed. "Mom called me."

"Are you okay?"

"Yeah." He carried the cleaning supplies to the kitchen and started putting them away. "She said it was just a mild heart attack. He's going to have to cut back on fried foods and start exercising, but otherwise he's fine."

Clearly, Randy had been more level-minded during his conversation with Mom. I couldn't remember anything past the part about Daddy not even wanting me to know.

"You didn't think a little heart attack would take out such a stubborn old coot, did you?"

"Randy!" I cried, aghast.

"Oh please, him having a heart attack didn't change the truth." Closing the cupboard beneath the sink, he turned to face me, a serious look in his eyes. "But it did change my perspective."

He took a sip of the sweet tea I'd left on the counter. "It made me think about how short life is. And how much of my time I've wasted on Laura Jane."

"Good," I wanted to say, but I just let him continue.

"If she's happier with someone else, then I'm not going to get in her way. And I'm not going to let that get in my way." He blushed like a tomato. "I'm going to ask Kit out."

Thank the Lord.

What a difference a day made. Yesterday he was lying around in bed, grumpy and depressed. Today he was cleaning the bathroom and asking girls out.

Unable to restrain myself, I threw my arms around him in a big bear hug. "Glad to have you back, baby brother." I even kissed him on the cheek, despite his efforts to avoid my lips. "I've missed you."

His blush darkened.

"If I clean your bedroom will you promise never to do that again," he grumbled.

I knew he was teasing.

"This calls for a celebration," I insisted. "How would you like to go to a gallery opening?"

"What kind of gallery?" he asked, untangling himself from my arms.

"An art gallery."

He made a sour face. "Do I have to pretend to like it?"

"Maybe," I teased. "But you can impress Kit with your artistic sensitivity."

"Ha!" he called after me as I headed to my room.

"Call Kit while I get changed," I told him. "I'll call Chris." I slammed the door, then peeked back out to add, "And find something more fashionable to wear than jeans and a t-shirt."

A couch cushion thudded against my door as I pulled it shut.

I just laughed.

It felt good to have the real Randy back.

AFTER LAYING a hand on every item in my wardrobe, I finally settled on a pale pink satin halter dress with a full skirt that hit just below my knee. With the help of a push-up demi bra, I had delicious cleavage to show off in the deep v-neck.

I paired the dress with crystal-studded, peony pink slingbacks that shaped my legs into Betty Grable-worthy curves and a silver sequined clutch.

At my vanity I touched up my makeup to get pout-perfect lips and just-blushed cheeks, put on a pair of dangly silver earrings, and pinned my hair up into a tousled French twist.

I checked out my image in the full-length mirror on the back of my bedroom door. More daring than usual, but maybe it was time to shake things up. Not too shabby for a girl from Cypress Springs.

When I emerged—half an hour after going in—Kit and Chris had already arrived.

Chris let out a low whistle.

"Looking good, sugar."

"Damn, Bethany," Kit exclaimed, "you look amazing."

"You two should take pictures," Randy suggested. "It's not often she brings out the big guns."

I threw him a you're-lucky-I'm-in-a-good-mood grin.

"Too bad it's going to be wasted on my brother and a gallery full of gay men." I looked at Chris and batted my eyelashes. "Sure you won't be changing your orientation any time soon?"

His clear blue eyes narrowed with searing intensity. Everywhere he looked I burned. He'd never watched me so intently —except for that night in my car.

With a quick shake of his head he looked away. He ran a hand through his hair and I thought I heard him groan.

Kit laughed out loud.

She seemed in a really good mood herself.

"Get a clue, Bethany," Randy snarked. "Chris isn't—"

"Ready to go?" Chris interrupted over whatever Randy was saying.

A look passed between the two men that I couldn't read. Like a stare-down between two dogs waiting to see which would flinch first, which would become the dominant animal.

Kit, still laughing, grabbed me by the arm and dragged me towards the door.

"Men," she managed between laughs. "They are deranged creatures, no matter their sexual preference."

Then she burst out in another round of laughter, leaving me with the sinking feeling that I was missing something very important.

Women, I thought, were sometimes equally deranged.

SEVENTEEN

WHITE WALL GALLERY was only a few blocks from my building. I'd never been, but had walked past their opening galas on several occasions. Well, more like walked *around* them since the parties almost always spilled out onto the street. More people always showed up than could fit in the modest space, and they eventually opened the doors and let the crowd take over half the block. Everybody who was anybody—or wanted to be—attended their openings, in full on evening regalia.

Tonight was no exception to their all-out glitz and glamour.

Danial's boyfriend must have been very talented.

Or very well connected.

Champagne flowed freely, delivered on exotic wooden trays by tuxedoed waiters. The cream of society was there—the latest generation of those venerable old money names and a few of the hottest celebrities.

No wonder the *OSG* cast was there. They were the next big thing.

I grinned and took a sip of sweet champagne.

Kit, looking very celebrity herself in a simple white strapless dress and sexy strappy sandals that added four inches to her five-two height, sipped her own champagne.

Randy, never more than a few feet away from her, had donned black pants and a black t-shirt. Very celeb-casual. And, if a girl can say so about her brother without sounding like an Arkansas hillbilly, hot as hell.

"They make a cute couple." Chris kept his voice low enough that neither of our siblings heard him. "Think he'll ever get over that ex of his?"

I grinned. "He already has."

"Well then," Chris said, clinking his champagne flute to mine, "tonight should be very interesting."

As if it weren't already.

A film crew from the local news had been weaving through the crowd all night, trying to catch shots of celebrities and socialites *ooh*ing and *ahh*ing over Naldo-the-boyfriend's work. When they found out the cast of an upcoming hit show—months before the premiere and already the media buzzed with their impending stardom—were in attendance, they insisted on filming interviews with all five guys.

So far Chris had avoided the reporter. For a new celebrity, he sure seemed uninterested in the glory of fame. Which only made me love him more.

Oh my Lord. Did I just confess that I lo—

"Here she comes again," Chris announced before disappearing into the crowd.

I was trying to spy where he'd escaped to, still reeling from my mental admission, when the reporter walked up. "Wasn't Chris Thompson standing here a moment ago?" she asked.

I shook myself back into the moment. Chris would not

appreciate my sending the reporter trailing after him. Especially if I mentioned why I was so distracted in the first place.

Shrugging noncommittally, I replied, "Haven't seen him."

She scowled, her over-tweezed brows pinching together in a nasty frown. I was tempted to suggest Botox.

Instead, I smiled seAlexandrialy and took another sip of champagne.

"I think he's at the bar," Kit offered.

The reporter motioned to the cameraman and pushed her way through the crowd, despite the fact that Chris wasn't at any of the three bars in the gallery. At least she was gone.

"He's not going to get away without talking to her." Kit handed Randy her empty glass—he headed for the nearest bartender. "She's a bulldog."

"You don't think your brother's clever enough to outwit a determined woman?"

Kit raised her brows. "Is yours?"

I sighed as Randy returned with a fresh glass of champagne Kit hadn't had to ask for. "No," I admitted. "Sadly no."

Randy scowled, clearly sensing there had been some discussion at his expense, so I changed the subject.

"Anyone seen Evan?"

"I saw him with Danial earlier," Kit offered.

"He was just at the bar," Randy added.

"And now he's right behind you."

I jumped at the sound of Evan's voice and tried to look happy to see him. "There you are." I patted his shoulder. "I was wondering if you were still here."

He stepped closer so no one else could hear our conversation.

"You can drop the act," he said with a smile. "I know you

better than that. You wanted to check up on me. Maybe see if I was here with a *woman*."

I gasped. He couldn't have known what I'd been up to all this time. "I don't know what you're—"

"You don't have to explain," he interrupted. "I know you're trying to catch me 'being straight' or something."

"I absolutely am not!" I declared, feigning insult.

I knew I wound up sounding guilty.

He leaned in to whisper, "But you won't catch me."

There was something arrogant about the way he said it that made me mad. Like he knew what I'd been trying to do all along and had been extra careful about watching his step. He'd been countering my every move like some elaborate chess match.

Fine. The gloves were off. I threw down the façade of innocence, and accused, "Because you know I'm watching you and you're taking precautions."

"No," he argued. "Because—"

"Alright, who told that reporter where I was hiding?" Chris demanded as he returned to our group. "I thought we were all in on the conspiracy."

Kit and Randy didn't appear to notice his return, intent on their own heated conversation.

"That reminds me," Evan said, looking suddenly uncomfortable, "I need to go give my interview. Catch you later."

As he slipped away into the crowd I stomped my foot in frustration. I had been so close to getting a confession. One more push and he would have cracked. I could see, smell, taste, and feel it. All I missed was hearing it.

Within my grasp, but out of my reach.

Aaargh!

"Angry, sugar?" Chris asked.

Angry was an understatement.

"I'm ready to get out of here."

I looked around, anxious to leave, but Randy and Kit were nowhere in sight. Must have disappeared at the same time Evan escaped.

"Darn it," I growled. "Where did they go?"

"They're adults," Chris countered. "If you need to go, we'll go. They know how to get home."

I nodded, grateful for Chris's insight.

Chris smiled and we set off at a hurried pace—well, me hurrying, Chris keeping up—walking the three blocks to my building in silence. It wasn't until we were waiting for my elevator that he asked, "Want to tell me what happened?"

My anger and frustration bubbled to the surface in an emotional mess.

Everything tried to come out at once.

"He— He just— He—" I growled in frustration. "He knows I'm onto him and now it's all a big game. I'll never catch him."

His voice low, he asked, "Hasn't it always been a game?"

"Not like this."

The elevator arrived. I marched in and punched the button.

"I think you should consider the possibility," Chris ventured, "that Evan really is—"

"Don't!" I stopped him. "Don't say it."

He sighed deeply but didn't continue.

My mind raced as the elevator ascended. Subtle attempts weren't going to work. I needed to try something drastic. Something desperate.

"I need to up the stakes," I said as we reached my floor and the doors slid open.

"You're taking this too far," he argued. "You need to accept the fact that Evan really is—"

"No. He's not." He couldn't be. "I just have to dig deeper."

Chris remained silent as I unlocked my door, but I could tell he had something he wanted to say. When I pushed open the door and headed inside, expecting him to follow, he surprised me by waiting in the hall.

"Why?" he asked when I turned to look. "Tell me why this is so important to you."

Because. Because I needed Evan to be straight. I needed him to be one genuine failure on my dating record. That might not make sense, but I needed one relationship to have failed because we weren't compatible and not because I'd picked yet another gay guy to date. I needed a relationship that failed on its own merits—or lack thereof—rather than one doomed to failure before it even began.

I needed the reassurance that this wasn't an inherent and inescapable flaw.

It might not make sense to anyone but me, but I needed it more than anything else.

There was no way I could explain this desperation.

"You wouldn't understand."

His blue eyes darkened with sadness. "Try me."

"I ..." I started, but nothing more would come out.

Chris shook his head, then turned and walked away.

My heart broke into a billion little shards. Great, Chris was the one thing I needed almost as much as proving Evan wasn't gay. And I managed to drive him away.

"Way to round out the day, Lange."

I swept the door closed and headed for a long, hot soak in

the tub, unable to dredge up any excitement at the memory of its sparkling enamel.

♥

"I'M SORRY," I said when Chris opened his dressing room door the next morning. Handing him the bouquet of daisies I held behind my back, I added, "These are for you."

He walked away without saying a word.

Was he rejecting my apology? I was almost ready to cry when he returned with a small gift-wrapped box in his hand.

"I'm sorry," he explained. "Friends don't need to know motives. They just need to help you."

Then I did cry.

"That's the sweetest thing." I threw my arms around his neck and hugged him as my eyes watered and the tears spilled out over my cheeks. "I was miserable all night, thinking I'd lost you."

He leaned back and wiped at my watery tears.

"I never should have walked away. I'm not the kind that gives up." He nodded his head toward the box in my hand. "Open that."

Eyes blurred by tears, I pulled off the silver ribbon and matching paper and opened the little velvet box inside. There, on a bed of pale pink velvet, was a heart-shaped silver charm that read, *Friends First*.

A flood of tears filled my eyes at the inscription. I pulled him back into a hug, reveling in the feel of his arms wrapped around me.

Those words said everything.

No matter what else happened, we would always be

friends. First, foremost, and always. For the first time in my life I was genuine friends with a man without being romantically involved. And it felt good.

This was how love should feel.

And if romantic love was out of my reach, true friendship was a pretty terrific consolation prize.

"You two need to get over it and have sex," Bryce drawled as he walked by on the way to his dressing room. "When you have a moment, sweetheart, we need to decide where to shop for Lyle."

He blithely disappeared into his room.

Chris and I laughed in each other's arms.

"I'd better get to work," I said, wiping away my second wave of tears with my right hand while Chris attached the charm to the bracelet on my left wrist. "Who knows what Bryce'll do without adult supervision."

Charm in place, Chris took my hand between his and gave me a squeeze.

"I just want to make sure you know," Chris dipped his head to look me directly in the eyes, "whatever you need from me, you've got."

"Thanks." The tears threatened again, but I kept them back. Mom always said you should keep some in reserve in case you really needed them. "I love you, you know."

And I meant it. With all my heart.

"I know," he said, smiling. "I love you, too."

As a friend. It went unsaid, but it was still there.

At this point, that would have to be enough.

"Cut the mushy crap," Bryce shouted through his open door. "We've got work to do, clothes to buy, straight men to save."

"Go." Chris gave me a playful shove in Bryce's direction. "I'll see you later."

"Yeah," I replied. "Later."

"Hurry up, bi—"

"I'm coming already," I shouted back at Bryce. "Stop mouthing off before you say something I'll have to make you pay for later."

"Bring it on, sweetheart." He stuck his head out the door and waggled his eyebrows at me. "Bring it on."

"Oh," I said, channeling my inner cheerleader, "I'll bring it."

When I looked back, Chris had disappeared into his dressing room.

How was it possible for my heart to feel so full and so empty at the same time?

❤

LYLE TRANSFORMED from cyber-geek to super sleek. He stepped out of the dressing room at Bradford's—hair already cropped to a flattering length and gelled to a trendy spike and beard trimmed to a rugged stubble—dressed in a dusky blue button-down shirt and black slacks from Vanny-O and looking like a heartthrob.

A major overhaul from the closetful of metal and punk T-shirts and ratty black jeans Bryce had found in his closet that morning.

His e-girlfriend had better watch out.

"We did good, sweetheart," Bryce said as the film crew packed up to leave. "I've never been so proud of a straight guy in my life."

The best part was how eager Lyle had been to make the change. It was like he knew there was something major lacking in his appearance, but he didn't know how to fix it. Almost everything Bryce suggested was a big hit. He had been willing to try everything once.

"He certainly let us do our will," I replied. "I never thought he'd go for that turquoise tie. Everything in his closet was either black or olive drab."

Now, with an armload of shopping bags, his closet would be full of bright blues and cool greens that would make his remarkable eyes stand out even more dramatically.

Bryce leaned in to whisper, "I'm glad he didn't recognize you."

That made two of us.

"It's amazing what a difference a ponytail makes."

My mother would have rolled over in her grave—if she were dead—to know her daughter had her hair in a ponytail. Growing up I wasn't allowed to leave the house without well-teased hair *a la* Dolly Parton. I had been the only girl in ballet class whose hair wasn't in a bun.

"Bryce," Cassie shouted from the service elevator, "get your butt in this car. We've got to get to the apartment for the homecoming shot. Bethany, you coming?"

And risk Lyle recognizing me when he saw me in the familiar background of his building? "Not this time."

Cassie waved and allowed the elevator doors to almost close as Bryce tried to step on. From the look of malicious mischief on her face it had not been an accident. The doors popped back open, Bryce stepped inside, and they all disappeared behind a wall of gleaming metal.

Finding myself alone in a fabulous department store I did

what any self-respecting, fashion-conscious person would do: I shopped.

♥

THE IDEA CAME to me in the outerwear section at Bradford's —amidst the plaids and peplums. Near the back wall there was a display of trends for the coming Fall. One of the mannequins wore a plain tan trench coat paired with sexy heels.

Very hot.

Curious, I'd peeked beneath the lapel and found the mannequin in the buff underneath.

By the time I got home I'd planned the entire enterprise. It started with me putting on the trench coat over some skimpy lingerie and—

"Thank God you're home." Randy pounced on me the second I walked in the door.

The look on his face was one of sheer terror.

Daddy!

"What happened?" I demanded, afraid to hear the answer.

Grabbing me by the hand, he dragged me across the room to the suitcase laid open on the floor—he'd refused my offer of some closet space on the grounds that he wouldn't be on my couch long enough to need any. His clothes lay strewn all over everything. The floor, the couch, the replica Tiffany floor lamp in the corner.

"Kit and I are going out tonight." He gave me a pointed look. "On a *date*. What should I wear?"

What should he—

"Randall James Lange." I punched him in the shoulder. "You had me terrified and picking out mourning clothes."

"What?" He looked at me like I was the crazy one.

"*Grrr*. Never mind." I pushed him aside and evaluated his clothing selection—spread out as it was.

If he hadn't terrified the life out of me in the first place I would have been nothing but overjoyed at this turn of events. Randy had asked Kit out, she'd accepted, and now he was getting ready for a date. It had been a long time since he'd had to worry about impressing a new woman. I was glad the new woman was Kit.

There was no woman better prepared to be the rebound girl. No woman more capable of surviving the rebound curse.

"Where are you taking her?" I asked.

"Taking her?" Randy echoed. "I've been in the city a couple weeks. I wouldn't know where to look. *She's* taking *me* to some bar called Razzmajazz."

I pictured the casual martini bar in the uber-trendy Lower East Side. An eclectic mix of styles and classes mixed in a jazzy atmosphere where black leather couches had replaced tables and the barstools were upholstered in leopard print.

The kind of place where, to make an impression, you dressed down to dress up.

"You can't go wrong with jeans and a button-down shirt."

I selected a pair of well-worn jeans with a little fraying at the hems and an ice blue short-sleeve shirt that would make his eyes sparkle.

If dressing Lyle had taught me anything, it was that the eyes made the man.

"Here." I threw the clothes at him, my heart finally returning to a normal pulse after the frantic thoughts of Daddy his thoughtless words had caused. "Wear these and a plain white tee with those oxfords I sent you for Christmas last year."

Randy's gaze lowered to the clothes in his hands and he blushed.

"If you don't have *those*," I said, feigning insult, "any black dress shoes will do."

"Thanks, Bets."

He smiled with relief and went to the bathroom to get ready.

Though my heart calmed, my hands still shook from the adrenaline of the fear-induced panic attack. For the space of several seconds, I truly thought Daddy had died. And my heart had stopped. Just like that. Just stopped.

Sinking onto the couch, I pulled out my phone and, after scrolling to the L section of my address book, dialed Mom's cell.

"Julia Lange," she said pleasantly.

I sighed with relief. "Hi, Mom."

"Bethany?"

Like she had another daughter.

She sounded surprised, which wasn't out of the question since I usually only called on birthdays and holidays and in emergencies. Sometimes that seemed like enough. Today it seemed like neglect.

"Yes, it's me." It had been so long I almost didn't know what to say. "How... What... I just called to check on Daddy."

I heard her sigh with relief. Since it wasn't a birthday or a holiday she probably thought it was an emergency.

"Oh honey, he's doing fine. The doctors released him

yesterday and he's resting at home. I'm at the grocery store right now buying fiber-rich foods."

Thank the Lord.

"That's good," I said because she paused and I needed to say something.

Nothing else came to mind.

This was a big mistake, I should never have called. No wonder I didn't call more often. It always wound up awkward and I never knew what to say.

"Well, I just wanted to check on him," I began, unable to stop the cascade of words flowing from my mouth, "and since he's doing fine I guess I'll go since I don't have anything else to—"

"Your father loves you."

I sucked in a sharp breath mid-ramble and made myself exhale slowly to keep from hyperventilating. Sometimes Mom knew just which button to push.

"I know, Mom," I said.

But I didn't. Not really. If he loved me why didn't he ever call me? Why didn't he come visit me in New York? Why didn't he at least pretend to support my choices? Why hadn't he even wanted me to know he was in the hospital?

"He only wants you to be happy," Mom said.

"I am happy." Mostly. "Why can't he see that?"

"Maybe you should try telling him that."

"I have tried. I—"

"You've been stubborn and defiant," Mom interrupted with an impatience she'd never shown before. The strain of Daddy's illness must have taken its toll on her temper. "You two are more alike than either of you will admit."

Ha! That was a joke. Daddy and I were nothing alike. We'd

been at odds since the day I'd turned twelve and asked to get a second piercing in my ears. He'd said, "No." I'd gotten it anyway.

That was when our relationship began to die. Two decades spent fighting and rebelling. Choosing Business and Marketing instead of Home Ec senior year. Getting into Columbia when he thought I should go to Auburn. Moving to New York when he thought I should stay in Atlanta. Everything from what I wore out the door to who I took to prom to whether or not I made a showing at church on Sunday. Everything became a battle.

We were nothing alike.

"No, we—"

"Talk to him, Bethany," she said in a tired voice. "Make things right."

There was so much pain beneath the quiet request. The pain of a woman caught between two people she loved for a lifetime. For the first time I realized how hard this must have been for her. How does a woman choose between her husband and her child?

She couldn't. And she shouldn't have to.

Settling everything with Daddy was the right thing to do.

But I couldn't.

"I—" Couldn't take that step? Couldn't make the first move? Couldn't sacrifice my pride? "Mom, I can't."

With a sadness I'd never heard in her she said goodbye and hung up.

I'd said I couldn't do it. But the truth was I wouldn't. Because I loved him too much.

What if he didn't love me back?

EIGHTEEN

BETWEEN EPISODES 103 and 104 we had a week-long break in the shooting schedule so Trevor and Steven could show the first episodes to focus groups.

I spent my mornings at Walk-In Closet, going over inventory and sales reports with Kit, who had everything under tight control—including Randy. He looked happier than I ever remembered. Even if it didn't work out, I knew that Kit was the best thing that could have happened to him.

The show wasn't set to air for another six months, but already the shop was reaping the benefits. It had been mentioned in several press releases about the show, some of which had been picked up by national media. The show itself had bought several thousand dollars' worth of product—for cast and participant wardrobes. And every time they filmed a segment in the shop walk-in traffic boomed with rubberneckers.

Seemed like no one could walk by without stopping in to find out if any celebrities were filming. Once inside, they almost always did a little shopping before they left.

So, with business booming and Kit on top of all the details, I had free time on my hands for the first time in years.

I spent most of it thinking about my last ditch plan to prove Evan's straightness—and trying not to think about Chris's *non-straightness*.

I had all the requisite elements: trench coat, skimpy lingerie, sexy heels. All I needed was someone to hold my hand until the moment of truth.

"Morning, sugar," Chris said as he walked into the shop. "Ready for a day out on the town?"

"Absolutely," I replied.

Outwardly smiling, inside I was secretly shaking at the prospect of asking Chris to accompany me. He had said he would be there for me, help me with whatever I needed no matter the motivation. But we hadn't mentioned Evan since the night of the exhibit opening. Maybe he'd changed his mind.

"Where should we go?" he asked.

"The Met," I answered automatically.

My freshman year at Columbia we had an art history assignment that consisted of finding a work of art in the Met to study for the entire semester. I had taken the M4 bus across the top of the park and down 5th Avenue, gotten out at the stop before the Met, and paid my admission. I wandered half the museum before winding up in the European Paintings section at the top of the grand staircase. It only took seconds for me to fall in love with *Allegory of the Planets and Continents*.

There was a bench right in front of the massive painting and I could sit there for hours drawing, meditating, or just marveling that this miraculous work of art was merely Giovanni Battista Tiepolo's sketch for a palatial ceiling mural.

A fact both inspiring and intimidating. Most people couldn't aspire to so masterful a finished product.

That wooden bench was my escape from the buzzing world of Manhattan life. My own private retreat on days when I couldn't get an appointment at the spa or afford a trip up the Hudson.

That was where I asked Chris to help me seduce Evan.

"I have a plan," I explained as we sat at the bench.

"For what?" he asked.

He stared at the painting intently, as if it hypnotized him as much as it had me my first visit.

"For proving Evan is straight."

To his credit, he didn't flinch or frown. "How?"

"Seduction."

He tore his gaze off the painting to stare at me.

"What do you mean?"

"I mean," I said, "I'm going to seduce Evan."

Chris slowly turned his whole body to face me. His eyes were dark and unreadable, but I had an idea what he was thinking.

He thought I was crazy. Desperate. Stupid.

I was all those things and the only way I had come up with to stop being crazy, desperate, and stupid was to prove Evan was straight. Until then it was like I had no control over my own mind.

"Did you just say that you're going to—"

"Seduce Evan. Yes, that's what I said."

Shaking his head like he couldn't have heard me right, he said, "Are you—"

"Crazy?" I finished for him. "Yes, but I don't have any other choice. I'm out of options."

"You can't seduce him," Chris argued. "You can't just show up and expect him to take you to bed. For crying out loud, he's gay!"

The security guard in the corner of the roomed glared at us for making too much noise.

"No, he's not," I replied calmly. "And I'm not going to bed with him."

"Of course you're not," Chris said. "He's gay."

I chose to ignore his broken record argument.

"I'm going to seduce him just enough to prove my point," I explained. Then, taking a deep breath, I said, "I'd like you to come with me. So I know you're waiting outside. For moral support."

I waited expectantly.

"I ..."

When it looked like he was going to say no, I hurried to add, "But if you won't then don't worry about it and I'll go by myself."

His eyebrows, squeezed together in a scowl, started twitching.

"It's okay," I said, letting him off the hook. "I'll be fine. I'll just—"

"I'll go." He didn't look happy about it. He didn't even look convinced that he'd said it. "I think this is the dumbest thing I've ever heard, but I'll go. I told you I'd be there for whatever you needed and I won't back out. If you want me there—" He sighed. "—I will be."

Leaning into him, I wrapped my arms around his waist and laid my head on his chest. He didn't return the hug, but I knew it was a sacrifice for him to agree.

I hadn't expected a miracle.

Just knowing that he meant it when he said he'd stand by me made this place even more precious. I didn't even mind the twinge of sadness that tightened around my heart when I wished it was Chris I planned to seduce and not Evan.

♥

THERE WAS a cast and crew meeting at the studio Friday afternoon to discuss the results of the focus group. We all gathered around a giant conference table while Trevor and Steven gushed over the positive feedback.

The focus group, made up mostly of soccer moms and middle-aged housewives, loved everything about the show—the cast, the concept ... everything. They were smitten.

"This is going to be a huge hit, people," Trevor said. "Their only suggestions were that we visit their homes to makeover their husbands, boyfriends, fathers, and brothers."

"I hope you're all ready for super-stardom," Steven added, the comment directed to the cast.

Everyone clapped and cheered, but my mind was focused on what I had planned for that night. All I could think about was how I was going to seduce my ex-boyfriend and whether it was going to work.

What would I do if it didn't?

When the meeting broke, Chris and I went to his apartment near Union Square—which was closer to Evan's and free of nosy younger brothers—to get ready. Somehow it felt weird that I'd never been to his apartment. It seemed like there wasn't anything I didn't know about Chris.

Yet his home surprised me.

He had told me about his tiny studio, but I assumed he

would have upgraded. Considering my compensation for working on the show, his had to be even better. But the space we walked into was a cramped, one-room apartment with a sofa bed covered in wrinkled clothes and rumpled sheets.

My cheeks flamed at thoughts of what could happen on those sheets.

"Sorry it's a mess," he said. "I'm almost never here."

"It's…" I struggled to find the right word. "Charming."

Chris laughed. "All right," he said. "If that's what you want to call it."

As I spun to finish my tour, I saw precisely why Chris had rented this studio. Half the square footage was the kitchen. It wasn't huge by any means but the appliances gleamed and the counters were spotless. Clearly he had prioritized his cleaning efforts.

I set my tote and purse down on the counter

"You can change in the bathroom." He motioned to an open door opposite the kitchen. "It's clear, I promise."

I checked the time on my phone. There was still time. In a few short hours, when darkness fell, I would don the lingerie and trench coat, strap on the sandals, and carry out my seduction.

The thought left an aching emptiness in the pit of my stomach.

I wasn't backing out, but second thoughts were not out of order.

"How about we watch some TV before the, um…" He couldn't seem to find the words. "Before we go."

I nodded, unable to speak as nerves set in. He shoved the clothes off the sofa bed, pulled the comforter over the sheets, and grabbed the remote as he settled in against the back. I climbed on next to him, nestled against his side, and relaxed instantly. He turned on the TV, clicking at the remote until he found the Gourmet Channel.

"Might as well do a little research," he said with a small laugh.

I laughed, too. In that instant I was happy. Truly happy. I didn't need to be anywhere else or do anything but exist right here. I didn't need to prove anything to anyone, not even me. This was what contentment felt like.

My head drooped against Chris's shoulder and I felt him wrap an arm around me and give me a squeeze as I drifted to sleep.

When he gently woke me some time later it was dark outside and he asked, "Ready to go?"

Do or die time.

Bliss forgotten, I steeled my reserve to do what had to be done. If I let the happiness of a single moment stop me I would spend the rest of my life wondering what would have happened if I'd gone through with it. If I ever wanted to find happiness with someone—more than just the friend Chris would forever be—I needed to answer this question for myself.

"Yeah," I said, wiping to sleep out of my eyes. "I'll go get changed."

I stumbled off in search of the bathroom, tote in hand. As I stripped and changed into the pink lacy lingerie in the surprisingly clean space, I heard Chris pacing outside the door, proving he wasn't as okay with this as he'd seemed.

"Are you sure you want to do this?" he asked.

I laughed. "Would you rather do it?" After all, he had

claimed he was attracted to Evan enough to want to ask him out. "Because we would know the truth either way."

Belting the honeydew green trench around my waist, I opened the door to an unamused Chris.

"Ha, ha," he was saying. "Very fun—"

His mouth dropped open when he saw me.

"You—you—you can't go out dressed like that!"

"I can," I said, walking to the couch and sitting down to strap on my shoes, "and I will."

He stayed silent while I buckled first one shoe then the other, but I could feel his displeasure. I'd explained the plan to him fully, so he shouldn't be surprised at my costume. I tried to tell myself it was nice to have someone so concerned over my actions, but I'd hated my parents for that in high school and I wasn't about to thank Chris for doing the same now.

I picked up my purse, tossed Chris my keys, and said, "I'm ready."

Even if he didn't look happy, he caught my keys and led the way to my car across the street. On the short drive I concentrated on keeping my nervous stomach under control. No need to spill lunch—half a Waldorf salad from a deli near the studio—all over my car. Chris didn't say a word until we pulled up in front of Evan's building.

"Are you sure?" he asked.

I nodded. "I'm sure," I said before he could ignite some doubts in my quivering belly.

I planted a quick kiss on his cheek, told him not to worry, and jumped out of the car.

My hands were shaking so much I didn't think I could manage pressing the buzzer. Not that I knew what I was going to say to explain my presence anyway.

Right as I walked up the stoop, a polite older gentleman exited, holding the door for me as I struggled to stay upright in stilettos while my legs wobbled. As I walked past I thanked him. His attention, however, was on the deep V between the lapels of the coat where the pink lace of my teddy peeked out.

What a letch!

Before disappearing into the entry hall, I turned and waved to Chris, who was fuming from across the street. He must have seen the man gawking at my chest.

With a deep breath to calm my nerves, I pressed the elevator call button and, startled when the doors opened immediately, stepped on board.

I spent the ride up focusing on my breathing. It wouldn't do any good if I passed out from hyperventilation before I even got to his door. The elevator lurched to a stop at the third floor, the doors sliding open with a creak.

I gave myself a mental You Can Do It pep talk and stepped into the hall.

Before I had a chance to think—and maybe talk myself out of the whole thing—I pressed the buzzer next to his door.

I heard shuffling inside.

With jerky movements I unknotted the belt on the trench coat and pulled apart the pale green canvas panels.

Metal scraped against metal.

He was unlocking the door.

Hands on my hips bracing the coat open, feet apart in swimsuit model stance, pink lingerie prominently displayed, I schooled my features into a seductive come-hither look.

The door swung open noiselessly.

"Hello, Evan."

NINETEEN

"BETHANY?" Evan looked back over his bare shoulder. "What are you doing here?"

I thought that would be obvious. And with him wearing only a towel, like he'd just gotten out of the shower, he looked ready.

"What do you think I'm doing here?" I tried in my sexiest voice.

"I think," he said, stepping forward to guide me into the hall and pulling the door halfway shut behind him, "that we need to talk."

"Talking," I said, not budging, "was not what I had in mind."

His failed attempt to back me into the hall brought him within inches. I lifted my hands to his chest and leaned into him. He jumped back so quickly he knocked the door wide open and I stumbled in after him.

Encouraged to see his towel slip lower, I started to shrug out of the trench coat. I had it down to my elbows when Evan ordered, "Stop."

He approached, grabbed my coat by the lapels, and lifted it back up over my shoulders.

"Bethy," he said quietly as he tugged the coat closed over my lingerie, "I think you should meet—"

"Hello," a deep male voice said.

Peering around Evan I saw a tall, olive-skinned man standing in the doorway to Evan's bedroom. Like Evan, he was clad only in a towel.

"—my partner," Evan finished. "Louis."

Louis smiled and waved.

I stood there, dumbstruck.

Um, ah. "Well butter my butt and call me a biscuit."

Drat. Those deep Southern roots came out at the worst times, like when my world crashed in around me.

He was gay. Evan was actually, truly, in-the-flesh gay.

More flesh than I needed to see.

A sound resembling one of Chicken's agitated squawks came out of my mouth. What could I say to that? Even if my mind suddenly started working again—at least well enough to form a coherent sentence—I didn't think there was an appropriate response to the situation.

Hallmark didn't have a sorry-I-thought-you-were-straight-when-all-along-you-had-a-secret-male-boyfriend card.

I fled, tripping down the hall in my four-inch heels and unconsciously taking the stairs instead of waiting for the elevator. As the stairwell door closed behind me, I heard Evan call out, "We should talk about this."

But my unsteady feet carried me down the two flights of stairs, each clack of my shoes reverberating up the shaft with a deafening echo. At the ground floor I burst into the entrance hall, rushed out the front door onto the street, and ran all the way to the car.

Chris sat sideways in the back with his legs stretched out—as far as they could stretch in the narrow car—across the seat. When he saw me approach he lurched up.

I reached the door before he could get to the lock button and I jerked on the handle repeatedly, willing it to open.

Open, open, open!

"Let go of the handle," he commanded.

I did.

With nothing to focus my frustrations on, tears filled my eyes. My breathing quickened and I could feel myself begin to hyperventilate.

Just when I was about to lose control the lock knob popped up and Chris swung the door open from the inside. He flipped the lever that sent the passenger seat sliding forward and started to climb out of the car.

I pushed him back and climbed over him into the back seat. He quickly reached out to pull the door shut before turning his attention to me.

"What happened?" he demanded. "Did he hurt you? If he laid a hand on you I'll—"

"He d-didn't h-hurt me," I stammered, not caring that tears streamed down my sure-to-be-splotchy cheeks and instantly my nose plugged up. "H-h-he's—"

I wailed, unable to say the words out loud.

Chris pulled me against him, smoothing his hands up and down my back as he whispered soothing words in my ear and let me blubber on his shoulder.

I wasn't sure how long he held me like that, but when I

regained control of my raging emotions—at least enough to stop weeping—I managed to say, "He's gay. He's really gay."

Chris could have said, "I told you so," but he just hugged me closer.

"I know, sugar," he whispered.

He cupped my head in his hand, cradled me close like a baby, and pressed a kiss to my temple.

"You'll be fine," he promised. "I'm here for you."

"No I won't be fine," I said, shaking my head. Panic rose in my heart. "I'll never be fine. My love life is a disaster. Boy, can I pick 'em. Evan's gay, you're gay."

"Bethany—" he said, his voice firm.

"Everyone's gay." I sounded hysterical, but I couldn't stop.

"—I'm not—"

"Hell," I shouted with one last burst of fire, "maybe I'm gay!"

"—gay."

What!?

"What?"

"I'm not gay," he repeated.

I tried to jerk away, but he held me tight against him.

A billion things raced through my mind.

This wasn't possible. This had to be some extreme form of delusion. I'd finally reached the breaking point and had graduated from poor judgment and desperation to auditory hallucinations. This was the beginning of the end.

"You are," I insisted, trying to hold onto my sanity.

"No," he replied evenly. "I'm not."

He had to be lying. He felt bad that I was having a complete mental breakdown in his arms and this was the only thing he could think to say to make me feel better.

After all we'd been through, after all I'd told him—confessed to him—he had to be gay.

But doubts tickled. Memories surfaced. Of that morning in my silk pajamas. Of that kiss, right here in the back seat of my car. What if he *wasn't* gay?

If it was true—if Chris really was straight—why hadn't he told me?

All the chances he'd had to tell me and hadn't. All the times I'd told him I wished he weren't gay. All the times I battled my own attraction because this time I was *not* going to fall for a gay guy.

This was too much.

"Aaargh!" I screamed and struggled against him.

Fists pounding against his chest, I released a lifetime—or at least a few months' worth—of bottled up anger. It wasn't fair. Why couldn't I ever see what was in front of me? Why did it take a serious slap in the face for me to see—actually *see* —people?

No, not people. Just men.

Why did I have so much trouble reading men? Was this my curse?

My fire died, turning to pain.

Chris held me tight, and tighter still when I started sobbing with my whole body. I was such a fool. First I fell for gay men pretending to be straight. Now I'd graduated to falling for straight men pretending to be gay. Was anyone as messed up as me?

"Shhh, sugar," Chris whispered. "Come back here."

Lowering my arms, I felt the jingle of my charm bracelet against my wrist. I thought of the charm he'd given me, of his devotion despite being unable to reveal his true self.

Something I should have seen all along.

My heart softened and I stopped fighting. Tightening my arms around his waist, I relaxed into him. He continued to massage his hands up and down my back. I felt him turn his head so we were cheek to cheek.

At the first pressure of his lips—on my forehead, on my eyelid, on my cheek—my heart raced into double-time.

Battling the instinct to pull out of his arms—convincing myself it was really true, he really was straight, was no easy feat—I leaned back to look into his eyes.

The clear blue depths sparkled nearly silver in the center. And not just from the mercury vapor streetlight. They sparkled with interest, with excitement, mirroring the attraction I'd been battling for what felt like forever.

All the worries in my mind fled and I sank into him with a relief I'd never thought to feel. For the first time in eons I was on the same page as the man in front of me.

It felt darn good.

Then his lips touched mine—this time I knew he meant it— and I knew nothing could ever feel bad again.

I WOKE up in a strange bed, surrounded by unfamiliar bedding and a radiating heat. It took me a few seconds to remember where I was and then convince myself it was all real.

"Morning, sugar," Chris said, his voice rumbling in his chest beneath my chin.

"Morning yourself." I lifted my head to look at him,

reclining back against a pile of steel gray pillows like a man content with his lot in life.

"Do you believe it today?" he asked with a smile.

"No," I answered.

He chuckled. "We're going to have to work on your trust issues." He flipped me onto my back, covering me with his body. "But if you need another round of proof, who am I to argue?"

His head descended, lips hovering a millimeter above mine when the phone rang.

"Damn," he said, planting a quick kiss on my mouth before rolling over to answer the phone. "Yo."

I grumbled at his desertion, but snuggled happily back into the covers to doze a little longer.

"No," Chris said. "I haven't."

As he listened, I heard my phone ding with an incoming text message. I stuck my hand out, feeling for where I'd left it on the nightstand.

"I'll look right now." Chris punched off his phone. "Damn."

"What's wrong?" I asked, but as I read the text from Cassie, I knew.

Daily reports one of guys not gay. Mtg at three.

I shook my head. "Is this for real?"

Chris cursed at his phone, then turned the screen so I could read the headline.

Counterfeit Queer Exposed!

The subtitle was even worse.

A cast member on the next hot gay makeover show, One Straight Guy at a Time, isn't gay after all.

Quickly scanning the article I was relieved to see it didn't name names—left Chris's identity secret. Neither did it name the anonymous source who claimed to be the straight cast member's former fiancé.

I looked at him. "How did they find out?"

"I have no idea." He ran a hand over his hair. "I've been so careful."

"Who else knows?" I asked. "I mean, do you have any exes who might want to get back at you or anything?"

He shook his head. "I haven't dated anyone in a while. And my last girlfriend still sends me Christmas cards. I've been so focused on my career since I got to New York that I've barely had time for friends, let alone dating."

Rolling to the edge of the bed, he leaned over his knees and hung his head in his hands. I reached out to rub a reassuring hand over his back. "It'll be okay."

"It won't," he insisted. "God, I knew I shouldn't have gone through with this. I hate lying and this is some kind of epic karma for doing it on such a big scale."

I didn't know what to say to make him feel better, so I wrapped my arms around him from behind. He rested his hand on my forearm and squeezed.

"Who would have done this?" he asked. "It doesn't make any sense."

My phone dinged again with another text. Chris's phone buzzed at the same time. We ignored the messages until another came through. And another. Several messages in rapid succession.

A quick check told me it was the cast freaking out. Adam, Danial, and Even were going into full-on panic via group message.

Adam: *I heard the studio hired private eyes*

Danial: *Me too*

Adam: *They're going to sue for breach of contract*

Danial: *For millions in damages $$$*

Evan: *Was this you, Bethy?*

Adam: *Bethy? Lol!*

Danial: *Why would Bethany do this?*

Evan: *Bethany?*

This was the last thing Chris needed to see, so I silenced both our phones.

"I'm going to find out what happened," I told him.

He half-shrugged and shook his head, then pushed to his feet. "I'm getting a shower."

I watched helpless as he walked into the bathroom. I felt bad for him. As much as I'd been furious at Evan for lying—which he wasn't—I suddenly realized how hard it could be on someone to pretend to be something they weren't.

Chris wasn't a bad guy. He'd just been in a tough situation and took an opportunity when it fell into his lap. I'd done the same thing when I agreed to work on the show. I could hardly blame him for doing the same. And I was determined to find out how the paper had found out.

I started with Cassie. She knew absolutely everything about her production. I dialed her cell, figuring that she might not be at the studio this early.

She picked up, but instead of greeting me, her voice in the background was saying, "I have no comment. I've told you three times I have no comment. I'm not going to have a comment no matter how many times you ask me the same question."

"Cassie?"

"You can call the studio press office if you want a more formal no comment statement." She sighed heavily, and then, "Bethany?"

"Yes," I said. "I got your text." And twenty-seven from the guys. "Are you okay?"

She groaned. "What an awful day."

"I know," I ventured. "That's what I wanted to talk to you about."

"You and every reporter in the Tri-State area."

"What happened?" I asked.

"You've got me," she replied. "The phone calls started even before I got to work. One of the reporters from *The Daily* got my unlisted cell number and called at five-thirty."

Must have been a slow news week.

Then again, the show had been getting serious publicity while still in the early phases of production. No wonder the media was so quick to glom onto such a juicy tidbit.

"Do you, um,—" I swallowed. "—know which guy they're talking about?"

"None, as far as I know." She read one of the headlines out loud. "It's tabloid drivel. It doesn't have to be true if it can make waves."

"It *is The Daily*," I said. "They're usually pretty thorough about checking their sources."

"You know something." Cassie's voice rose an octave as she spoke. "It's Evan, isn't it!? You got the proof he was straight and called the paper and—"

"No!" I said. "It's not Evan. I, um, actually proved myself wrong on that one."

"Then what?" she persisted. "I know you, Bethany Lange, and you've got a secret. I can hear it in your voice."

"No, I—" I looked at the bathroom door, not wanting to lie to her but not willing to throw Chris under the bus. "Nothing I can share."

I was already walking the thin gray line between friendship and business. Throw in the love of my life, and I was all screwed up.

No matter how much I wanted to tell her, my friend, about Chris and me I couldn't.

"Nothing that would make a difference now," I promised. Someone had already, and telling Cassie about me and Chris now couldn't help the situation.

"You can tell me, you know," she said softly. "Friend to friend."

I was tempted, but this wasn't a decision I could make without consulting Chris. He had more to lose.

If he hadn't already lost it.

"I will," I said. "As soon as all this blows over."

"That may be sooner than we'd like." She groaned. "You saw my message about meeting this afternoon?"

"Is that bad?" I asked.

She shrugged. "Who knows? They're executives. Unpredictable by nature."

That didn't sound good.

"I'm going to find out what happened, Cassie."

"All I know," she said, sounding like she was in pain, "is what was in the papers. The scum from *The Inquisitor* let it slip that the source had been stalking the guy on location during shooting."

That wasn't much to go on, but at least it was something.

"Okay, thanks," I said. "I'll see you this afternoon."

"Let me know what you find out."

I ended the call and stared at my phone, still lighting up with texts from the rest of the cast. Adam, Danial, and Evan were taking panic to a whole new level.

Watching the onslaught of messages scroll by, something clicked into place. Something that had been niggling at the back of my mind for weeks. Ever since—

"Oh my God."

"What?" Chris asked from the open bathroom doorway.

For a moment I couldn't speak. A mostly naked Chris with a towel around his waist and water droplets glistening in his hair made it nearly impossible to think. But the haunted look in his eyes reminded me why this was so important.

"I have to go," I blurted, jumping out of bed.

I didn't want to get his hopes up if I was wrong, but I was pretty certain I wasn't. In a flash, I had pulled on yesterday's clothes, yanked my hair into a messy knot, and was out the door and on my way to the studio.

♥

BRYCE'S DOOR WAS SHUT. A rarity. He was more of an extreme sharer than a secret keeper.

I considered knocking, but decided against it. The element of surprise could be a major benefit.

He was on the phone, talking in fervent hushed tones.

"The newspapers?" he exclaimed. "I can't believe you did that!"

His back was to the door and he didn't realize I'd entered until I said, "Tell the redhead hello for me."

"Aaack!" he shrieked, dropping the phone as he fell out of his chair.

"I'm sorry," I said, not meaning it. "Was that meant to be a private conversation? There are so many secrets around here I can't seem to keep them *straight*."

His jaw dropped—maybe at my biting comment. He picked himself and the phone up off the floor.

"I'll call you later, Molly," he said into the phone. "I can't talk right now."

As he set his phone on his desk he watched me warily.

Brazen Bryce was nowhere in sight.

"Sooo," I drawled, "her name is Molly. I almost feel like I know her, we've both been spending so much time with you lately."

He looked miserable. Part of me wanted to gloat, to lord this knowledge over him because I'd been the one to uncover the truth. But the same look haunted his eyes that I had seen in Chris's this morning. He felt bad enough already.

I took pity on him. "Tell me about it."

"We were engaged," he said, rubbing his hands over his face. "That was why I auditioned. I wanted to be able to give her the wedding of her dreams." He looked at me with red-rimmed eyes. "I didn't want her to know what I was doing. When I got cast for the show I broke up with her. I tried to tell her it was only temporary, that I just couldn't tell her why. She thought I was seeing another woman."

What was it with guys not telling girls why they were really breaking up? It only led to problems later.

"She figured out what was going on," he continued, "and instead of talking to me she went to the press."

He leaped up from the chair and started pacing around the room, shoving his hands through his shaggy blonde hair.

"All she had to do was wait," he insisted. "Just a few more

months, just to see how the show went. If it was a success I wasn't going to renew my contract. If it failed then no big loss. I did it all for her."

A soft knock sounded at the door, but Bryce was so agitated he didn't notice.

"I love her," he growled, "but sometimes she won't listen to reason. I don't care for myself. But I feel awful she ruined this for everyone else."

The door swung open. Cassie stood in the doorway, a stormy look on her face. She had caught the tail end of his tirade.

"I don't know what the heck is going on at this studio," she said, "but you both need to be at the meeting this afternoon. Three o'clock." She gave Bryce a pointed look. "Don't be late."

After waiting a second to give us an opportunity to answer her questioning look—which we both chose not to do—she shook her head and left.

"Bryce," I began, thankful for Cassie's interruption because he had calmed down considerably, "you need to make things right."

"I know," he said. "I'll apologize to the cast—"

"No." I laid a hand on his arm. "You need to make things right with Molly."

Brows knitted in confusion, he eyed me like I'd suggested he pair plaid with paisley. I smiled—the kind of smile Mom used to give when she was granting permission to do something I thought I'd never get to do.

"You love her," I explained. "You need to fix this."

Bryce's face cracked with a giant smile. Was this how Mom always felt when I'd reacted so joyously to her unexpected permission?

"You're right!" he cried.

He gave me a quick hug, grabbed his jacket, and ran out the door. Leaving me with happy thoughts of Mom. Which led to sad thoughts of Daddy.

Maybe I needed to take my own advice. Bryce wasn't the only one who needed to make things right. It was time I grew up and swallowed a big dose of pride.

I dialed Dad's cell phone on my way out of the studio—heading home to change into something more professional than last Chris's baggy clothes for the network meeting. His phone went right to voicemail.

I tried Home. Answering machine.

Mom's cell. Voicemail.

As I descended into the subway I tucked my phone away. I would just have to try again later.

♥

BETWEEN TREKKING out to Brooklyn and back—including a delay on the subway when it stopped under the East River for ten minutes in total darkness—it was two o'clock when I got home. I couldn't show up at the meeting in day-old clothes. Bursting in the front door, I dashed through the hall and skidded into my room.

I searched through the contents of my closet, settling on a periwinkle sheath dress and a matching cardigan.

There was a knock at my bedroom door.

"I'm in a rush, Randy," I called. "What do you need?"

I unzipped and dropped my skirt.

"Bethany," my mother's voice said, "your brother isn't here."

I lurched forward, my skirt catching around my ankles and sending me pitching across the floor. Scrambling to my feet, I ran to the door and jerked it open.

"Mom?!"

She was standing there—in all her ivory ladylikeness—in my hallway, with my intimidating father at her side. I couldn't do more than blink for several long seconds.

"Daddy?" I asked, breathless.

He looked stern and unhappy, but beneath that he looked older. Older than even the last Christmas picture.

The heart attack must have taken a toll.

When he didn't say a word, Mom kept talking.

"Randall was here when we arrived," she said, seamlessly filling the silence as she always did. "He took us to see your store when he went to work. It is a lovely boutique."

I watched Daddy nervously.

"His little girlfriend seems very ..." She searched for an appropriate term to describe Kit. "Modern."

About that time I realized I was standing there in a wrinkled white oxford shirt and my red lace undies.

"If you could just—" I felt my cheeks flame. "I'll be out in a moment."

And then I shut the door in their faces.

Ten minutes later I had pulled myself together into some semblance of a ladylike appearance. My makeup was practically non-existent, but I didn't have time. I had to get uptown for the network meeting. As soon as I found out why my parents were here.

They were sitting on my couch, looking uncomfortable. But then they always looked uncomfortable.

"Can I get you something to drink?" I offered, falling back on my gracious hostess upbringing.

"No," Daddy said. "Thank you."

I hovered at the edge of the rug that delineated the living room area. Daddy rose and walked to where I stood.

"Bethany, I—" he began. He looked over his shoulder to Mom, who gave him a reassuring nod. With a big sigh, he said, "I'm sorry, baby."

Next thing I knew, his arms were around me. For a solid sixteen seconds I stood frozen in shock. My father was not the sort to display affection physically. Hell, he didn't display affection in any way.

"I'm a stubborn old man," he continued, "and I don't know if I can mend all my fences." His voice broke a little at the end. "But I'd like to try."

And I'd thought all my tears for the week had been exhausted.

"Oh, Daddy," I cried, wrapping my arms around his waist and squeezing him tighter than a lid stuck on a pickle jar. "I've missed you so much."

"I've missed you, too, baby girl."

At this point my mother joined the hug, wrapping her arms around us both and shedding her own tears. I couldn't remember the last time we'd shared a family hug—maybe not since before Randy was born.

"We should go see Randy," I said. Then remembered why I'd hurried home. "Damn, I can't. I have to get to a meeting."

Mom flinched at my use of profanity.

Daddy laughed.

I said, "Why don't you come with? We can go out for a late lunch after."

With no time to wait for an answer, I grabbed them both by the wrist and headed for the door. Everything was finally going to fall into place—I would make sure it did.

TWENTY

THE NETWORK OFFICES were on the top floor of a Midtown skyscraper. My parents and I ran into Adam and Danial in the lobby waiting for the elevator. They were still freaking out over what was going to happen to the show and whether there would be legal repercussions.

I tried to reassure them, but in truth I didn't know what they would do. Like Cassie said, they were unpredictable executives. They might shrug off the issue. Or they might blackball everyone involved.

Since they'd gone to the effort of calling the meeting, maybe that meant they weren't about to forget the whole thing.

The express elevator whizzed us to the fiftieth floor in seconds. A severe-looking receptionist—complete with librarian glasses and skin-tight bun—met us in the lobby.

Leaving Mom and Daddy to the cushy leather chairs in the waiting area, Adam, Danial, and I followed obediently as the receptionist led us to the meeting room. Cassie, Evan, Trevor, and Steven were already there, along with several crew members, the other consultants, and three grim-faced executives clustered at the far end of an expansive conference table.

With what felt like all eyes on me, I barely noticed the view of Central Park from the wall of windows lining the length of the room. I took the seat next to Cassie, who was nibbling furiously on the eraser end of a pencil.

No one said a word.

When the door opened again, everyone looked up.

Chris didn't look at anyone, not even me. Head down, he walked around the far side of the table, lowering into the chair opposite mine. I frowned, willing him to look at me. I wanted him to tell him everything would be okay, that it wasn't his fault.

Still, he didn't look at me.

"Is everyone here, Miss Bishop?" Grim-Face #1 asked.

"No," Cassie answered, sounding more nervous than I'd ever seen her, "we're still waiting on—"

"I'm here, I'm here," Bryce announced, marching into the room and to the head of the table. Resting both hands on the gleaming wooden surface, he said, "Let's get this out of the way. I'm straight and that headline was about me."

Next to me, Cassie groaned. I had a feeling she was hoping to smooth over the whole situation, play it off as a media hoax and move on with the show.

Chris finally looked up—first at Bryce and then at me. He raised his brows in question. I smiled and nodded.

He visibly relaxed.

"B-but—" Danial stammered.

Adam interrupted, "I thought it was about me."

Someone gasped.

"No," Danial said, finding his voice. "It was about me."

Chris laughed out loud. "Me too."

"I knew you weren't gay," Bryce exclaimed.

Soon, everyone except the grim-faced three was laughing. Even Cassie had given up being mad and was trying valiantly to hold in a giggle or two.

Grim-Face #2 growled, "Is *anyone* in this blasted cast gay?"

Evan raised his hand. "I am."

Oh, the irony—don't think I couldn't see it.

"This is a disaster." Grim-Face #3—the grimmest of all and therefore, I assumed, the highest ranking—threw up his arms in defeat. He pushed back from the table—the other two followed suit immediately—and addressed the assembled group. "Clearly this is beyond salvation. The show is canceled."

He turned and stalked out of the room.

One Grim-Face followed on his heels saying, "Consider yourselves lucky we don't intend to sue."

He gave each of the cast members—except Evan—a stern look before turning to Cassie and saying, "Miss Bishop, we would like to see you in the President's office. Now."

Cassie followed him, turning back as she reached the door to say, "Wish me luck."

For the longest time, everyone just sat there.

No one moved.

No one spoke.

It was like we were collectively holding our breath.

Then Bryce walked around the table and tapped me on the shoulder. "I need to talk to you."

His action broke the trance and suddenly everyone was talking at once. I moved closer to Bryce.

"I'm going to re-propose to Molly," he said.

"That's great," I replied, stepping out of the way so others could get by.

"I just wanted to thank you."

He hugged me and now that he wasn't gay it felt a little awkward. Like I was only now aware of the fact that he was a man. Then I remembered, this was Bryce. Gay or straight he was the same silly, outrageous, fondling guy.

"You're welcome," I said as I hugged him back. "And good luck. From what I've seen of Molly, you're going to need it."

"Will I ever." He laughed. "I'd better go. She's waiting for me."

I watched him jog out of the room, hurrying to meet his future. I turned to look for mine.

Chris was gone. Why had he slipped out so quickly, and without saying anything? Maybe I could catch him at the elevators.

Evan was waiting for me in the hall.

"Bethany," he said when I walked out. "We need to talk."

Um, ah, well. "Go ahead."

"I wanted to apologize for—" He bit his lip, thinking. "—for not telling you the truth when we broke up."

"It's okay," I said, a little startled to realize I meant it. "Really. I'm fine about it now."

"No, it's not okay," he insisted. "I should have told you because you deserved better. You saved me and I lied to you."

"Saved you?" What was he talking about?

"You helped me realize what I was hiding inside," he said. "You made me accept that I was gay."

"Great," I said, my mood dimming, "glad to know I'm an A-plus turner. If you ever run across any straight men you want to date, send them my way. I'll have them on your team in no time."

"You always had the oddest sense of humor." Evan laughed, then took my hands in his. "You saved me by being wonderful. I woke up one morning, looked at you, and thought, 'Evan, if you can't love a woman as beautiful, caring, and wonderful as Bethany, then something is not right in your life.' It took me a while to figure out what, but I did and now I'm happier than I've ever been."

He made it sound a whole lot better than I'd ever imagined. Still, I had one question. "What was with all the secrecy?" I asked. "At the bar and, um—" I caught myself from saying something revealing about my recent stalking-like activities. "—other stuff."

Evan blushed.

"It's Louis," he explained. "He's an aide in the Mayor's office—the very *conservative* Mayor's office—and he hadn't come out yet. We couldn't meet openly until he made his announcement, which he did yesterday." He grinned. "It was kind of fun, actually. We would go out and sit next to each other at the bar, like we were strangers. I felt like a spy."

Now I knew why Louis had looked familiar the night I tried to seduce Even. He had been the man sitting next to Evan at *Geoffrey's* when Kit and Chris and I had followed him there. Not that I knew anything about feeling like a spy…

"I almost forgot," he cried. "We're getting married. I'm sending out the formal invites next week."

"That's wonderful," I said, truly happy for him. "Just make sure you mail it to my apartment. I'm having a disagreement with my mailman at the shop."

♥

CHRIS WAS LONG GONE by the time I was done with Evan. Mom and Daddy were standing when I got back to the waiting area. Even though the show had been canceled and my guy—could I call him mine after only one night?—I couldn't help smiling.

My parents were in the city, and for the first time in a very, very, *very* long time things were right with them. Randy was over Laura Jane and onto Kit, who might chew him up and spit him out but he would come out smiling. Bryce was going to propose to Molly, again, and Evan was going to marry Louis. Everyone was getting their happily ever after.

And, once I found Chris, I would get mine too.

"You look happy," Daddy said.

"I am, Daddy," I answered. "I really am."

"I'm glad you realized," he said, "you don't have to make everyone else happy before yourself."

"I've realized—" I pressed the elevator call button. "—that sometimes things have to work themselves out."

Mom looked confused. "But what about—"

"Hush, Julia," Daddy interrupted. "That will take care of itself, too."

As we stepped into the elevator, knowing not to get in the middle of something between my parents, I asked, "Ready for lunch?"

They both smiled and nodded without saying a word.

Which should have been my first clue.

Leading the way, I crossed the gleaming lobby and pushed out into the glorious sunshine. A beautiful day.

Funny how a day could start out perfect and wind up

taking so many twists and turns. For that matter, my life had taken a lot of twists and turns in the past few weeks. And almost all of them for the good.

Now I only had one last twist to find.

"Ah-hem."

I turned to the sound.

Chris stood there, a timid grin on his face and a gift-wrapped box on his outstretched palm. Everything else forgotten, I ran forward and threw my arms around his neck.

"You didn't leave," I exclaimed.

"No," he said. "I didn't leave."

There was something in his voice—a serious undertone—that made me step back. He pressed the gift box into my hands.

"Before you open that," he said, "I have to apologize."

I started to argue, but he waved me off.

"I've spent the last several weeks falling for you." He smiled as he tucked a strand of hair behind my ear.

As far as apologies went, this was a winner.

"What I did—" He dropped his hand. "—lying to you, to the producers and the cast, it wasn't fair to anyone. You shouldn't forgive me."

"But I—"

"Let me finish," he said, and I did. "Lying to you was worse than anything Evan did, because I *knew* I was lying. I know how much that hurt you. You shouldn't forgive. But if you do..."

He nodded at the gift box in my hand.

I pulled at the silver paper, not knowing what to expect. Inside was a little velvet box just like the last one he gave me. As I opened the lid the hinge creaked.

Another heart-shaped charm lay on the pink velvet lining. This one read, *Lovers Forever*.

Lifting my shaking arm, I held out my bracelet. Chris took the charm and carefully attached it next to the last one. Together, the two hearts read, *Friends First, Lovers Forever*.

My eyes stung.

I couldn't risk looking at him or I wouldn't be able to speak.

"You're right," I said. "You shouldn't have lied, not to anyone. But—" I shook my head when my voice started to crack. "But I understand why you did. And I think I understand now why I kept being drawn to gay men."

"What is that?" he asked, lifting my chin so I had to look at him.

"What was the point of dating anyone attainable," I explained, "until I met you?"

He grinned and I couldn't help grinning in return.

"I love you," he whispered.

I laughed, remembering the first time he'd said it and how I'd thought he'd never mean it the way he meant it now.

"I love you, too."

"Good," he whispered. "Because the next velvet box you open won't hold a charm."

I laughed again because I couldn't keep all my joy inside.

"Are you two gonna get a room," Kit shouted from the row of benches lining the side of the plaza where she sat with Randy and Mom and Daddy, "or are we going to lunch? I was promised food."

My arms around Chris, I smiled through my tears.

"Lunch," I shouted back, then whispered to Chris, "we can get a room later."

Arm in arm we followed the rest of our group in search of food. A funny thought occurred to me and I stopped suddenly.

"What if you turn out gay?" I teased.

"I won't," he promised.

"But what if?" I persisted. "It's not like I have the best track record."

"I promise, sugar," he said, "the only thing in my closet is clothes."

Dear reader,

Straight Stalk was born of my crush on Thom Filicia from the original version of Queer Eye. One day I thought, *I wish Thom wasn't gay*. Then almost immediately thought, *What if Thom* **wasn't** *gay?!*

I think you can see where that idea led…

Straight Stalk, in turn, ended up providing the inspiration for my first YA book, Oh. My. Gods., but that's a tale for another book.

The City Chicks series continues with born-and-bred New Yorker Cassie's story in *Trying Texas*. Turn the page for a sneak peek…

To get insider extras, exclusive giveaways, and breaking news, visit teralynnchilds.com/subscribe to join my mailing list.

TRYING TEXAS
Chapter 1

I must have done something terrible in a past life to deserve this kind of punishment. Really terrible. Like clubbed baby seals and knocked down old ladies in the street terrible.

As I stared out the front window at the long, never-ending stretch of highway, I had to fight the overwhelming urge to fling myself out of the moving SUV. The gray strip of blacktop seemed to go on into infinity. Pure, unabashed nothingness. Isolation surrounded by dust, cows, and—

"Was that a tumbleweed?" I demanded.

Eddie stared straight ahead, eyes on the road like a hypnotized zombie. "Uh-huh."

Had we really been in New York just this morning? It didn't seem possible. My six a.m. caffeine injection and everything bagel with shmear from the deli around the corner from my apartment felt like a lifetime ago. Twelve lifetimes.

As a native Manhattanite, Los Angeles was normally as uncivilized as I was willing to get—and that was only for the few short years of film school because my undergrad advisor thought I should "broaden my experience base" before entering the industry.

But even though New York was half-a-continent closer at the moment than when I had been in California, I'd never felt farther away. I had no idea how much nothingness actually filled the country between the two coasts. I'd never been one of those snotty New Yorkers who considered everything between us and L.A. to be nothing more than a flyover state, but I was starting to think maybe they were right.

Did people actually live here?

Dallas hadn't scared me. It was a big city, after all, with shopping and culture and every amenity a die-hard city girl could want. There had been skyscrapers and traffic noise. Grit, pollution, and panderers at busy intersections. A drugstore with ample supply of my more-necessary-than-ever heartburn medicine.

Sure, the attendant at the car rental desk had a thick accent and said *y'all* a lot—a *lot*—but that was almost charming. I'd actually thought to myself, *Maybe Texas won't be so bad after all.*

But this? This was a different world—a different universe.

A couple hundred miles west from one of the busiest airports in the world in one of the largest metro areas in the country, and I might as well have been on the moon.

Was this even the same planet?

"How long since you had signal?" Eddie asked.

I glanced down at my phone, clutched desperately in my fist.

"Half an hour," I replied. "At least."

Since leaving Fort Worth city limits I'd seen more cows than cars and more abandoned tractors than cell towers. Four hours in the car and I hadn't seen a fast food place in the last two. I was starting to forget what drive-thru coffee looked like.

This was *literally* the middle of nowhere.

Eddie swerved suddenly, sending me shoulder-first into the passenger door of our rental SUV.

"What the hell?" I demanded, pulling myself back upright.

"There was an armadillo in the road."

I stared at him incredulously as I rubbed my bruised arm. "An *armadillo*?"

He made a face.

First a tumbleweed, and now an armadillo? Those had to be against traffic laws or something.

"How much longer?" I whined.

"According to the GPS," he said, "about twenty minutes."

I dropped my head back against the seat. "Thank God."

"Oh, my bad," he correct. "We exit the freeway in twenty minutes. It's another thirty-five after that until we're in Rocky Gulch."

If Eddie knew how badly I wanted to stab him in the neck with a pen right now, he would probably pull over and make me get out of the car.

If he knew how badly I wanted to stab myself in the neck with a pen, he would probably hand me a sharp ballpoint.

I settled for digging the bottle of antacids out of my purse and chomping two chewable cherry tablets. As much as I didn't want to *be* in the middle of nowhere, I wanted to *die* in the middle of nowhere even less.

As we chased the sun toward the horizon, I thought back over the series of events that somehow culminated in my exile to America's answer to Siberia, aka the desert dry plains of central Texas.

In my own defense, I couldn't have known. I wasn't in charge of the casting decisions, and even if I had been, I couldn't possibly have known that four of the five cast members on our gay makeover reality show, *One Straight Guy at a Time*, were in fact not gay at all. I wasn't a mind reader and my gaydar was apparently set on oblivious. How was this my fault?

Still, as the least senior producer involved, when the big boss set out the chopping block, my neck was the first one offered up in sacrifice.

I should have been grateful that Bud Gorman was giving me a second chance.

My mission was simple. If I could produce the rough pilot of a new show, *Try It On*, with a next-to-nothing budget and only a cameraman for crew, without incident, he would consider—*consider*—putting me back on the list. And the list was where I wanted to be. Where I *needed* to be. Being on the list was Plan A for climbing the ladder of career success, all the way to an Emmy, an Oscar, and a Golden Globe at the very top. Being off the list was... well, I refused to consider that possibility. There was no Plan B.

I was under no misconception that this was anything less than a sudden death probation. I *had* to make *Try It On* a success.

Try It On was one of those reality shows where seemingly normal and sane people—and I used those terms in the most liberal sense—gave up their ordinary lives to experience something completely different. Episodes in the works included a stay at home mom who would live the life of a Park Avenue princess, a school teacher who would play the part of Broadway star, and a motorcycle shop owner who would try to hack it as a park ranger. What made *Try It On* different from the five-thousand other shows with the same general premise was the amount of time participants committed to their trial lives—an entire month.

Filed under the why-would-anyone-do-something-so-dumb category of TV shows, as far as I was concerned, but a gig was a gig and I needed to get back on Bud's good side. My career in television was ready to take off and I needed to stay on the right track.

Even if that meant I had to spend the next thirty days in exile from civilization.

"Chocolate?" Eddie asked.

"Sure." I sat up a little straighter in my seat and held out my hand. "Thanks."

He scowled at me sideway. "As in do you have any?"

"Oh." I slumped. "No. Not even a breath mint."

"My boyfriend always has chocolate." Eddie pursed his lips. "Then again, he's more of a girl than you are."

I punched him in the arm. "If I had known we were traversing the Kalahari, I would have grabbed a jumbo bag of candy bars along with my antacid."

When Bud told me I could choose my own cameraman for the pilot from the selection of lens jockeys with horse riding experience—a very necessary skill for someone expected to capture every moment of life of a working ranch—I been relieved to see Eddie Monroe on the list.

He was the size of a taxi—and not an ordinary four-passenger sedan taxi, one of the giant minivan ones reserved for swarms of tourists with more luggage than sense. He was fast as a panther, though, and had the ability to make me laugh in almost any situation, which was why I'd blurted his name on the spot.

We'd been through more disastrous productions together than I cared to remember. He saved me from a trip to the ER on *Apes with Knives*, managed to make a hardened cage fighter cry on *Into the Octagon*, and deftly avoided the advances of a dozen drunk coeds—whose gaydar was as faulty as mine—on *Spring Break Strip Poker*. On top of all that, the man was a regular Houdini with a camera.

I knew that if I was going to be stuck in the middle of nowhere for a month, the only way to make the experience bearable would be to bring along someone who knew how to get the best shots in the worst conditions and who I could actually tolerate for long periods of time.

Lord knew, there was nothing else about this wasteland that was inviting me to hang out any longer than I absolutely had to.

I popped another antacid and quietly knocked my head against the window.

Eddie stopped the car in front of the dusty blue Victorian house with a three-story turret and dormers in the roof. A streetlight out front cast an amber glow that turned the white trim into gold. A carved, painted sign in the yard declared this the *Yellow Rose Bunkhouse Bed and Breakfast*.

A picture-perfect image that looked straight off a movie set. Hopefully not one with a psycho serial killer hiding inside.

"Not bad," I said as I climbed out of the car. "I'll go get us checked in."

The sidewalk and front path were lined with small purple flowers with centers that were almost the same color as the house itself. When I got to the front door, I hesitated. I'd never stayed in a bed and breakfast before. It was kind of a hotel, but it looked like a house. What was the protocol for this time of night? Was I supposed to knock or just walk right in?

I tried the handle and found it unlocked.

In the end, I decided on a hybrid approach. I knocked on the door while opening it and walking inside.

"Hello?" I whisper-shouted to the empty front hall.

There was a table to the left with an open book, like a guest register. Otherwise, it looked completely residential. A pair of doorways opened off the hall to either side. One led to a dining room, with a big wooden table and a dozen mix-and-matched chairs. The other was hidden by a decorative folding screen, painted with a cattle drive scene straight out of the Wild West.

This really looked like someone's house. Maybe the sign out front was a mistake. Maybe I missed an arrow or something. I needed to get out of there before I was arrested for breaking and entering. Or at least entering.

"Welcome to the Yellow Rose Bunkhouse," a cheerful voice whispered behind me.

I covered my mouth to hold in a shriek as I spun around to find an older woman, mid-to-late-sixties probably, with a broad smile on her round face and a pile of gray hair curled into a loose bun. She wore plain blue pants and pale blue blouse beneath a brightly-colored floral apron.

Blue seemed to be the color of the day—or night, as it were.

"Can I help you?" she asked, her smile unwavering.

"I'm Cassie Bishop," I replied, keeping my voice as low as

hers. I stepped forward and offered her my hand. "I'm with Go Gorman Studios."

Her head tilted slightly to one side and her smile grew twice as big. She stepped forward, bypassing my offered hand to pull me into tight hug.

"It's so nice to meet you, Cassie," she said as she patted me on the back. "I'm Sue-Anne Arnold. I'm the chief cook and bottle-washer here."

"It's a beautiful…" I struggled to choose the right word. Hotel? House? Bed and breakfast? I decided to avoid the confusion altogether. "It's beautiful."

"Did you just come by to check out the property?" she asked.

Property! That was appropriately neutral.

"No, we're ready to check in."

Her eyes widened and for some reason that made my heart beat a little faster.

"I'm sorry, but —" She wrung her hands helplessly. "—we have no vacancy tonight. The Filcher-Farmer wedding is next weekend and they have the entire place booked. We're full."

"Full?" She couldn't be serious. "We have a reservation."

"Yes," she replied. "For next month."

"For next—?" I shook my head. "No, that's not possible."

She gestured at me to follow her and then turned and walked deeper into the house. We went down the hallway, past the staircase, through an open doorway, and into a cozy white kitchen. Sue-Anne crossed to the round kitchen table where a laptop was open. She sat down and started punching in keys.

A moment later, she called me over.

"Here, look," she said pointing at the screen.

I leaned down to read the open email from Bud's assistant, Marian, making the arrangements for our reservations. The date in the original email was one month off.

That was just what I wanted to hear after a long day of travel. I got up a four o'clock this morning to finish packing and had been trying to get to the middle of Texas—Rocky Gulch, to be exact—ever since.

First, our itinerary indicated a flight out of LaGuardia, only to get there and be told we were flying out of Newark. One high-speed cab ride later, we arrived just as the flight was canceled. After being bumped from three flights—thanks to awful thunderstorms blanketing the Midwest—we finally got routed through Atlanta, Chicago, and Denver, before catching the last flight into Dallas.

What should have been a short, direct flight had turned into an all-day mess.

It was after midnight back in New York.

Exhaustion and frustration hit me full force.

I shoved a hand into my curls. "Crap."

"Language dear," she said gently.

Fine, there had to be another option. We would just have to find another place to stay.

"Sorry," I offered lamely. "It's been a long day. Can you recommend another place to stay in town?"

Her laugh tinkled like bells on a Christmas tree. "There isn't one."

I scowled. She couldn't be serious.

"I'm sorry, but Rocky Gulch isn't terribly metropolitan. The Yellow Rose is the only lodging in town." At least she sounded genuinely sorry. "If I had a cot or a bedroll to spare I'd make room. Even the sofas in the parlor are full of little ones tonight."

I sighed. "How far is the next closest hotel?"

"That'd be two exits down on the highway," she offered. "Near to an hour away I'd imagine."

"An hour?" I couldn't hide my shock.

How was it possible that the closest thing to a hotel in this town was full *and* the next closest place to stay was over an hour away?

This production was already a nightmare, and filming hadn't even started.

"I'm so sorry, dear." She reached out and patted my hand.

I took a deep breath and let it out very slowly. "It's fine. We'll make it work."

She pushed to her feet and crossed to the counter, where a rack full of freshly-baked treats sat cooling. She placed a pair of muffins at the center of a blue bandana and then wrapped them up. Tied them with a bow and everything.

"Here," she said, handing me the bundle, "take these for the road."

I gave her a weak smile. "Thanks."

Sue-Anne followed me to the front door and waved as I climbed back into the rental car. As soon as the door clicked shut, I let out a string of sailor-worthy swear words.

Eddie stared at me. He wasn't entire used to this kind of rant from me, but usually it took at least a couple days of shooting for something to so completely upend my calm.

Today I was ahead of the curve.

When I finished, he cleared his throat. "How'd it go?"

I glared at him. "Bud's idiot assistant reserved the wrong dates."

Marian tried hard. At least, I thought she tried hard. Maybe she was just really good at pretending to try hard. Clearly she was *not* good at actual work.

On any production you have to roll with the punches. Avoidable punches are a little more painful to swallow.

"So, let me guess," he said. "No room at the inn?"

"There's a wedding this weekend." I forced my fists to unclench. "The entire bed and breakfast is full and the next closest hotel is an hour away, back on the freeway."

Eddie shook his head. Then sniffed the air. "Do I smell blueberries?"

I handed him the muffin bundle. If he could be appeased by a pair of muffins, who was I to deny him?

Letting my head drop back against the seat, I considered our options.

Choice one, we drive *all* the way back to the hotel on the freeway. But even if they had rooms available—clearly not a sure thing, given my current luck—we would have to drive *all* the way back here in the morning. The shoot was scheduled to begin a seven, which would mean getting up at the butt-crack of dawn. Again.

I groaned at the thought. It was already nearly midnight. If I didn't get a good night's sleep, things could get ugly.

"These are amazing," Eddie exclaimed. He held out a muffin to me. "You sure you don't want one?"

I shook my head. All I wanted was sleep.

Choice two, we… what? Stayed here?

I twisted around in my seat. The car rental company had upgraded us to a full-size SUV. The thing was a least a few square feet larger than my apartment. The passenger seat felt like a luxurious recliner and the back seat looked like a darn comfy sofa bed.

"Hey Eddie," I asked, "how would you feel about spending a night in the car?"

Ready to read the rest? Get *Trying Texas* now.

ABOUT THE AUTHOR

TERA LYNN CHILDS is the RITA-award-winning young adult author of the mythology-based Oh. My. Gods. series, the Forgive My Fins mermaid romance series, the kick-butt monster-hunting Sweet Venom trilogy, and the Darkly Fae series. She also wrote the City Chicks chick lit romance series and co-wrote the Hero Agenda and Creative HeArts series. Tera lives nowhere in particular and spends her time writing wherever she can find a comfy chair and a steady stream of caffeinated beverages. Find her online at *teralynnchilds.com*.

MORE BY TLC

the City Chicks series

Eye Candy

Straight Stalk

Trying Texas

City Chicks (Volume 1)

♥

the Creative HeArts series

Ten Things Sloane Hates About Tru

Falling for the Girl Next Door

♥

the Darkly Fae series

When Magic Sleeps

When Magic Dares

When Magic Burns

When Magic Falls

When Magic Wakes

♥

the Oh. My. Gods. series

Oh. My. Gods.

Goddess Boot Camp

Goddess in Time

the Forgive My Fins series

Forgive My Fins

Fins Are Forever

Just For Fins

Pretty in Pearls

the Sweet Venom trilogy

Sweet Venom

Sweet Shadows

Sweet Legacy

the Hero Agenda series

w/ Tracy Deebs

Powerless

Relentless

www.ingramcontent.com/pod-product-compliance
Lightning Source LLC
Chambersburg PA
CBHW021001120726
47905CB00009B/2792